Ice in the Blood

Kevin Wignall

First Published 2023 by Hamsun Press

1

The only cute things about Bobo were his nickname and the dimple that appeared in one cheek when he smiled. At a stretch, maybe the smile itself—even at thirty, he looked like a goofy teenager who knew he wasn't the best at anything or the most attractive, but was just happy to be at the party. That was how he looked when he smiled—cute—and it was a lie.

Bobo wasn't a cute person. He'd probably only ever killed two people—he'd stabbed a guy in the neck with a broken bottle in a bar fight back in Minsk, and a girl he'd picked up on the street in Brussels had never been seen again, presumed dead—but he'd hurt a far larger number, in many different ways.

He'd trafficked people, drugs, animals and armaments, before finally joining Vitali Petrov's payroll as another slab of protective muscle. He knew how to use it, too—he'd spent a year learning Krav Maga in Tel Aviv in his early twenties and had trained and sparred for an hour or two every day ever since.

Bobo liked to use escorts, but he also liked to abuse them, so Kissari was probably the only pimp on the whole of the Cote D'Azur—maybe in the whole of France—who'd let

Bobo loose on his girls. The escorts themselves didn't like it, naturally, but nor did they have much choice.

Tonight's girl was called Polina—blonde, tall, wearing strappy heels and a flimsy gold dress, a look designed to signal glamor and sex appeal to a certain kind of man, the kind of man who wouldn't notice and wouldn't care that she clearly didn't want to be here, not in Room 302 of the Grand Hotel, not in Cotignac-sur-Mer, not in this life.

She looked resigned rather than nervous as she walked into the room ahead of him, a pretty good idea what she might be expected to endure over the claustrophobic hour or so that lay ahead of her. She switched on an alluring smile as she started to turn toward him, but it didn't last long.

Bobo shoved her hard in the back and her face crumpled, shocked by the power of it as she stumbled forward off the heels and crashed onto the bed. It had been a shove, nothing more, but it was clear from her expression that she knew how dangerous this man was. Still she was trying to act, to make him think she was okay with this, that she'd make him happy any way he wanted.

Bobo stepped forward, looking down at her as he loosened his belt and pulled it free with a snap. He spat a word out in Russian, not clear, not even clear to Polina, though she smiled nervously, and on any other day, that smile wouldn't have made any difference to the outcome of what happened here tonight.

Jay Lewis was seven years older than Bobo, knew how to look after himself but had better things to do every day than spend an hour training and sparring. In a fight, there wouldn't be much of a competition, but Jay didn't much care for fighting.

He stepped out of the bathroom and shot Bobo between the shoulder blades. Polina jumped in shock at the noise, pushing herself up the bed. Bobo staggered forward, turned, looked at Jay with recognition and confusion, then fell to the floor, his head cracking and becoming wedged against the foot of the bed. There was no need for a second shot.

Jay looked at the girl and said, "Okay?"

She nodded, but said, "Why did it make so much noise?"

He wasn't sure what she meant at first, then followed her gaze to the gun with its silencer.

Jay smiled. "Not like how it is in the movies, huh?" She shook her head. "Don't worry, even if someone heard, they won't think anything of it." He walked back into the bathroom, picked up the package and by the time he came out again she was off the bed and standing looking down at the body. She showed no emotion.

He handed her the package. "Canadian passport, bank card, cash, airline ticket. You're on the 07.10 out of Nice."

He glanced at his watch. "You're checked into the Novotel near the airport—you'll find the keycard and the room number in there. There's a train from Cotignac in forty minutes. You need to change your clothes and be on that train, then take a cab from Nice-Ville."

She nodded, taking it all in. "My suitcase is down in the lobby. I can change in the restroom and leave through the back. And I have the dye for my hair like you said. I do that when I get to the hotel."

"Good." She'd remembered everything he'd told her to do and was treating it seriously, which was important, because if she didn't get away, his game was as good as over down here and the last six months would have been wasted.

"Thank you." For the first time, she looked overcome. "You don't know how much this means to me."

He could believe that, but he hardly deserved her gratitude.

"If it hadn't been you it would have been another girl."

"I know." There was no self-pity, which in turn made him hope for a better life for her.

"What will you do? In Canada?"

"I want to be a hairdresser. I trained for a year, before I came here."

It was such a modest dream and yet she seemed almost afraid of saying the words aloud in case those hopes crumbled to nothing out in the open. And Jay realized for the first time that, quite by chance, he'd done something good here this evening, other than killing Bobo.

"I hope you do it, Polina. You deserve more than this."

"Thank you." She glanced at the floor. "Why did you hate him so much?"

"Bobo? I didn't hate him. He just had the wrong kind of face, that's all."

"He was an animal. All the girls said so."

"Yeah." Jay looked down at the body—all that useless cruelty reduced to an awkwardly positioned carcass. "You do understand, once you get to Canada, this is a new life for you? Become a hairdresser, build something new, but don't contact anyone from your past ever again. If you do, the man he worked for will come after you and he'll kill you."

"I understand." She slipped the package into her purse and walked toward the door, but stopped then and looked back at him. "Why are you wearing a tuxedo?"

"I'm on my way to the casino."

She smiled, then laughed a little. At first he thought she might be laughing at the absurdity of it, that he could kill a man before going off to the casino. But young as she was, she knew well enough that the glamor of casinos and luxury hotels and exclusive bars and private yachts was illusory, a veneer that concealed so much violence and filth beneath. No, in truth, she was probably laughing simply because it reminded her that she was free, and that with any luck, she would never have to go to a casino again.

Two days later, Jay took an early dinner at the Yacht Club with Amandine. It was early on her account—she had a gallery opening she'd promised to attend—but it worked for him too.

As she got up to leave, she kissed him quickly and said, "Might you call by later?"

"Sure. I probably won't be able to stay the night, but…"

"When do you ever?"

"Would you want me to?"

She gave him a seductive smile and said, "I want what you want, Jay."

She turned on her heel without waiting for a response and he watched her glide across the room. A couple of people who knew her smiled or said hello as she passed, a few others who didn't turned and looked in her direction anyway, drawn by the high cheekbones and flawless skin, the hair worn in an artfully casual chignon, the linen dress that somehow always remained uncreased. She got noticed, always.

The set-up between Amandine and Jay suited her as much as it did him. They enjoyed each other's company, had some fun, nothing too complicated, and he wasn't there in the morning cluttering up her perfect apartment. He wouldn't have been with her if he'd thought she wanted something more permanent, but it was as she'd said—she wanted what he wanted.

Jay's eyes were still on the door when he saw Stas come in. Even in the evening, the Yacht Club's smart dress code was interpreted in a raffish mix-and-match kind of way, mostly old money that didn't need to try too hard. As a result, Stas looked laughably out of place in his overpriced sleek gray suit, black shirt and black silk tie.

He crossed the restaurant with a muscular swagger that might have impressed people elsewhere, then sat in the chair that Amandine had just vacated and looked at Jay with a questioning expression, as if he were the one whose evening had been disturbed.

A waiter came over, but Stas turned to him and said, "Leave us alone."

It was issued like a threat, and the kid backtracked quickly, looking rattled—he'd only been there a few weeks. Jay would have to find him before he left, apologize, give him a decent tip. As if Jay needed any more reasons to despise Stas, he hated people being rude to wait staff.

"What can I do for you, Stas?"

"Did you find anything?"

"About Bobo?" He took out his phone and pulled up the stills from the security cameras in the corridor outside Room 302. He showed him the first. "This is the girl leaving, within a few minutes of arriving with Bobo. She was clearly in on it." He swiped to the next shot. "Then this guy leaves ten minutes later."

Stas took the phone and looked closely at the image, frowning. "He looks like an Arab."

"I thought the same, Arabic, North African. You don't recognize him?"

"No. Do you?"

"If I did I wouldn't be asking you. There's another picture from the camera at the service entrance. Doesn't show much. A second guy on a motorbike, no plates. Our man there gets on the back of the bike and they ride off."

Stas looked deep in contemplation, but his thoughts were so visibly slow that Jay almost filled in the blanks for him. Finally, though, it all appeared to fall into place.

"Before you came here, there was a Moroccan girl—"

"No, it was just after I got here. Bobo almost killed her, right? Messed her up so bad that Kissari let her go. Didn't she head back to... Tangier or somewhere?"

"Yes, Tangier. Good." He handed the phone back to Jay, looking pleased with himself as if he'd worked it out all on his own. "Arabs. That's who did this. And that means we'll never find them. So! I'll tell Mr. Petrov we can forget about it."

Stas and Bobo hadn't much liked each other, which probably went some way to explaining Stas's eagerness to draw a line under this. That said, it probably wouldn't have occurred to him anyway that some of the security stills might be fakes.

"Don't you think Bobo's uncle might want us to try at least?"

Bobo's uncle was a general in the Belarussian army. It was the uncle who'd made sure the murder in the bar in Minsk had been deemed self-defense. And unbeknown to uncle or nephew, the same family connection had been Jay's motive for putting a bullet between the younger man's shoulder blades.

Stas looked unconcerned. "Bobo's uncle is a patriot. When the time comes, he'll support the coup."

Jay made a show of accepting his assurance, even though in his experience, patriotism was the most fragile of flowers.

"I made some enquiries about the girl, too, spoke to Kissari. No sign. He thinks she probably didn't get far— they probably killed her and got rid of the body."

"So they saved us the trouble. These women, they think they can treat us how they like." He grimaced, looking full of hate. "Scum."

The irony of that assessment would have been lost on Stas, even though Bobo's sexual violence had been an open secret. Stas himself didn't use prostitutes. Apparently he had a wife back in Minsk whom he rarely saw, and as far as Jay knew, there was no one else taking her place down here.

Stas took his own phone out now and brought up a picture of a guy talking to a crew member from one of the yachts in the marina. He put the phone down in front of Jay.

"A CIA man came into town yesterday. You know him?"

The guy in the picture looked mid to late twenties, dark hair, clean cut, wearing a white polo shirt and cream chinos. To the casual observer, he would have looked a good fit for the marina, an Italian maybe, from one of the yachts. To Jay, the whole look screamed "CIA".

"No. I left five years ago—this guy was probably still in college."

He handed back the phone and Stas looked at him with contempt.

"So you don't know anything?"

"Not about him. Even if I hadn't left before he joined, it's a big agency."

Stas shook his head, a theatrical gesture of disbelief as he said, "It beats me why Mr Petrov pays you for security advice, when you really don't know very much about anything."

"So why don't you persuade him to get rid of me, save him some money?"

"I might just do that."

"Good. Then when the coup fails because he didn't have me advising him, he'll know who to blame."

Jay was overplaying his hand but it didn't seem to matter.

Stas muttered a couple of words in Russian—or possibly Belarussian—that Jay didn't understand, then said, "The coup will succeed, with or without you."

"Vitali doesn't think so."

"Maybe. But he wants to know who this man is and what he's doing here, whether it's good for us or bad." He stood, towering over Jay with what was presumably meant to be an air of menace. "So find out. Do your job."

Stas left without saying another word, earning dismissive stares from the other diners. It wasn't just the clothes, more that his face didn't fit somehow. It really didn't fit at all.

On the other hand, Jay was annoyed with himself that he'd heard about this new arrival from Stas. Jay had been living a pretty good life in Cotignac-sur-Mer these last six months, most of it at Vitali Petrov's expense, and it was true what Stas had said—he wasn't doing much of a job as security adviser if he was the last to know about the CIA sending a foot-soldier down here.

Of course, little did Stas know, but that was the least of the ways in which Jay wasn't doing his job as Vitali Petrov's security adviser. It was nowhere close to even being the start of it.

3

Jay didn't have to wait long to find out about the CIA guy. He'd popped into Zinc later that evening to have a drink with Lucien, the owner, and was sitting at the bar when the new arrival came in and took the stool next to him.

Lucien broke away from the conversation and said, "Yes, Monsieur, what can I get for you?"

"Could I get a Negroni?"

"Of course, coming right up."

Lucien made busy and a short while later the guy turned to Jay and said, "Hey, how's it going?"

Jay looked around the bar. It was pretty busy, but none of the other barstools was taken and yet the guy had chosen to sit right next to him.

"Going well, thanks for asking. New in town?"

The guy smiled in response, reached into his pocket and pulled out a business card which he handed over.

"Pretty much. Rich McKenzie. I'm a yacht broker."

Jay glanced down at the expensively weighty card in his hand, then back at Rich McKenzie. He was nondescript bar for a small white scar on his chin, striking against his tan. Without the scar Jay wasn't sure he'd have been able to pick McKenzie from a lineup an hour from now.

Jay placed the card on the bar. "I left the agency five years ago, Rich. I miss some things about it. But I don't miss engaging in the kind of conversation you were planning on having right now. I know who you are, you know who I am, so why don't we cut straight to what you're doing here?"

Rich stared back at him, probably trying to judge how to play this, but then Lucien came back to them and placed the drink on the bar.

"One Negroni, Monsieur."

"Thanks." He took a sip, buying himself a little time, then said to Jay, "You, of all people, should know that the US Government doesn't need to explain its presence anywhere. That said, I'm expecting to be here for at least the next few weeks. Something's afoot."

"Something's *afoot*?" He smiled at the old-fashioned turn of phrase. "Well that's good to know, Rich, but I'm a civilian, so I'm not entirely sure what it might have to do with me."

Lucien placed a silver tray on the bar with McKenzie's check. He glanced down at it, took some notes from his wallet and tossed them onto the tray.

"It might have something to do with your employer, Vitali Petrov."

"You mean my client. I don't have an employer, not anymore."

He looked on the verge of saying one thing, but stopped himself and shook his head, saying, "You think you're so smart, don't you?"

"I don't know about when you joined, Rich, but being smart was a prerequisite in my time."

Rich stood abruptly, a little too close for Jay's liking as he said, "I have to level with you, Lewis, I don't much like people who benefit from the Agency's training program, then go work in the private sector. It just goes against my scruples. But we all know something big is coming, and when it does, your *client* will not be happy if you haven't offered your full cooperation." He pointed at the card. "That's my cellphone number, but I'm sure I'll see you around."

He headed for the door and left Jay wondering what this meant. Vitali hadn't told Jay the date, but he reckoned they were getting close, only a week or two out from the planned coup. Vitali had been making his plans for years,

Jay for the last six months, and he didn't much like the idea of someone at Langley screwing it all up now.

Lucien walked over and looked with disappointment at the barely touched drink.

Jay looked at it too and said, "What a waste of a good Negroni."

Lucien took the glass from the bar as he said, "He's the CIA guy?"

"You heard?"

"A few rumors. If you want to go incognito in Cotignac-sur-Mer, don't pretend to be a yacht broker."

Jay laughed and Lucien walked away with the drink and the silver tray.

Jay turned on his stool and looked back across the bar. His eye caught an attractive face, a brunette sitting in the corner booth looking down at a laptop. It wasn't the kind of place that people usually sat and worked, especially in the evening. But then Jay realized he knew her—Amandine had introduced her to him at a cocktail evening at the Yacht Club last week, Harriet Baverstock (*friends call me Harry*).

She was English, had been here a week or two, and worked in… something financial, either wealth management or asset management? He couldn't remember, and actually couldn't remember a single thing about her, which should have been a clue in itself. He thought of Rich McKenzie and the mysterious something that was "afoot", and he reasoned that if Langley had sent someone down here, London probably had too.

He picked up his drink and strolled over to her table. To some extent, this was at least Jay doing his job. If the CIA and MI6 were down here he needed to know if they were planning to support Petrov's coup—that seemed most likely, but it was hard to be certain when he was so out of that particular loop—or if they were only here as passive observers. He certainly doubted they had plans to undermine it. So he needed to find out, but more than that, after dealing with Stas and Rich McKenzie in one evening, Jay simply felt like seeing a friendly face.

She looked up from the screen and he said, "Miss Baverstock, I don't know if you remember, but we met last week, at the Yacht Club?"

She grimaced slightly. "Miss Baverstock makes me sound like a primary school teacher. And not only do I remember, but I *thought* we were on first name terms?"

"Of course." He gestured to the seat opposite. "Am I disturbing you?"

"Not at all. A welcome diversion."

She closed the laptop and pushed it to one side. She had a glass in front of her and a large bottle of Evian. He remembered thinking her attractive at their first meeting, but seeing her again there was undoubtedly an extra appeal he hadn't noticed before.

Jay sat and said, "It's unusual to see people working in here."

"Just a change of scene from the hotel."

"Where are you staying?"

"The Bellevue."

"Very nice. I like the restaurant there."

As if responding to that mention of his social life, she said, "Your girlfriend not with you this evening?"

"No, she's at a gallery opening and... we're um, we're not really a couple, in any formal sense."

"I can't possibly think why you would tell me that."

She was smiling at him, an unmistakably flirtatious glint in her eye. He smiled back, taking the hit, but he noticed that for all her playfulness, she wasn't missing anything from this back corner table.

"So, Harry, I'm sure you guys told me last week, but how did you and Amandine meet?"

"Yes, I'm sure we did tell you. It was at the spa. We got talking. I'd only just arrived in town so Amandine was giving me the lowdown."

He nodded, but didn't reply for a few seconds and she looked at him quizzically as if amused by his silence. She was really quite beautiful, and he was certain he wasn't fooling himself in feeling a low-level chemistry between them. Even so, he was determined he wasn't about to get played.

Finally, Jay said, "I've been out too long: I'm getting rusty. I should have made you from the start."

"I'm sorry, I'm not following."

"Oh, I think you are. Does Rich McKenzie know MI6 has someone down here?"

She maintained a bemused expression for a little while, but he could see her calculating, too. She'd made sure to meet Amandine at the spa as a way of getting to Jay, which meant she was also down here because of Petrov. Jay could just tell that she was shrewd enough to make the smart play now.

"Not yet, he doesn't. I'm here more as observer than active participant."

"And what is it that you're observing?"

She gave him a barely-there smile, as if to say he should know better than to ask.

"Okay, I respect that. Clearly it involves Vitali Petrov, or you wouldn't have made sure to meet Amandine as a way of meeting me. So I guess at some point you're hoping to gather intel from me on the coup he's planning in Belarus, and I'm not ruling that out. But whatever it is that's brought you people down here, if it involves a threat to Vitali, I really need to know about it."

"Goodness, you really are rusty, or did you always like to put all your cards on the table right from the start?"

"I just like that I no longer have to talk like a civil servant."

"I find it hard to believe you ever talked like one, and that whole loose cannon thing is *so* out of vogue right now."

"Maybe that's why I quit."

"So that you could carry on living in the past?" Even her teasing had a flirtatious edge to it. "You do have quite the life down here, don't you, Jay? Truth be told, I'm rather envious. But for what it's worth, I don't foresee any threat to Vitali Petrov from our side, so I don't think you need cancel your membership at the Yacht Club just yet."

"That's good to hear. Even better if you're gonna be staying around for a few weeks—just as an observer, of course."

There was that same glint in her eye as she said, "If I do become a participant, I'm sure you'll be the first to know."

Jay smiled, in part because there was now no question in his mind that she was flirting with him, but also because of what she'd said. She hadn't told him much, but she'd told him enough.

Vitali Petrov—Jay's client—was planning to overthrow the regime in Minsk, ushering in a bright new dawn of democracy and tolerance, and it now seemed that Western governments were starting to offer at least their tacit support. Nothing overt, of course—isolating Russia a little further was one thing, but nobody wanted to be seen goading the bear.

That was why Rich McKenzie had approached Jay, because as Petrov's security adviser he was perfectly placed to act as a clandestine bridge between them. That's why Harry had wanted to meet him too. They were lining up deep behind the scenes to support regime change.

So Jay's charmed life probably *was* under threat, because unbeknown to any of them, he had only one job to do down here, and that was to ensure that Vitali Petrov's coup failed and that Belarus remained an ally of Russia. And he hadn't spent six months patiently working towards that goal for other people to come in and undo it all so close to the end.

4

Jay bumped into Amandine later at Chez Felix. He kept his word in not staying the night, but it was almost dawn by the time he got back to his apartment. He stepped out onto the balcony and looked down, the town and the sea before him still in darkness, but the first luminescence showing in the eastern sky.

Reluctantly, he left the cool stillness behind and went to bed, but he woke naturally by ten, showered and headed out to Pascale's for breakfast. As he left the apartment building he noticed a woman and a boy getting out of a taxi on the other side of the street, the driver pulling their baggage from the trunk. He guessed it was getting to the start of full vacation season, something he hadn't experienced yet in the six months he'd been here.

He walked through the dark interior of Pascale's and out onto the small terrace which offered a view over terracotta rooftops to the sweeping blue on blue of the Mediterranean, studded here and there with white sails and sleek superyachts and a lone fishing boat.

A couple sat on the far side of the terrace, but otherwise it was empty, the mid-morning lull. Simone, the young waitress, brought him his coffee and croissant, and then as she walked back inside he heard her say good morning to a new customer, first in French, then in English. He could hear some movement of chairs in there, what sounded like an unnecessarily complex negotiation over their order—a woman, with an American accent—but silence finally descended again as he finished eating his croissant.

Then the woman appeared at the doorway onto the terrace. She was probably about his age, slim, reddish-blonde hair. She was pretty, but looked stressed out and slightly wild around the eyes. He recognized her now as the woman he'd seen getting out of a cab up the street. Jay guessed their accommodation wasn't ready so they'd come to Pascale's.

She looked like the kind of person who turned everything into a drama so he avoided catching her eye, concentrating instead on his coffee. She glanced back in through the door, presumably at the kid, then walked out onto the terrace.

"You mind if I sit down?"

Her voice was a little shaky, but she was talking to Jay, and he didn't see any easy way out of it, so he gestured toward the chair opposite and said, "Please."

She pulled the chair out and sat. She had a large manilla envelope in one hand which she put on the table now. He could see her damp handprint on the paper.

She stared at him for an uncomfortable second, then said, "You don't remember me, do you, Jay?"

He did a quick calculation. This wasn't a professional encounter. He'd just seen her get out of a taxi with a kid and suitcases. So it was just a coincidence, so he could relax. But he also had no idea who she was. He studied her face. She was pretty, striking blue eyes, but...

"Eleven years ago, 2008, Guatemala City. Is it coming back to you?"

The name came to him immediately.

"Megan?" Even though he'd remembered with the prompt, she didn't look the same somehow and he couldn't quite pin down how she'd changed. "Megan...?"

"Anderson."

"Of course." She'd been working for a charity there that helped street kids. He'd been in Guatemala doing what he did back then, only for a few months, but they'd spent most of those few months together. They'd had some fun, too, although it hadn't ended well, as he recalled. "Wow. What are the chances? What brings you here?"

She rested her hand on the envelope but didn't answer, staring at him for a while as if she hadn't understood the question. He waited, and after a lengthy pause she started to speak again.

"I know it ended pretty badly in Guatemala, Jay. Between us. I learned... I learned things about you, things I didn't like. I should have known, I guess, but I never quite... The shock of it, you know? I thought you were there to help people, like I was, but you weren't, you were there to hurt people. To hurt the Guatemalans."

Hurt the Guatemalans?

Jay took a sip of coffee as a way of stalling. It was the only way he could stop himself from laughing, and he didn't want to laugh at her. But this was the most surreal conversation, and it was far too early in the day.

Once he was composed again, he said, "Sure, I remember. But you know, like I said at the time, I was working for the government, and sometimes working for the government you have to do unpleasant things. Trust me, Megan, no one was sorrier than I was that it ended the way it did between us."

That was a lie, of course—he'd hardly given it any thought at the time or in the years since—but she was nodding like it was a nervous tic. He remembered she'd been heavily dependent on Prozac in Guatemala and yet would still get so overwrought that he'd once made the mistake of asking if she was in the best field of work for the sake of her own mental health. She stood now, walked to the door and looked in to check on the boy, then came and sat down again.

When she still didn't speak, Jay said, "So, I guess you're on vacation? I saw you up the street with your boy.

Obviously, I didn't realize it was you, or I would have come say hello."

"I didn't want to be in touch with you. I just didn't." There was a tremor in her voice. Jay wasn't sure what to say, but this was getting less amusing by the second. "I didn't want Owen to be exposed. I thought, without that influence, he could be normal. But he never was, not really, even when he was small. I just couldn't… reach him. Not the way I wanted. And then, the final straw, the whole…"

She seemed to be talking to herself now rather than to Jay. And he had absolutely no idea what she was talking about. He was actually wondering how quickly he could extricate himself from this chance reunion. He took his phone from his pocket and looked at it.

"Listen, Megan, it's great seeing you again, and maybe we can catch up while you're in town, if you're not too busy, but, I have to um—"

She looked at him now as if he were the one talking nonsense.

"Jay, I'm not here on vacation. My God, I would never come somewhere like this by choice. It's just so… I'm here because, Owen…" She ground to a halt, then held her hands up as if she were about to pull her own hair. "He's *your child*!"

Finally, she'd said something that made sense, but it raised too many questions, all at once. Above all—the one that mattered most to Jay in the moment—was how she'd found him. Because it was clear now that this wasn't a chance encounter, but that she'd come here looking for Jay, and that was a real concern, because she should never have been able to find him.

He almost asked her outright, but he knew that wasn't the first response most people would expect from a man who'd just been told he'd fathered a child.

"Are you sure? I mean…"

She smiled to herself. She'd briefly found her composure.

"He just turned ten. I didn't sleep with anyone for over a year before I met you, and I didn't sleep with anyone after you left. Of course, it's in your nature to assume I might be lying, because of who you are, but one look at him is all the DNA test you'll need. He looks *just* like you, Jay. And…" She looked momentarily overcome with some memory or other, and Jay in turn had a vivid flashback of the despondency and sense of hopelessness that had dragged her down repeatedly during their time together. "I so wanted him to be different. It's why I never contacted you—like I'd have known how to do that anyway. I thought, if he wasn't exposed to that kind of…" She sighed, then headed onto a different track. "Whatever's wrong with you, it's in him. And I feel terrible, like I've failed as a mother, but the older he gets, the harder it becomes. What else can I say? He's not my child, he's yours, and that's all there is to it."

He glanced toward the door himself, wanting to see the boy, to be sure of what she was saying. It was easy enough for Megan to claim he looked just like Jay, but if she planned to make him honor some kind of paternal obligations—and why else would she be here—he needed more than her word that the child was his.

He was about to offer some sympathetic but empty words, but she was already busy taking the paperwork out of the envelope. Her hands were trembling enough to make him wonder if she was on some kind of medication now.

"It's all here. I had it all done properly." As she shuffled through the papers, a passport fell to the ground. Jay picked it up and put it back on the table. That small gesture seemed to stop her short, and she fixed those startling blue eyes on Jay. "I'm a good person, and I tried, Lord knows I tried, but he…" She looked like someone in the throes of a serious breakdown. He remembered again, how frantic she'd get back in Guatemala, obsessing about how they couldn't help all the street kids, becoming so overwhelmed by the world's problems that she'd struggle to help herself. She put the pile of papers back on the table and he put his hand on top of hers which seemed to calm her instantly.

"Megan, I don't understand. What are you trying to tell me?"

"He's yours." She said it like it should have been obvious to him. "I tried, I really did, but… he nearly *killed* a boy Jay. Think about that. I can't take it anymore, I just can't. So that's it, he's yours now."

Her meaning finally became clear and it was so insane that, in a reflex, he withdrew his hand.

"Megan. This is crazy. You can't just abandon your kid. I mean, that's what you're talking about, isn't it?"

"I'm not abandoning anybody. I gave birth to him, I raised him for ten years, but I failed, and so… I'm not abandoning him, I'm handing him over to his father."

Now Jay did laugh. "Seriously?"

"Of course, seriously. I'm not asking you to do more than you should. And I'm not giving you a choice, Jay. Why should I? I know the things you did in Guatemala—some of it, at least. I could make life *very* uncomfortable for you."

She was threatening him, which finally, was something that made sense to Jay.

"Megan, you need to be very careful with what you're saying right now."

"Oh, I've been careful, don't you worry about that. You always thought I was crazy, because you don't understand people who care, but I'm not crazy. I've left a sworn affidavit with my attorney. If anything happens to me, then—"

"What? You honestly think I would hurt you?" He made a point of sounding offended, shocked, but he knew she was in the ballpark even if she didn't know it for sure herself.

Megan shook her head, "No! No, of course I don't, but you have to understand…" She closed her eyes, took a deep breath. "Is it hot out here?" It wasn't, but before he could answer, she said, "Where's the restroom?"

"Inside, take a right, all the way to the back."

She stood, but pointed at the pile of papers, saying, "You should take a look through those. It's all pretty straightforward. And it makes sense, when you look at it properly."

"Um…" Jay wasn't sure what to say. They weren't done with this yet, whether she knew it or not, but his first question came back to him now. "How did you find me, Megan?"

"I know it's a lot to take in, but take a look. Any questions, I'll try to answer them when I get back from the bathroom."

"Megan, how did you find me?"

She shook her head, looked to the door, then back to Jay. "I didn't. Owen did." She smiled sadly. "Like I said, as much as I wanted it to be otherwise, he's not my child. He never was."

She walked inside and Jay picked up the pile of papers. It didn't take him long, either, to realize she was deadly serious about this. There were witnessed documents naming him as the father and handing over full custody to Jay—he had no way of knowing how much weight they carried in law, but it showed her intent clearly enough. There was the birth certificate, too, without Jay's name on it.

It didn't seem like the work of someone in the midst of some kind of mental health episode, but he had to admit he didn't have much knowledge of these things, and had been ill-equipped to understand her troubles back when they'd been a couple. He remembered, too, that she'd possessed a remarkable ability to deal with bureaucracy and government departments even as she'd struggled to get out of bed in the mornings. In that sense, maybe one of the few things they'd had in common was an ability to compartmentalize.

He put the pile back into the envelope, all except for the passport which he opened now. It was Owen's and as he saw the photograph, he reeled a little, because she'd been telling the truth about the physical similarity. Somewhere in storage, Jay had pictures of himself from around the same age—before his own world had fallen apart—and this could easily have been one of them.

He slipped the passport in with the other papers, then looked at his phone as it vibrated with a message. It was from Benny, confirming the meeting later this afternoon in Nice. He sent a quick reply, saying he'd be there. And that meant, of course, that he'd have to extricate himself from this situation with Megan by two.

He checked the time now, then looked to the door, wondering what was taking her, and then he felt his stomach hollow out.

Simone came out, heading toward the couple across the terrace, but Jay called her over first.

"Simone, the lady who was here, is she still…"

"She left."

"Left… you mean she's gone?"

"Yes."

"And the boy?"

"No." She looked nervous. "But, she said you would… she said you knew."

"Sure. My mistake, don't worry about it."

He stood—his thoughts spiraling—and picked up the envelope, and he had to admit to a certain amount of admiration. Even in the midst of the crisis she was going through, she'd still managed to play him, and to play him well and truly. But this wasn't the end of it, because he knew one thing with total certainty—there was absolutely no room in his life right now for a child.

5

Jay picked up the envelope and walked over to the door. The boy was sitting at a table on the far side of the café with an empty plate in front of him and what looked like a milkshake. A large suitcase was set to the other side of the table, with a small backpack sitting on top of it.

The boy looked completely composed, studying something on the table in front of him whilst simultaneously sucking on the straw. His hair was fairer than Jay's, but again, he could see even from here that there was no question about his parentage.

Jay walked in and as he got close, the boy looked up.

"Hello, Owen."

"Hello." He had blue eyes, though not quite the same blue as Megan's—Jay's own mother's eyes had been blue, but he couldn't clearly remember the way she'd looked, so maybe it was just a fancy to think Owen's eyes resembled hers.

"I'm Jay."

The boy held out his hand and without thinking, Jay shook it, immediately ambushed by how small it felt in his own, the soft warm palm, the bony little fingers.

He saw now that the piece of paper on the table was the check. A blue wallet sat open next to it, and coins and notes were spread out on the table.

"What's that you're looking at there?"

"Oh, it's the check. I've never been to France before, so I don't know what kind of tip I should give. Mom says you should always be a generous tipper."

"Good advice. Do you know where your mom is now?"

"She's gone home. She said I have to live here now, because I hurt Isaac Gleick."

His composure was impressive, maybe even just a little unsettling, given that he'd just been effectively abandoned by his mother and left with a complete stranger who just happened to be his biological father.

Jay looked to the door out onto the street, wondering if he had time to catch her, stop her. It seemed unlikely given the minutes he'd spent looking through the documents while she was already running from both of them.

"Where's home, Owen?"

"Denver, Colorado."

"Do you have a cellphone?"

He looked solemn as he said, "I did, but Mom took it off of me because of what I did to Isaac Gleick, and then she said it probably wouldn't work in France, so it was pointless me having it back."

That sounded like a deliberate ploy to Jay, shutting down the means of getting in touch with her. He started to think through his own options. He still had contacts, people he could call. He could probably get her intercepted before she ever boarded a plane. But then what?

And he felt for the kid. It wouldn't work for the boy to be part of Jay's life, not now, probably not ever, so he'd have to come to some other arrangement—and quickly—but he didn't want Owen left feeling that neither parent wanted him, even if it happened to be the truth.

"Tipping is complicated in Europe. In some countries you round it up, others they add service to the bill, and some places they don't expect you to tip at all."

"Really?" He looked as if Jay had said something outlandish.

"Sure, like Switzerland. They pay the staff well, and, that's how it is. You can still round up, but it's no big deal."

"So, would I just round this up to six dollars? I mean, six euro?"

Jay leaned in closer to look at the check. "Yeah, usually." He pulled another chair over and sat down. "But how about we make it my treat today. I guess you know I'm your dad?"

He nodded. "What should I call you?"

"You can call me Jay. I mean, it's a bit weird to call me Dad when you've only just met me. That wasn't my choice by the way. I worked for the government back when I knew your mom, and she…"

He tried to think how best to put it into words that a ten year old would understand.

"Mom said you're an evil son of a bitch."

That would do it.

"Well, I guess that's one possible assessment, although I'd prefer it if you didn't use language like that. It's not very pleasant."

"Sorry." The apology was given without sulkiness, but rather like someone acknowledging he didn't yet know the norms of this new world in which he found himself—how much to tip, what to call the father he'd never met before, what constituted acceptable language.

"It's okay, you weren't to know." He checked the time. Marion would be at the apartment, and maybe that offered a possible solution for the afternoon at least. "I have some meetings later, but for now, how about we get out of here and go see my apartment."

"Okay." He started to put his money back into his little wallet.

Jay went and found Simone. She was talking to the couple out there on the terrace but as soon as he appeared in the doorway she walked over to him and he paid her.

She smiled and said, "It's all good?" She tipped her head toward the café.

"Yeah, it's all good."

"He's your son?"

"Yeah, she told you?"

Simone laughed, shaking her head. "She didn't need to!"

"No, I guess not. See you tomorrow, Simone."

"Bye, Jay."

When he walked back through, Owen was standing next to his suitcase and Jay was thrown again by how small the boy was, and by the obligation Megan had dropped in his lap. It seemed too much responsibility.

As Jay reached him, Owen looked up and said, "You're really tall."

"Well I'm taller than you." He smiled, letting him know he was teasing. Jay had been small for his age too, before a sudden growth spurt at thirteen had seen him overtake most of his peers. "You'll get bigger. Come on, I'll take the case, you bring your backpack."

They set off, but even wheeling the case, Jay could tell it was heavy and that only seemed to reinforce the terrible thing that had been done to this boy here today. His whole world was in this case, because Megan had decided he was never going back. Jay couldn't contemplate the kind of mental anguish that might have caused her to behave like that.

As if reading his mind, Owen said, "Don't you wanna know what I did to Isaac Gleick?"

"Is it important?"

"Mom said it was. She said it was the final straw. I nearly got arrested."

"You did not!"

"I so did."

Jay laughed. "Sure, if you wanna tell me, I'd like to hear."

Owen took a deep breath. "Okay. So, Isaac is in the same grade as me, but it's like he got held back a whole bunch of years, because he's really big, and he's mean, too. So, this day, he was picking on Marty Shaw who's like, the *smallest* kid in the whole of 4th grade. He was putting him in a headlock and twisting his ears and stuff. And Marty was crying, but Isaac just kept laughing at him and calling him a baby. So I told him to leave Marty alone, and Isaac asked me what I was gonna do about it, which actually, was a pretty good question. But then Mr Carradine came along, so Isaac let Marty go, but he pointed at me and said he'd get me next and it'd be much worse."

"Were you scared?"

"Kind of. I knew he meant it. He's a complete psycho."

"Okay. So what did you do?"

"When it got to lunch, I knew he'd come looking for me, so I waited by the top of the stairs—I knew he had to come that way because the cafeteria is downstairs. Anyway, he was with these other kids he always hangs around with and he saw me, and I heard him say, 'Watch this', and he came toward me. I won't tell you what he called me because you told me you don't like bad language."

Jay said, "That's fine. I can probably guess the kind of thing anyway."

"So he came at me fast, like he was gonna hit me, but I held onto the railing really hard with one hand and I reached out with the other and *pulled* him toward me and threw him down the stairs, just like that. It was pretty easy actually."

"That's good thinking, to use his own momentum against him. It's the basis of jujitsu."

"I did not know that." He looked up at Jay, apparently genuinely impressed. "Anyway, it was pretty bad. He broke his arm and his... scalpel?"

"Scapula?"

"That's it! And his head was bleeding and he got a concussion and all kinds of stuff like that. They said I could've killed him, so they kicked me out of school and Mom said it was the last straw. And that's why she brought me here."

"Well, that's not such a bad result, is it?" He pointed. "This is my building."

They walked into the lobby and as they waited for the elevator, Owen said, "Aren't you angry? Mom was really angry."

"Could you beat this kid Isaac in a fair fight?"

"No!" He laughed, like it was a ridiculous idea. "He'd have kicked the... I mean, no, it would not have ended well."

"Well then." They stepped into the elevator and Jay pressed for the top floor. "You looked out for someone who was weaker than you when everyone else was too afraid. That's a good thing. You understood the consequences that would follow, and you used strategic thinking to overcome a bully who was bigger and stronger than you. Ideally, you would have done it in a way that caused less damage, and it's true, you could have killed him, but I think on balance, you made the right call. Sounds like the jerk deserved it."

Owen looked up at him, a surprised and joyous smile as he said, "Thanks, Jay."

He smiled back at him. He liked this kid. And yes, on reflection, approving of excessive force to overcome a bully probably wasn't most people's idea of good parenting, but Jay couldn't think of any alternate course of action Owen might have taken in the circumstances. On another level, too, looking at his smile, Jay wondered when this kid had last been told he'd done something right.

The elevator doors opened and he pointed left and said, "We're just along here."

He opened the door and wheeled the case into the small hallway. He could hear Marion in the bedroom, so he pointed to the door into the open plan living room and kitchen.

"I just need to speak to Marion, so why don't you take a look in the living room, go out on the balcony." Feeling the urge to redress his earlier irresponsible parenting, he added, "Don't climb on the railing."

"Okay. Who's Marion?"

"She's my housekeeper. She tidies the place, handles my laundry, keeps my fridge stocked with essentials. I don't do much cooking." Saying it out loud made him realize that his lifestyle really wasn't a great one for a child to be part of, even briefly. He pointed and said, "You can leave your backpack here for now."

"Okay." He slipped off the backpack and put it on top of the case, then looked up at Jay with another smile, this one maybe a little nervous, like the strangeness of the situation had just hit him.

Jay watched him walk into the living room, then he turned and went into his bedroom where Marion had just finished changing the bedding.

She looked up and said, "Hello, Jay."

"Hey, Marion, you wouldn't happen to be free this afternoon?" She was already starting to shake her head, but he continued regardless. "I have to go into Nice, but my son just turned up unexpectedly and I need someone to—"

"You have a son?"

"Yeah, I didn't know about him until… well until just now as it happens, but he's staying for a while. It's kind of complicated."

"I can't today, sorry, but… he's staying *here*, with *you*?"

She sounded incredulous, and Jay was slightly stung. It wasn't like he was partying with drugs and hookers. But he guessed she had some idea of the kind of work he did, and a better one of the resolutely self-oriented lifestyle he lived.

"Would you like to meet him?"

"Yes!" She said it as if he shouldn't have even needed to ask.

They walked through into the living room. Owen was out on the balcony, looking out over the town to the blue of the sea below. He turned and walked in when he heard them.

"Owen, this is Marion."

"Hello." He looked unsure whether to hold his hand out as he had for Jay, but the decision was made for him. Marion looked immediately smitten and took a hold of him, then ruffled his hair, muttering in French the whole time. Owen looked uncomfortable with the physical attention, but happy after the fact.

"What a beautiful boy," she said, turning to Jay. "Maybe Amandine could look after him this afternoon?"

She looked doubtful even before she'd finished asking the question. Amandine was not obviously child-friendly. But then nor had Jay been before this morning. Even so, Marion seemed to discount it.

"Why don't you take him with you?"

"I can't, I have…" He thought ahead, though, to his two meetings, and it wasn't like anything would happen that might be unsuitable for a child to witness. A child was pretty good cover, too. "You know what, you're right, I'll take him with me. It'll be fun."

Marion looked less certain, suggesting that was taking it too far, but she didn't voice her reservations, and said only, "Then, maybe you can show him his room and I'll make some lunch—a baguette—and you can sit on the balcony and eat before you go."

"Sounds like a plan."

He turned and smiled at Owen. He'd show him the spare room, then they'd have lunch, and hopefully he'd get the answer to the most pressing question right now—how had a ten year old from Denver somehow managed to track Jay down to this apartment in Cotignac-sur-Mer?

6

Looking at the spare room now with Owen by his side, Jay saw it with fresh eyes—a bare white-walled space with a couch against one wall and nothing else.

But Owen pointed at the couch, unfazed as he said, "Is that a futon?"

"Yeah. I mean, we could get you a proper bed if you'd prefer that."

"I like futons. It's a couch, but it turns into a bed."

"Sure, so, we'll get you a duvet and stuff today. Um, your bathroom is through that door there."

Owen looked up at him. "No! Way! I have my own bathroom? That's so cool!"

Jay found himself bemused by what constituted cool to a ten year old.

"Great, and you have a closet there. And we can get a few more things, maybe a chair and a desk…" He was trying to think of his own childhood bedroom. "Maybe just some stuff to make it look more like a boy's room."

Owen looked around at the white walls, the window looking onto the street and the building across the way, and said, "I think it's okay."

"Good."

Jay was actually thinking he was going to a lot of trouble for what he imagined would be a short term arrangement. Megan was apparently in the middle of some sort of crisis, but those things she'd said, she couldn't have meant them.

He thought back to the young woman he'd known, who'd get so upset by the plight of the poor in Guatemala. True, her sorrow and anger had sometimes manifested itself in troubling ways, but he still struggled to see her as the kind of person who'd just turn her back on her own child like this. She'd change her mind, return for him, but at the very least, Jay also had to accept that Owen would end up being a part of his life from now on, however occasionally.

"Want me to help unpack your case?"

Owen nodded and Jay wheeled it across to the built-in closet and turned the case on its side before opening it. He started to hand him the neatly folded piles of clothes, t-shirts and sweaters, pants, a coat, socks and underwear, sneakers, so many things, a whole little life.

Owen saw it simply as a task to undertake, but Jay found himself becoming forlorn. He thought back to his own father, trying to normalize a new domestic routine with Jay after his mom died, when he was only two years older than

Owen was now. He'd always been hard on his father's memory when he thought about him, but even though this was a completely different situation, he saw afresh now how tough it must have been for him.

When they were done, he lifted the empty case onto the top shelf inside the closet and then Marion called and they walked through onto the balcony where she'd laid out the simple lunch on the table. There was a glass of wine for Jay, juice for Owen, a baguette for each of them.

Marion looked at it and said apologetically, "We don't have much in. I'll bring more tomorrow. You like ham and cheese?"

"Yes, thank you."

She smiled, closing her eyes for a second and putting her hand on her heart.

She turned to Jay then and said, "Today is difficult, but other days, perhaps, if you need to go out in the evening, I can come. Or my niece, Juliette—she's seventeen."

"Thanks, Marion, I might have to take you up on that."

She kissed Owen on the top of his head, then left.

Once the front door had closed, Owen said, "Am I gonna be in the way?"

He was astute. Jay didn't think he'd been that tuned in to the adult world when he was ten.

"Not at all. I have work to do. I'm a security consultant, which doesn't take up a lot of time, but the hours can be strange. Otherwise, it'll be fine." Even as he spoke, he thought of Rich McKenzie and Harriet Baverstock, the imminent coup, and how things might be about to change up a gear, but he'd have to worry about that as and when. "You know, here in France, it's normal for kids to be out late at night, have dinner with their parents, things like that."

Owen looked ready to respond, but then became distracted by a plane flying in low just off the shore. Jay turned and saw what it was.

"You're gonna love this. See that plane? It's for putting out fires. They're probably just training today, but the pilot's gonna bring it right down and scoop up a whole load of water into the belly of the plane."

"No way!"

"Yes way. Just watch."

They watched as the plane dropped down and skimmed the surface of the sea before climbing again. Owen was silent, but when Jay glanced at him, he saw his mouth was hanging open.

"Keep watching. They don't need the water today, so when they get high enough they'll just drop it all out into the ocean and then they'll come around again."

The plane dropped its cargo like a sudden cloud burst out at sea, and now Owen laughed.

"That's so cool! Do they ever catch fish by mistake?"

"I guess they must." Owen contemplated that, and Jay said, "Owen, I need to ask you a question. I asked your mom how she found me, and she said she didn't, that you found me. Is that true?" He'd just taken a bite out of his baguette, so he simply nodded. "Okay, it's fine, you haven't done anything wrong, but I do need to know how you managed to do that."

Owen made a show of the fact that he was still chewing, then took a drink to swallow what was in his mouth.

"Walden."

"Excuse me?"

"This kid I know, Walden. He's like, thirteen, and he's a really great kid, but he's so completely on the spectrum. He's a total genius with computers. I asked him to find you, so he did, on the dark web."

So much for secrecy. Jay was disturbed that he could be found so easily, dark web or otherwise.

"Why did you do that?"

He looked sheepish, his eyes a little downcast as he said, "I knew Mom was looking for you and couldn't find you.

She didn't want me anymore, and you were the only person she could send me to."

"What about her parents?"

Even as he asked, he had a vague memory that Megan's relationship with her parents had been tense, at best.

"She doesn't speak to them. I think they might be old. They live in Wisconsin."

"Okay, but you should be really careful on the web, and so should Walden. Are you still in touch with him?"

He looked dejected. "I know how to get in touch with him, but I don't have a cellphone anymore, or a computer."

"That's easy enough to fix. Maybe tomorrow—there's a store here in town. But you know, your mom was wrong to put you in that position. Doesn't matter how angry she was, she was just plain wrong."

"It wasn't *her* fault." He sounded defensive, which Jay guessed was only natural. He turned then, as if looking for the fire plane which had disappeared over the headland. "I mean, I know she doesn't love me, but she's still my mom."

"I'm sure she loves you."

Although, if Jay were honest with himself, he couldn't know that for a fact. Yes, she'd been passionate about the street kids and poverty and the environment and a whole load of other things, but passion and love weren't the same things, something he'd witnessed often enough. What had he really known of her beyond those superficial impressions?

Owen offered a little shake of the head in response anyway, looking stoic. Jay noticed a single tear running down his cheek, but Owen cleared his throat and brushed it away, as if embarrassed.

"Owen, it's okay for you to cry. This is a crazy situation, for both of us, so if you feel like crying, you cry."

He shook his head again. "Mom says boys shouldn't cry."

"*What*? That's insane. Of course boys should cry."

"Do you?"

Jay thought back to the last time he'd cried, when he was two years older than Owen was now. He remembered the doctor responding by putting his hand on Jay's shoulder, and how that hand had felt like an intrusion rather than a comfort.

"Not for a long time, but that doesn't mean anything. Fact is, your mom isn't here right now, so we make the rules. From now on, if you wanna cry, you cry."

"But I don't want to. It's just… I don't know what I did wrong."

And there was the wound at the heart of this child. He'd been abandoned by his mother, made to feel like it was his fault, left in this strange country with a strange man. Old enough to blame himself, too young to excuse himself, he was left bereft and confused.

"Well… you did get kicked out of school for throwing someone down the stairs." Owen laughed, which was better, much better. "You did nothing wrong. No matter what we do, some people just won't like us. Well that's their problem, not ours."

"What about Mom?"

How did he even begin to answer that?

"Would you rather be with her now?"

Owen looked deep in thought, and Jay guessed that had been the wrong question. Of course he'd rather be with his mother right now, no matter how strained things had been between them.

But then, to his surprise, Owen said, "I'm not sure. Like, I know I'll miss her, but…"

Maybe things had been even more strained than Jay realized.

"I know, it's difficult. So let's not think about it. We're in a beautiful place. You can have a lot of fun here."

"What about school?"

"You wanna go to school?"

"Not really."

"Then don't worry about it. School's out in a few weeks back home anyway. We can worry about school in the fall. But this afternoon, we're going into Nice. It's a short ride on the train. You can meet a captain in the French police."

"What kind of gun will he have?"

"A SIG Sauer. Why, do you like guns?"

"Not especially. I like first person shooter games."

"Like on a console?"

"Yeah. I had a PlayStation, but I couldn't bring it with me."

He didn't sound aggrieved, stating the fact plainly instead, like it was just one of those things, but Jay said, "We'll have to see about getting you one of those, too."

"Wow. Now *that* would be awesome, but it isn't even like my birthday or Christmas for a long time."

"True, but I missed all your birthdays and Christmases up until now, so."

Owen smiled, trying to restrain himself, but clearly overjoyed at the prospect of being reconnected with his favorite tech devices and his first person shooters.

Even so, before they left, Jay went into the bedroom and locked his own guns in the strong box.

7

As they walked to the station, Owen said, "Did you grow up here?"

Jay looked around, imagining what it would be like to live here as a child, as a teenager. The kids he saw about the place seemed to be living pretty idyllic lives, but a few weeks ago he'd been chatting to a young barman at the Bellevue who was desperate to escape—*people are always sad when they're leaving*, he'd said, *but they're going back to so many amazing places, and I'm stuck here.*

Jay had felt much the same throughout his teenage years, despite living somewhere most people would have considered equally idyllic.

"No, I grew up in a town called West Bedford, New York. Kind of a commuter town, I guess."

"A computer town?"

"Commuter, someone who travels to work. A lot of people who lived there would travel to work in New York City. It was pretty affluent. You know what affluent means?" Owen shook his head. "It means there weren't many poor people. It was a nice area."

"Were you rich?"

"Richer than most, I guess, but normal for West Bedford. My dad was a cardio-vascular surgeon, my mom was a writer for a magazine."

"Are they dead?"

Jay looked at him askance. "What made you ask that?"

"Just that you're talking about them like they're dead."

"Am I?" He was intrigued by Owen's all too accurate reading of his words. "Well, yeah, they're dead. My mom got sick and died when I was twelve."

"What did she get sick with?"

"Breast cancer. You know what that is?"

Owen nodded, the expression of a man of the world. "Mrs Pavesi got breast cancer. She didn't die but all her hair fell out."

"Yeah, that happens." Jay thought momentarily of his mom assuring him her hair would grow back, that it had only fallen out because the chemotherapy was working so hard to make her better. But it hadn't grown back, not properly, and within a year of that promise she was dead.

He was waiting for the inevitable question about how Jay's dad had died, and was wondering how best to explain it to a child, but Owen's mind had flitted to something else.

"Is it far, to the railroad station?"

"No, it's just up the hill there—you can see the roof. Why, are you tired?"

"No." He said no more at first and they walked quietly, in step with the early afternoon silence, just the sound of Owen's sneakers lightly hitting the sidewalk. Then he said, "Do you have a car?"

"Sure. It's in the garage under the building."

"What kind is it?"

"A Mercedes."

"Oh, cool. So why are we taking the train?"

"It's just easier for getting into Nice, and quicker—the road gets jammed a lot of the time."

"Mom has a Toyota RAV4, but it's pretty old, I think."

"What does your mom do, Owen?"

"She works for a charity, helping illegal immigrants." That shouldn't have been a surprise, but Jay was struggling to see how she could square that lifelong commitment to helping the disadvantaged with her decision to give up on her own child. She wasn't well, he was certain of that, and he wanted to make allowance for it, but couldn't, not really. "That's why she stopped speaking to her mom and dad. She says people like them are part of the problem."

"And she doesn't speak to them all?"

"She doesn't even let me speak to them. They send a package for me every birthday and another at Christmas, but Mom sends them back. She doesn't think I know about them—the packages—but I do. I don't think it's very nice to send gifts back, do you, Jay?"

"No, I don't. I guess… I don't know. I don't want to say anything bad about your mom, and hey, we don't know the whole story of why she doesn't speak to them."

"Because they're part of the problem," he said, repeating himself. "Like I am."

Jay looked at him and Owen looked up and shrugged.

"Do you get in trouble a lot? I mean, apart from throwing that kid down the stairs?"

"Kind of. But only for stupid stuff. Like, in school, I don't like when teachers tell you off for doing something when it wasn't you, so I tell them that. And I wasn't allowed to go on a field trip so I got Walden to hack the school's computer and cancel the booking for everyone else." Jay didn't say anything, but he felt a sneaking admiration for that ingenious piece of vengeance. "And I got kicked out of Junior Soccer Stars."

"Why, what did you do?"

"Coach Harding told me I didn't kick the ball hard enough. So I kicked it at his car and broke one of the mirrors."

Jay laughed. Owen looked up at him and laughed too.

"Well that showed him. Did you mean to do it?"

"*Yeah*? Because he was being such a… well, I just wanted to show him. But I pretended it was like an accident, and it was, kind of, because I was aiming at the car but I didn't know I'd hit the mirror."

"Did he believe you?"

"I'm not sure. He got really mad, and he called Mom right away to come pick me up. I thought he was gonna hit me but he didn't. Mom grounded me for a month. I wasn't even allowed to see Walden and he lives just along the block."

That had probably been wise under the circumstances— who knew what revenge he might have had Walden engineer for him.

"Did you get in trouble when you were a kid, Jay?"

"Not really. I didn't like rules and I didn't like being told what to do, but…" He'd also been given a lot of slack after his mom died, but looking back now, he realized he'd also been adept at manipulating people and situations—was that the only difference between him and Owen, that Jay had known how to make the system work in his favor? "I guess you just need to learn how to read people."

"Like a book?"

"Kind of. So you learn what other people want from you, and that's how you learn how to get what you want from them." He glanced down at him. He was nodding as if giving it serious thought, but he was clearly faking—Jay had confused him. "Also, sometimes, it's best to back away from trouble, but if you have no choice, you need to know how to defend yourself, preferably without throwing someone down the stairs. So, maybe if you're here for a while, I can teach you some self-defense, you know, like martial arts?"

"Seriously?" He looked ecstatic. "I wanted to do karate, but Mom wouldn't let me. She doesn't believe in violence."

Jay had discovered that to his cost a decade ago.

"Nor do I if I can help it, but sometimes, understanding violence is the best way of avoiding it."

Sometimes, of course, there was no way of avoiding it, and some people couldn't be reasoned with, or didn't deserve the effort. Most people were good and decent, given the chance, but there were enough who weren't that there would always be a need for violence.

That was all for another time. Right now, Owen was just ecstatic at the thought of being confident enough to take on a bully like Isaac Gleick in a fair fight. And Jay saw no reason to deny him that thrill by spelling out the messy reality of life.

8

Owen spent the brief train journey kneeling on the seat to look out of the window at the shimmering blue below and the occasional glimpses into trackside homes and people's lives.

He stayed close as they walked through the concourse at Nice-Ville, as if nervous of the bustle and the loiterers and the police and military presence. Jay wondered if he should take hold of Owen's hand, but he didn't have enough experience of children to know if ten year olds would consider themselves too grown up for that level of chaperoning. So they walked on as they were and he noticed the boy relaxing then, once they were out of the station and into the town.

He always met Benny in a traditional coffee shop on Avenue Durante. Jay had probably walked down the street ten times and yet he saw it now with fresh eyes as Owen drank it all in—the parked cars and the traffic and teenagers tearing past on scooters, the grand Belle Époque buildings and modern apartment complexes. A woman sitting drinking coffee on a balcony waved as Owen stared up at her and he shyly waved back.

Benny was already sitting in the coffee shop when they got there, at his regular table near the back, even though there was no one else in there. Tristan, the young guy who ran the place single-handed during the day, acknowledged Jay but did a double-take.

"My son," Jay said, and Tristan pulled a face, as if to say, *no kidding.*

Benny was looking equally intrigued. Seeing Jay with a child was obviously the last thing any of his regular contacts expected.

As they reached him, Jay said, "Long story, but this is my son, Owen. Owen, this is Benny, the police captain I was telling you about."

"Hello."

He held out his hand. Benny looked surprised by the formality, but shook hands all the same.

"Pleased to meet you, Owen."

"Me, too."

Jay guessed Owen didn't have any preconceptions of what a French detective might look like, so probably hadn't been expecting the stereotypical unshaven, overworked, slightly shabby guys that usually filled the role on screen anyway. But Benny was not that stereotype. He was sleek and well-groomed, wearing a polo shirt today that showed off his physique. Apart from the gun, he'd have probably made a more convincing yacht broker than Rich McKenzie.

Jay sat opposite and Owen sat next to him. Then Tristan came over with Jay's coffee and said to Owen, "How would you like some ice cream?"

Owen looked up at Jay and said, "Is that okay?"

"Of course."

Tristan smiled. "Great. Why don't you come over to the counter?" He winked at Jay then, and Jay nodded his thanks.

Once they were alone, Benny said, "Wow, you're really full of surprises."

Benny was hardly in a position to talk. He wore a wedding ring, but had never once mentioned a wife or children or anything about his domestic set-up, even in passing, and Jay could easily imagine that he never took the job home to them either. But then Jay could also see that the sudden appearance of Owen was dramatically out of keeping with his own man about town image.

"Trust me, this was as much of a surprise to me as it is to you. A woman I was seeing for a few months years ago showed up out of nowhere this morning while I was having breakfast at Pascale's, told me he's my son—"

"That's clearly true."

"Sure. But then she told me she was handing over custody. She went to the bathroom and never came back."

"She's gone?" He looked astonished.

"Just walked away."

"Incredible. You want me to…?"

"I'm not sure what good it would do, not right now. I guess if I let her cool down, maybe call her tomorrow once she's back home." He didn't have her number, of course—she'd made sure of that—but he doubted it would be too difficult to get her cell. "His mother seems to think he has a dark side, which she naturally thinks he inherited from me."

"He looks fine to me."

"Exactly, he seems like a sweet kid. My instinct is that this is more about her than it is about him, but then… she dumped me, too."

Benny shook his head, finding something amusing in the situation or Jay's description of it. Jay could hear Owen and Tristan talking over by the counter behind him, Owen laughing almost continually, sounding exactly like a sweet little kid.

"Did you kill Bobo?" That got Jay's attention. "Just between us, of course."

"Bobo got killed, that's all that matters."

Benny looked satisfied with that, and said, "It's difficult sometimes. We feel like we're always fighting a lost battle. But Bobo getting killed, that was a good day. How does Vitali Petrov feel about it?"

"Too soon to tell. But on that subject, the ship I mentioned last time—it'll arrive in Algiers tomorrow night, Taranto two days later."

Benny frowned, looking uncharacteristically uncomfortable. "I'm grateful for the assistance you've given us on this, Jay. The last two intercepts were really important. And I hate the thought of a shipment this big getting through. But I've been given orders from on high not to get involved anymore."

So, like Rich McKenzie had said, something big *was* afoot.

Owen suddenly giggled so infectiously that both Jay and Benny laughed a little too. That seemed appropriate, somehow.

"They say why?"

"They never say why. But for now it seems, they don't want to cause Petrov any more troubles, even if it means letting a billion euro worth of cocaine into Europe."

Jay wasn't sure how much Benny really knew about what was going on. Most of it probably fell outside his remit and he was shrewd enough not to get involved in something that wasn't his immediate concern.

Jay, on the other hand, knew that this shipment would provide Vitali Petrov with enough liquid cash to finance his planned coup. And because he talked at every opportunity about democracy and tackling corruption and a need for Belarus to pivot to the West, far too many people were willing to accept flooding Europe with cocaine as a price worth paying.

Jay said, "Don't worry about it. I might even be able to use the change of heart to my own advantage."

"I still feel like I've let you down."

"Not at all."

Benny sipped his coffee and studied the cup as he put it back down. "You know, I think we both know that things are coming to a head." He looked up again. "I just wonder, is this a good time for your boy to be here?"

They both looked over to the counter. Owen was perched on one of the high stools, his spindly little legs dangling. Tristan was on the other side of the bar and seemed to be showing him coin tricks. Owen was mesmerized, an expectant smile fixed in place.

"She'll change her mind, maybe even on the plane home. And I'm sure it'll be okay anyway. It's not like I don't know what I'm doing." Benny smiled, raising his eyebrows, and Jay said, "What?"

"Who are you really working for, Jay? It's clearly not Petrov, but… Who?"

"I'm working for me. Always me. And you know the old saying, Benny—no man can serve two masters."

"Hmm, I wonder."

Benny looked simultaneously intrigued and also happy to be kept in the dark. And right there, thought Jay, was one police captain who'd never become that grizzled stereotype, because he'd felt the need to ask the question, but deep down, he didn't want to know who Jay was really working for, and knew it was probably best for him if he didn't.

9

When they left, Tristan and Owen exchanged a complex, almost dancelike handshake that Tristan had apparently taught him over ice cream.

As they walked down the street, Owen was brimming with enthusiasm.

"Tristan was so cool. He showed me all these tricks with coins, like making them disappear and stuff and I watched *so* carefully but I still couldn't see how he was doing it. Can we go there again sometime?"

"Maybe. How was the ice cream?"

"It was okay. I had lemon and strawberry but they didn't have salted caramel—that's my favorite." As if only just noticing that they weren't walking back in the direction of the station, he said, "Where are we going next?"

"We're going to a grand old hotel called the Negresco— it's pretty famous. We're gonna have tea with someone from the Russian Consulate. Have you had tea before?"

"Sure. Walden's mom makes us tea all the time. They've got all these crazy names like Earl Grey and Gunpowder, but I kind of like them. Is he a spy?"

"Who, Walden?"

Owen laughed. "No! The Russian man. Is it a man?"

"Yeah, it's a man, and yeah, he's an intelligence officer. You know you can't talk about this, right?"

Owen fixed him with a solemn expression and said, "You can trust me, Jay."

"Good. It's not like you'll get in trouble, but it's best to keep these things quiet."

Apparently taking the advice at face value, Owen nodded, but didn't reply. He still drank in the sights of Nice as they walked toward the sea, but when they reached the Negresco, Owen was so unfazed that Jay wondered if he was used to staying in top-end hotels, unlikely as that seemed, given Megan's worldview.

It wasn't until they walked into the bar with its wood paneling and oil paintings that he seemed at all in awe of the place. Jay heard him whisper, "Wow", quietly, almost only mouthing the word.

The bar was busy but Jay walked over to the corner table with its high-backed chairs and sat down.

Owen pointed to the "Reserved" sign and said, "Doesn't that mean it's for someone else?"

"Usually, but this one's reserved for us."

Owen took that information on board and sat. He looked around, taking in the others patrons, the waiters, the bar staff.

"Will someone come and take our order?"

"Sure, but they'll wait for Georgy to arrive. Georgy Gumilev, that's the man we're meeting. We have to talk about some important things, so Georgy might speak in Russian or French—"

"Wow, do you speak Russian?"

"Enough to get by, but I speak French pretty good and so does Georgy, so he might speak French."

Owen thought that over and said, "I could sit somewhere else, if I'm in the way."

That was the second time he'd mentioned being in the way. Jay thought back to the year after his own mother's death, the numerous occasions when Jay's dad had realized he'd have to step up and change his own schedule to accommodate the son who'd been ferried around until then by his mom. His dad had never complained, but even back then, Jay had been able to see how much of an inconvenience it was, how much his dad was struggling, and so he'd voluntarily cut back on his own activities, claiming he no longer wanted to play this sport or attend that party.

Jay said. "Am I in *your* way?"

Owen screwed up his face and said, "*No!* Like how could you be?"

"Well, you can't be in my way, either. This is new for both of us, and we'll probably have to be flexible, but we can do this." He looked across to the doorway where Georgy had just appeared. He was an imposing figure—a still impressive physique masked by a well-cut suit, his gray hair cut short enough to hint at a military past—and yet Jay doubted any of the other customers in the bar had even noticed him come in. "Here's Georgy."

Owen turned to look but Georgy was on them before the boy spotted him. He shook Jay's hand with a smile, then turned and looked at an expectant Owen.

"Your son?"

"Yeah, this is Owen."

Georgy looked approvingly, patted the boy's head and sat down.

"So!"

He looked up as a waiter approached.

"Good afternoon, Monsieur Gumilev. Russian Caravan tea?" Owen's eyes lit up at the name. "And for the boy?"

Owen looked at Jay and said, "Could I have that, too?"

"Sure."

"Perfect. Russian Caravan for three."

Georgy smiled at Owen and said, "And maybe some pastries for the boy? You like the pastries, the cakes?"

Owen nodded, apparently overawed by Georgy's presence.

The waiter smiled indulgently. "Why don't you come and choose. I'll show you what we have."

As Owen got up from his chair, Georgy said, "Choose as many as you like." Owen headed off with the waiter and Georgy turned to Jay. "Charming. He reminds me of my grandson."

"I didn't know Owen existed until this morning."

"Ah, life is complicated. But this is a good complication to have, no?"

"I guess so."

Though in truth, Jay hadn't managed to fully absorb Owen's presence just yet. It was like they were playing a game, pretending to be father and son. If Jay thought too far ahead—thinking about the fact that Owen would sleep in his apartment tonight, and tomorrow and who knew how many more nights, thinking about being a parent and how he would even go about that—the whole scenario seemed ridiculous. How desperate or confused would a woman have to be to leave her child with someone she considered an "evil son of a bitch"?

Jay said, "I guess you've heard the CIA has someone in town."

"I wouldn't be doing my job if I hadn't." He smiled to himself. "We understand that the regime in Minsk is sending people down in the next day or two, presumably for a preemptive strike against Petrov. There are some former Alpha Group people involved. And Bogdanov owns a large property a few miles from here, so we think they might use that as a base. But they've gone very dark—we don't know exactly how many people they're sending or what their plans are."

"They don't trust Moscow?"

"Not so much that. After all, if we didn't support the regime in Belarus…" He didn't feel the need to finish the point. "I think this is more a case that they don't know who they can trust in Minsk itself."

"Do they know about me?"

"They know you're a security adviser to Vitali Petrov. So you will be a target, but I think on balance, it's better not to let them know the truth. Given how… *leaky* things seem to be among our Belarussian friends, we don't want Petrov finding out that you're not really on his side."

"That's like saying it's better to be hanged than shot."

"You know that's an old Russian saying?"

"Is it really?"

"No, I'm messing with you. But it sounds like it could be." Owen returned and sat down again. The waiter followed behind and placed a plate in front of him. Georgy looked impressed. "Just one pastry?" Owen nodded, seeming a little shy with Georgy. "Very good. Self-control is an admirable quality."

"Thank you."

He picked up the cake and started to eat, and then the waiter returned with the tea. Once it was all poured, Owen sipped at his and smiled to himself, and Jay could imagine he was thinking about telling his friend Walden about this strange new tea he'd tried. Not that Jay was entirely sure it was a good idea for Owen and Walden to be in touch with each other again, certainly not in the immediate future.

Georgy directed another approving glance at Owen, then turned back to Jay. Despite Jay's earlier prediction, he continued in English as if Owen weren't there.

"Bobo's uncle is already asking questions about what really happened to his nephew. He suspects Stas might have been behind it, which is plausible—they didn't like each other one little bit. He doesn't suspect Petrov himself yet, but we can continue to feed his doubts. And without him, the support of the army would be much less certain."

"That's promising. Less promising is that the latest shipment *will* get through, which means he'll have all the funding he needs."

"Ah."

Jay had been watching Owen. His concentration was fixed on the pastry, but Jay could tell he was listening, taking it all in. With Georgy's last response he glanced up, but lowered his eyes again quickly.

"Exactly," said Jay. "We still have the ultimate sanction if necessary, but I know you want to avoid that."

The ultimate sanction was killing Petrov, but it was politically more expedient for Petrov to fail than for him to be assassinated.

"There's still a great deal of chess to play before we get to that." He sipped his tea, placed the cup back on the saucer, his brows furrowed. "Your new domestic arrangements are perhaps not optimal at a time like this… but he's about the same age, I think, as Petrov's boy. That could be useful to you."

Owen didn't look up this time, even though he obviously knew he was being spoken about.

"I *had* thought of that. I'll be going up there in the morning. I'll take him with me."

"Good." Georgy looked indulgently at Owen, and said, "Imagine if we had started this young."

Jay nodded in agreement. But he was actually thinking they all started young in one way or another. The person Jay had become—no doubt the person Georgy had become, too—it was all seeded in the deep past of their childhoods.

He looked at Owen who was studiously pretending not to notice that he was now the subject of the conversation. And Jay even wondered if Megan had been right, that these qualities went back even farther, that for good or ill, the traits that defined them were there from birth.

10

They stopped off on the way back to the station and bought a duvet and some bedding. It was only a short train ride back to Cotignac-sur-Mer but Owen lay against the bag containing the duvet and immediately fell into what appeared a blissful, untroubled sleep.

Jay couldn't take his eyes off him, this boy who seemed simultaneously strange and familiar. Yes, in every real sense, he was self-evidently a stranger. Yet in some way he felt a connection, as if at some deep level Jay had always known he was there.

Above all, he felt another surge of sorrow for Owen, for what had happened to him. And again, Jay could not help but compare that sorrow with that of his own childhood, as much as he despised self-pity—that had been his father's weakness, not Jay's.

Jay thought he might have to wake him, so deep did his sleep appear, but as the train slowed on its approach to Cotignac, Owen awoke on his own. Jay wasn't sure if he saw a slight edge in the boy's eyes, a feral wariness that quickly vanished as Owen registered where he was. He was adapting to this new situation incredibly well, but that brief shift of expression made Jay wonder if some part of his cheery demeanor was an act. He dismissed the thought, fearing in turn that he was being influenced by Megan's crazy rambling from that morning.

Jay smiled and said, "Nearly home."

Owen nodded in response but didn't seem to have the energy for a reply.

As soon as they left the station, Owen reached up and took hold of Jay's free hand, apparently so tired that he needed that physical support. And his sneakers slapped more heavily now than they had earlier in the day. For the first time, as they walked with the boy's little hand in his, he felt like a father, the way he imagined other fathers to be.

Jay guessed he might have to let him sleep on the couch in the living room for tonight, reasoning Owen wouldn't be able to wait while Jay made up the bed. But Marion had somchow found the time to come back during the afternoon and Owen's room was transformed.

The futon had been opened out and made up with a duvet and pillows. There was a beanbag chair, a laundry hamper, a nightstand with a lamp on it, a couple of superhero posters on the walls. Owen took it all in with some sleepy proximity to amazement.

Jay said, "Are you hungry?"

Owen shook his head, his eyes drooping.

Jay squatted down so he was on the same level. "Okay, I know you're tired but you're almost there. Get your pajamas, brush your teeth, throw all your clothes in the laundry hamper. Can you do all that?"

"Okay," he said, sounding far away.

Owen walked to the closet, picked up his pajamas and went into the bathroom. Jay left him and put the new bedding—now demoted to spares thanks to Marion's efforts—into the closet in his own room. He glanced at the strong box as he did it, thinking of the guns, not wanting to think of them just yet, though he knew he wouldn't be able to walk about unarmed for much longer.

By the time he got back, Owen was piling his discarded clothes into the hamper. It hardly seemed possible, but he looked even younger in his pajamas as he plodded toward the futon and fell into it.

Jay crouched down again and pulled the duvet over him, then said, "Okay, I'll leave the bathroom light on and I'll leave the bedroom door open. I'm not going anywhere, so you just yell out if you need me. Okay?"

He nodded from the edge of sleep and sounded like a drunk as he said, "Goodnight, Jay."

"Goodnight, Owen."

The boy was gone, probably falling away into a world that was still familiar to him, of his mom and Walden and

Isaac Gleick and all the once-significant details of the life that had been his back in Colorado.

Jay closed the bathroom door over so just a sliver of light shone through. He did the same with the bedroom door, then poured himself a drink and walked out onto the balcony.

The sun was just setting, which only served to highlight the axis-shift in Jay's world since he'd sat here at the end of the previous night, watching the first hints of dawn creeping into the eastern sky.

The lights were beginning to come on below, and the soundscape was shifting into evening, a lull punctuated occasionally by high performance cars and bikes opening up, and by the shrill buzz of teenagers on scooters. It had been Jay's playground for the last six months, but for tonight at least, it was all a million miles away.

He sent a message to Marion, thanking her. Then he sent an email to Gillian Bryson, an old contact at Langley, explaining the situation to her and asking if she could get a couple of numbers for him—one for Megan, one for her attorney. Finally, he called Amandine, something he hardly ever did.

"Well, hello," she said, pleasantly surprised. "Don't tell me *you* are going to invite *me* to dinner."

It was true, he let her do all the running, although she didn't seem to mind, treating him like a stray or a wild animal that only came by to be fed.

"I'd love to, but… short version—it turns out I have a ten year old son, Owen, and his mother showed up today and left him with me."

There was a moment of stunned silence, like static on the line.

"He's there now, in your apartment?"

"Yeah."

"But for how long?"

Her tone was mildly aggrieved, as if Jay were acting unreasonably.

"I don't know. His mother, she… I can only assume she's had some kind of breakdown. She's flown back to America. She wants me to keep him, which I can't, obviously, not indefinitely. But it's not like I can throw him out on the street—he's ten."

As he spoke he had one ear trained on the apartment. He was pretty sure Owen wouldn't have heard him even if he'd been awake, which he almost certainly wasn't. Even so, Jay made a mental note to avoid saying things like that in future—whatever the reality, he didn't want Owen thinking he wasn't wanted.

"Goodness, Jay, this is a lot to take in."

"Tell me about it. I mean, he's a sweet kid. Maybe you can meet him tomorrow."

"I'm not so sure about that." She hadn't even paused, and Jay could understand that, because twenty-four hours ago, he probably would have responded in the same way. "You know, Jay, children are not really my thing."

"I get that. But you know, he's gonna be around now for…" How long? Even if Gillian came back with the numbers tonight, he probably couldn't call Megan until tomorrow. Nor had Megan seemed like someone about to change her mind, but even if she did, it might be days more, even a week, before she could come and collect Owen. "I think he'll be around for at least the next week. Maybe even longer."

Even as he said it, he knew that a week was too long, with things set to heat up in the days ahead. He felt the urgency of the situation, the need to reunite mother and son as soon as it was practically possible.

Another pause followed, this one briefer, before Amandine said decisively, "Of course, and it's important you spend time with him. He's your son, after all." There was a hard edge to her voice now. It made him realize that for all the time he'd spent in bed with this woman, there was no real intimacy between them. Backing up that newfound awareness, she sounded businesslike as she said,

"So maybe we should take a little break, until, well, you know, until we know where we are."

"Sure, that makes sense."

He wasn't even surprised. And yet he felt her stance said as much about him—or the person he'd been until that very morning, and possibly still was—as it did about Amandine.

"Actually, it could be good timing anyway. My sister asked me to visit her on Capri and I was in two minds. Perhaps I'll go."

"You should," he said. "And we'll see how things are when you get back and we'll take it from there."

Jay's mind was already racing, spurred by the mention of Capri into remembering that he needed to reroute a billion dollar shipment of cocaine that was headed right now for Algiers and then on toward Italy.

"Yes, I think it's best. Bye, Jay."

Her goodbye sounded final, and it perhaps said everything about the shallowness of their relationship that he felt a small degree of relief. He had more important things to think about in the coming days than his questionable relationship status, and in many respects, Owen wasn't even at the top of that list.

11

Jay got up at seven, but even then, the last hour or so of sleep had been fitful, imagining Owen would be awake and feeling lost. But when he looked in, the boy was sleeping soundly, sprawled out on his back.

Jay made himself some breakfast, noticing that Marion had also stocked up on cereal and other essentials. It was as if she'd singlehandedly set about turning this apartment into a home, although Jay guessed it would take more than breakfast cereal and superhero posters to do that, and he was pretty sure he didn't possess the extra qualities needed to complete the transformation.

It was well after nine when he finally heard movement, then the sound of the shower running in Owen's bathroom. The boy seemed precociously self-reliant for a ten year old, and when he finally came through he was dressed, even wearing his sneakers.

"Hello," he said, a hint of uncertainty about him.

"Morning, Owen. Did you sleep well?"

He smiled as if reminded of something noteworthy, and said, "Like, for so long. And I didn't wake up at all. But I didn't sleep on the plane, or maybe just a little. I was *really* tired, Jay."

"I'm sure you were—it was a long journey and a long day. So how about some breakfast? Marion bought different cereals."

He appeared hesitant and said, "Um, should I put my clothes from yesterday in the wash?"

"No, you can just leave them in the hamper." Jay struggled even to understand the question. "Do you usually wash your own clothes at home?"

"All the time. Mom says it's important for me to be able to look after myself. Because of the poor people. Or something. In Central America?"

Jay could kind of see where Megan was coming from, but it seemed extraordinary to put a child in that position, particularly when he was clearly too young to fully understand her reasoning. He was acutely conscious, too, that in the six years after his own mother had died, a total of four different women had kept house for his dad and him, two from Mexico, one from Honduras and one from El Salvador. Nor would his current lifestyle meet with Megan's approval.

"Well, there is a washing machine, but I'm not even sure if it works. Marion takes the laundry somewhere."

"Where does she take it?"

"I don't know."

Owen laughed, like Jay had said something outrageous, and all the way through breakfast, he kept giggling to himself, no doubt each time he thought of it.

When Marion arrived, Jay and Owen left, taking the elevator down to the parking garage. Jay pointed to the car and Owen automatically went to climb in the back.

"You can sit in the front."

"Really? Am I allowed?"

Jay shrugged. He had no idea what the rules were.

"We're not going very far."

As they pulled out of the garage, Owen stretched out imperiously on the leather seat, saying, "This is so cool. It's like a new car."

Jay said, "Yeah, it's pretty new, but I don't drive it much."

"No sh… I mean, no kidding! It even smells like a new car."

Jay smiled to himself. Among all her strictures, Megan had apparently still managed to raise Owen as a potty-mouth. Under the circumstances, he was showing incredible self-control in censoring himself for Jay's benefit.

They drove beyond the station and up the winding road that rose up into the hills immediately behind Cotignac-sur-Mer. The houses soon started to thin out, then to become more distant from the electric gates that protected them.

Jay pulled off the road, driving up to a solid metal gated entrance that didn't allow for any view at all of the house beyond. The cameras trained on the car were the only indication of a human presence.

After a few seconds, the gate slid open and Jay drove through into the lush gardens beyond. He stopped then, waiting for the four guards—two more than on his last visit—to wave him on. He wouldn't have gotten past the gate if he hadn't been known to them, but he still didn't want to drive past without their consent. He could see they were fidgety, expecting an attack, if not now, then sometime soon.

Owen stared out at the guards and said, "What kind of guns are they?"

"Heckler & Koch MP5s." He hadn't given this much thought to guns in over a decade. "Why, do you like them?"

"They look pretty cool. Are they good guns?"

Jay imagined Megan sitting in the back seat, patiently explaining that there were no good guns, and no good people who used them.

"Pretty good, in the right hands. I prefer a handgun myself."

"Me too." He looked at Jay. "I mean when I'm playing games."

"Yeah? Not when you're out shooting up the neighborhood?"

Owen laughed, a laugh which ironically made Jay think he needed to be more responsible in the things he said.

Then as they drove the hundred yards up the drive they got the first complete view of Petrov's Belle Epoque villa and Owen stopped laughing and said, "Wow! He must be like a billionaire."

"He's definitely that."

He pulled up and a valet came out to take the car from him, like they were arriving at some exclusive resort. The main door opened as they approached and one of Petrov's assistants—a young clean-cut guy who looked like a junior political aide, and whose name Jay had never learned—ushered them in.

"Good morning, Mr Lewis. Mr Petrov is expecting you in his study."

"Thanks."

They walked through the gaudily opulent entrance hall and the assistant opened the door into the study which had the look of being modeled on the library of a 19th Century British aristocrat, albeit without the sense of refuge—Jay doubted any of the leather-bound books lining the shelves had ever been opened, let alone read.

Petrov was sitting in one of the leather armchairs, his bulk wedged into it so that the leather looked like just another layer of his clothing. He spoke to the assistant in Russian, telling him to bring Alexei, his son.

Then he turned to Jay, gesturing to the armchair facing his.

"I heard you'd gained a son."

"News travels fast, Vitali." He sat down and pointed for Owen to sit on a nearby couch. "This is Owen."

Petrov looked at the boy.

"His mother is not here?"

"No, she left. Owen's staying with me for a little while."

Petrov nodded. Jay knew that his own wife was somewhere in this house, yet he'd never seen her. He'd only seen Alexei a couple of times in passing.

With that, the door opened and the strikingly blond Alexei Petrov came in. Vitali's heavy eyes lit up and he smiled with a level of indulgence Jay could never have imagined.

The boy came over and hugged his father. He was around the same height as Owen, though maybe a little heavier, but the way he acted around his father made him seem much younger. In turn, Petrov stroked his hair and kissed him, then held him by the shoulders and spoke quietly to him in Russian—Jay heard him mention Owen's name, but that was all.

Alexei was rapt as his father spoke, then turned and smiled at Owen.

"Hello, Owen. I'm Alexei."

"Hey, hello."

"Would you like to come see my room?"

"Um, sure." He looked to Jay who nodded, and then the two boys walked out with Alexei talking excitably. It made Jay wonder how often he got to mix with other kids.

Petrov looked on with remarkable tenderness as they left the room, then turned back to Jay and his expression regained its usual demeanor, an uncompromising rockface of somberness.

"Did you learn anything from the Russian?"

He was talking about Georgy Gumilev, because of course, the easiest way for Jay to cover his own duplicity had been to convince Petrov that he was playing Georgy.

"He was evasive about some of the details—I don't think he suspects me, but I'll need to be careful how much I push him."

"Hopefully not for too much longer. What *did* you learn from him?"

"As we suspected, Minsk is sending people down in the next few days. He said they'll probably use Bogdanov's villa as a base, which is what we anticipated. He was hazy about the numbers, but he let slip that some of them are former Alpha Group."

"Not current Alpha Group?"

"No, he specifically said they have some *former* Alpha Group people with them."

"Good." He didn't quite smile, but he came close. If the regime wasn't trusting this operation to current Alpha Group members, it suggested they were uncertain of their loyalty, which in turn made Petrov think he'd be able to rely on them himself when the coup was instigated.

"There's something else I need to tell you." Petrov raised one eyebrow a fraction. "Something kept troubling me about the last couple of shipments getting intercepted by the authorities. Sure, it happens, but I was still suspicious. I couldn't help wondering if somebody here was working against your interests."

"Who did you have in mind?"

"No one in particular, not yet. I thought Bobo was a possibility, or maybe…" He left it hanging, certain Petrov would know he was implicating Stas without saying it aloud. "Look, who can say? But that's why I've changed the shipment. It'll be offloaded in Algiers tonight, put on board a cargo plane and flown to Brindisi early in the morning. The only people who know about the change are me, our Italian contacts, and now you."

"Can you trust the Italians?"

"One hundred percent."

"Then you're taking a big risk, no? If the shipment is intercepted, it puts you in the frame."

"That's the kind of risk you're paying me to take. More importantly, if the police raid the ship when it gets to Taranto, they won't find anything, but we'll know that someone here can't be trusted."

Vitali took that on board and said, "Did we have the details of the ship before Bobo was killed?"

"No, confirmation came the morning after."

Petrov nodded, looking deep in thought. If the ship was raided, and it would be—even with Benny being forced to stand down, Jay had still seen to it that the Italian authorities had received a tip-off about the cargo coming into Taranto from Algiers—then Petrov would be left speculating about which one of his inner circle was working against him.

"I like the way you operate, Jay—no fuss, no drama, just efficiency. This I will remember, when my time comes, you have my word."

"Thank you, Vitali, I appreciate that."

"Good, so, let us go out onto the terrace. I've arranged coffee."

They got up and walked out together, with Petrov talking about his favorite subject, the state of politics in America. Jay indulged him and acted the part of the loyal retainer, even as he imagined telling Petrov the unpalatable truth, that if Jay did his job right, Vitali's time would never come, or at least, not as he liked to imagine it.

12

They were still sitting on the terrace when the two boys emerged from the house, a volatile bundle of noise and energy. Alexei hesitated when he saw his father in conversation, and Owen stopped in synch with him, but Petrov's face transformed again and he waved them over.

He spoke in English this time, saying, "Have you had fun?"

Alexei responded eagerly, and said, "Papa, can Owen come sailing tomorrow?"

"Of course, if you want him to, but we have to ask his father first." He turned to Jay. "Alexei begins to learn sailing tomorrow, private instructors, naturally. Would you have any objection to Owen joining him?"

Jay was conscious of Owen desperately hoping for an affirmative but at the same time looking ready for disappointment. It would probably never occur to him that Jay might want him to spend as much time as possible with Alexei Petrov.

"I think that's a great idea."

Owen beamed. Alexei threw his arms around Petrov and kissed him. As excited as Owen was, he looked at the display of affection, then threw a brief comical grimace at Jay.

"I'll have someone pick him up at ten if that works for you."

"That's fine. We'll be ready."

He stood and they said their goodbyes. Owen and Alexei tried the complex handshake Owen had learned the day before, but the choreography quickly faltered and the two boys burst into fits of giggles. Petrov looked at his son with an affectionate smile, as if he'd only just noticed how rarely he saw Alexei being a young boy.

As Jay and Owen drove away, Jay said, "What did you think of Alexei?"

"He was okay. He's pretty babyish, but once you get talking to him he's not so bad, and he has *so* much cool stuff. Seriously, Jay, I've never seen so many games and toys, and all these different electronic things, like, not just computers and consoles, but *all* kinds. It was pretty awesome actually."

"Which reminds me, we need to get you some of those things this afternoon."

"Even if I'm not staying?"

Was Jay so transparent?

"Sure, why not. You're okay about staying with me, right?"

"Yeah, but, I guess… I don't know. I guess Mom might change her mind and come get me. She does that sometimes—change her mind, I mean."

Jay was kind of banking on it, as much as he liked the boy.

"Who knows what'll happen, but you don't have to worry about it."

"Okay."

"Good. Did Alexei tell you anything about his dad?"

"Like, all kinds of stuff. He said they're going to move back to Minsk soon. That's in Russia, right?"

"It's the capital of Belarus, next to Russia."

"Oh. Well, he said his dad's gonna be the president, but his mom doesn't want them to go."

"Did you meet his mom?"

"No, but she doesn't want them to go to Minsk. She thinks they could get hurt if they go back. Would you have to go with them?"

"No, Vitali pays me a retainer for security advice and other things, but I don't work for him as such. I certainly have no plans to visit Minsk."

"Alexei said it's really cold there in the winter. Like, colder than Canada."

"Maybe, although, Canada gets pretty cold."

"I thought that, too." He pondered for a second, as if suddenly questioning the veracity of everything Alexei had said. "I'll try to find out more tomorrow."

"You don't have to do that. It's good that you have a friend, and that you get to go sailing tomorrow. You don't have to find out anything for me. Just enjoy yourself."

Owen looked up at him, and said, "But it's good, isn't it? If he tells me things about his dad, it's good for you?"

There was no escaping it, he was more astute than Jay could have imagined, and he was right, about the wider situation, and about Jay himself. Yes, Owen was a child— *his* child—and he really did want him just to enjoy himself, but he also couldn't deny that Owen was a resource. When Georgy had suggested Owen might be useful, given the similarity in age between him and Alexei, this was exactly what he'd been referring to and Jay had known that, too. So, apparently, had Owen.

"Honestly? It could help me a lot. But here's the thing, don't ask questions, just give him the space to talk."

"I don't understand."

"Okay, if you ask him when exactly he's going back to Minsk, he might remember that he's not really meant to talk about it, so he'll get suspicious and stop telling you stuff. By the sound of it, if you just let him talk, he'll tell you all kinds of things. And you can direct him if you need to. So, when you're sailing tomorrow, you can ask if he'll be able to go sailing when he's in Minsk. See, doesn't sound suspicious, but it gives him a reason to start talking about going back there."

"I *get it.* Yes. Okay."

He looked deep in thought for a while as he absorbed this exchange. Jay could imagine Megan's outraged reaction if she found out Jay had ostensibly been a father for twenty-four hours and was already using his new-found child as an asset. It wasn't quite like that, or not entirely, but Megan wouldn't see it that way.

He'd call her tonight anyway, and he fully expected her to be contrite now that she'd had time to consider what she'd done. He wouldn't tell her how difficult it might be to have Owen stay here, because he doubted that would sway her. Nor would he suggest Owen was missing her because he wasn't entirely convinced that was the case, not yet at least. But as he'd just suggested to Owen regarding his dealings with Alexei, so Jay would simply aim to give Megan enough space to see that this had been a mistake.

He'd bring her round, he was confident of that. But he glanced across at the boy, so small in the leather expanse of the passenger seat, and he hoped he was doing the right thing for him too. Not just right in the short term—getting him away from Cotignac before things got dangerous in the coming week or so—but also right in the long term. Jay wasn't father material, but on the little evidence he had, he wasn't convinced Megan was mother material either, and he suspected that Owen probably deserved better than the both of them.

13

As Jay had promised, they bought a whole bunch of tech in the afternoon—a cellphone, a laptop, a games console and a TV. Most of it they took home with them. The TV was delivered later in the afternoon, while Owen was sleeping.

Despite the mammoth sleep session of the previous night, the boy had visibly been in need of a siesta, but had assured Jay that this was not normal, that he didn't usually sleep much at all.

When he woke, they set everything up. Jay's only stipulation was that for now it was probably best he didn't get in touch with Walden, for a few weeks at least. Truth was, Jay thought any renewed contact between Owen and Walden was likely to result in some kind of activity that might reduce the chances of Megan taking him back.

Jay let him play for a little while on one of his new games, then said, "Okay, let's get ready and go for dinner."

Owen looked to the window, then back at Jay. "Seriously? It's nearly night-time."

"Like I told you, people down here take their kids out at night. You're not ready for bed, are you?"

"No, I only just woke up."

"Exactly. You can just throw a shirt on. Might be an idea to bring a sweater, too, in case it's cold on the way back."

"Are we walking?"

Jay guessed walking from place to place was a novelty for Owen. Despite its affluence, West Bedford had been a walking town by US standards. Denver, or at least Megan and Owen's part of it, clearly hadn't been.

"Yeah, we're walking, it's just down the hill a little way. So, give me ten minutes. If you're ready before me you can play some more on your games."

"Okay."

Jay went and jumped in the shower, dressed and came back through. He expected Owen to be deep in PlayStation territory but he was just coming out of the bathroom. He was wearing a long sleeve shirt, creased here and there, but in what appeared a studied way, with a sweater thrown over his shoulders and the arms tied loosely across his chest.

"Is this okay? I didn't know what to do with the sweater."

The kid had a natural style—he looked so much like something out of a photoshoot that Jay was worried he might be letting his son down.

"That's perfect. You look like a young gentleman."

Owen looked thrilled by the compliment, a response that once again saddened Jay in some small way—did no one pay him these small easy compliments, that he was smart, handsome, well-behaved, all the things people routinely said to kids to bolster their self-esteem?

"Let's hit the town."

They walked down to the Yacht Club. Despite Owen's earlier alarm, they were still in full daylight and the warmth of afternoon lingered on. They sat inside, but Owen looked with fascination beyond the diners on the marina-side terrace, gazing at the yachts and superyachts that lay moored beyond.

"Is that where I'll be going tomorrow?"

"I don't know. Possibly."

The waiter came over with the menus, the same waiter Stas had chased away a few days before. He said hello to Jay, then turned and smiled broadly at Owen and said, "Good evening, Sir. Your menu."

"Thank you."

Owen studied the menu, then looked up at Jay and said, "This is great. It's in French but they have the English written below."

Jay was surprised all over again by the kind of thing a child could be impressed by. His own childhood seemed so distant, it felt now as if he'd never been this full of incidental wonder.

The waiter came back and Owen said, "Please could I get the ham, and then, the pasta with truffle."

"Of course, Sir."

Jay said, "You know what truffle is?"

"Yeah, I had it once. It's kind of like a mushroom. They grow in the ground and they use dogs to find them. It's so cool."

The waiter looked on in approval, and Jay said, "I'll have the same."

"Of course. And a bottle of the Hermitage?"

"I think so. Owen, what would you like to drink?"

"Um…"

The waiter said, "Might I suggest some elderflower syrup with sparkling water and lots of ice—it's very refreshing."

"Okay, thanks."

Before the waiter could leave, Jay added, "And we'll need a small pause between the starter and the main. I have to make a phone call."

"Of course, Mr Lewis."

The waiter left and Owen looked around, taking in the surroundings, the quiet chatter, the sound of drinks being mixed at the bar.

"This place is great! Do you come here every night?"

"Not every night. I do come here a lot. I've only been living here six months."

Owen's mouth dropped open. "But everybody knows you."

"Yeah, it's that kind of place."

He could have corrected the boy, of course—it was the kind of place where everyone *thought* they knew him.

It was 8.30 by the time they finished their starters, and Jay wanted to call Denver before the lunch hour, so he pointed to the long verandah along the beach-side of the restaurant—empty at this time of evening—although people occasionally went out there to smoke.

"I need to make a call, but I'll be just out there. Will you be okay?"

"Totally." He pointed at his plate. "That ham was amazing."

Jay smiled, feeling treacherous, and walked out to the verandah. He looked down at the handful of people idling along the beach, enjoying the last of the sun, as he put in a call to the cellphone number Gillian Bryson had found for him—Megan's.

That was where he hit his first stumbling block. It was disconnected. He tried again to be sure. Then he called the other number, for *Bixby, Clementi & Wheeler*, Megan's attorneys.

This time he got an answer, and said, "Good afternoon, could I speak with Diana Clementi. My name's Jay Lewis. I'm calling about Megan and Owen Anderson."

"Thank you, Mr Lewis. Please hold. I'll just put you through to her secretary." He was put on a hushed muzak-free hold for a full minute before another voice, almost indistinguishable from the first, came on. "Good afternoon, Mr Lewis, I'm Ms. Clementi's secretary. She's just finishing up with a client, but I'm certain she'd be happy to speak with you, if you don't mind holding for just a minute or two?"

"Sure, that's fine, I'll hold, thanks."

"Thank you."

The hush resumed. He walked once up and down the verandah, then glanced in through the full height windows to check on Owen. He saw immediately that someone was sitting with him. At first glance, he imagined it was Amandine but then realized it was Harriet Baverstock. They were engaged in an animated conversation, with Harry laughing as Owen explained something.

Jay's first instinct was that Harry was getting information from him. But the more he looked and waited, the more he thought it was exactly what it appeared, a simple joyous conversation between an adult and a child. Watching it unfold left him feeling even more unsuited to the role he'd been handed.

"Sorry to keep you, Mr Lewis, what can I do for you?"

He snapped his attention back and turned to face the beach again as he said, "Ms. Clementi?"

"Please, call me Diana."

"Okay, thanks, Diana. I believe my… um, Megan Anderson, she's a client of yours."

"That's correct."

"And I have the documents your office prepared for her, so I'm guessing you know she's left Owen with me."

Her tone was deliberate when she answered. "I knew that was her plan, but I wasn't privy to her intended timetable.

Naturally, I'm pleased you've managed to come to a suitable arrangement."

"A suitable arrangement? Diana, she showed up here in the South of France, told me about Owen, gave me a package of documents. Then she went to the bathroom and never came back."

There was a pause. "I see. I wasn't aware that you were living overseas. Not that it has any direct bearing."

"Really? That's your takeaway from this? That I live overseas?"

"I'm sure you'll understand, Mr Lewis, that there's a very limited amount I can say about the situation. Megan is my client, you are not. I can express my concern and my sympathy about the nature of the handover as you describe it, but there's little more I can add. You'd have to discuss it with Megan herself."

"Which I'd like to do, but I just tried her cellphone and it seems to be disconnected."

"Yes, I was aware of that. She also anticipated that you might contact me, and authorized me to tell you that she's gone off grid, effective immediately, no phone, and a PO Box for her mailing address. She felt she needed to undertake such measures to ensure you couldn't track her down."

"And you consider that… normal?"

"Sadly, Mr Lewis, I deal with a lot of clients who are escaping from abusive partners—not that I'm suggesting you are in that category, but it means I do consider such extreme measures normal. And the fact that you managed to track down her cellphone number, something I didn't even have, suggests that her concerns were well-founded."

Jay sighed. He glanced in again at Owen and Harry, still chatting away like old friends, looking light years away from where Jay was right now.

"Diana, I just want what's best for Owen. He's a ten year old boy, and I work in a security environment, hardly a suitable life for a child. I get that Megan seems to have had some sort of… I'm happy to help, of course I am, now that I know about him, but I think—"

"Mr Lewis, let me save you the trouble. She won't have him back. Even if you were able to contact her, I feel it's important for you to understand… the strength and… intractability of her feelings on this matter. She simply won't have him back, I'm one hundred percent certain of it."

"What about his grandparents?"

It was Diana Clementi's turn to sigh.

"She has specifically refused to grant them access, citing the psychological abuse she says she experienced in her own childhood and adolescence."

Jay wasn't even sure where to begin with that one, but he didn't need to because she continued to speak.

"Look, Mr Lewis… I have no doubt you understand that I'm very limited in what I can say to you, but let me put it like this… You said you want what's best for Owen, and in my considered opinion, as an attorney, but also as a parent, Owen is far better with you than in any of the alternate scenarios you might imagine, even if they were all possible, which they're not."

"How can you say that, Diana? You don't know anything about me."

"That's true. All I know is that you worked for the government back when you knew Megan. Nothing else." Her tone became freighted with meaning as she added, "And yet still, I stand by what I said. Owen is almost certainly better off with you."

"I see."

Megan hadn't been cruel to Owen, he was convinced of that. So was this just Diana Clementi's view of Megan's mental stability? And amazingly, he found himself getting defensive on Megan's behalf—maybe it was just a dry-as-dust attorney reacting against someone who was passionate, emotional… someone who could leave her child on the other side of the world, with no means of him ever finding a way back.

"I'm sorry I wasn't able to help you more, Mr Lewis. But I wish you well. I know Owen has had some issues, but if it's any consolation, my interactions with the boy didn't support the portrayal painted by Megan—"

"You're saying it's all in her mind? That she's unwell?"

"No I'm not. And you must know I wouldn't comment on such things, even if I were to believe them. What I am saying is that with the right support and stability, I'm confident Owen will thrive."

"So am I. I'm just not convinced that I'm the person to offer him that stability. I'm happy to play a part in his life, but... Look, I can't go into the details, so can I just ask you to contact Megan, ask her if she'll reconsider, or if she'll allow him to go her parents."

"I'm more than happy to put that to her, Mr Lewis, but I have to forewarn you, it's highly unlikely."

"But you'll try?"

"Uneasy as it makes me, I will try, and I'll contact you on this number if she relents."

"Thank you, and thanks for your time."

He ended the call and looked out at the beach. There were still a dozen or so people strolling along, mainly couples of all ages, enjoying the peace and the relative cool now that the sun was finally falling low behind the headland in the west.

He was acutely aware that this final roll of the dice was unlikely to yield results, and he wasn't even sure what would be best for Owen anyway. Diana Clementi couldn't tell him the full truth of why she felt the way she did, and Jay couldn't tell her exactly why his life was never likely to provide the support and stability Owen apparently needed.

One thing Jay knew for sure, his own life was so lacking in child-friendly qualities that he couldn't even think of anyone he could call on to ask for help. And until he *could* think of another solution—or unless a miracle occurred and Megan gave approval for the boy to stay with his "psychologically abusive" grandparents—it looked like Jay was Owen's only option.

14

He walked back in and Harry stopped talking and looked up, saying, "Sorry to intrude, I'll leave you two alone."

"Not at all. Um, how did you…"

"Oh, I was just coming in as you went out to make your call, and I have eyes so I was able to deduce that Owen's your son. Thought you wouldn't be terribly upset about me introducing myself."

She stood now, her eyes fixed on his, a lively quality to her gaze that he was afraid he might be misinterpreting.

"No, I don't mind at all. Are you here to eat? You're welcome to join us."

"I fear I've intruded enough, but thank you."

"I think it's better than eating on your own." They both looked down at Owen and he looked back at them as if to say he was only stating the obvious. "I mean, unless you'd prefer that."

She smiled at him. "Well, as long as I'm not cramping your style."

Jay waved to the waiter who came over without being asked and arranged another place at the table. Harry ordered a main course of lamb, but accepted the offer to share Jay's wine.

Once they were all sitting with Jay facing the pair of them, Harry said, "Owen was telling me he's going sailing tomorrow, but was very mysterious about who he was going with."

Owen looked up at him. "I didn't know if I was allowed to tell."

Harry threw a teasing glance at Jay, and said, "So discreet for one so young, like a little spy." She nudged Owen conspiratorially and he smiled, but looked flattered too.

"Well, discretion's the better part of valor. But I think it's okay for you to know on this occasion. He's sailing with Alexei Petrov."

"Ah, of course, hence the secrecy." She turned to Owen. "Do you like him?"

"Yeah, he's okay. I only just arrived, so I don't really have any friends."

"*Excuse* me! I thought we were getting on so well."

He frowned. "Harry! I mean friends my own age."

She pulled a face at him and they both laughed. Jay was mystified, that this chemistry could have emerged between them almost instantaneously. Even as the meal went on, the two of them just seemed a natural fit with each other. It also made Jay wonder if he'd been imagining the chemistry between himself and Harry—quite possibly she was like this with everyone.

When Owen went to the bathroom, Harry said, "What an adorable child."

"Thanks. I only met him for the first time yesterday."

"Oh, I know. I got the whole hysterical lowdown about Isaac Gleick and the cops, then coming here, his mother absconding. Did you even know about him?"

"Not at all. And I'm not sure what to do about him, either. The phone call just now was with his mom's attorney. She doesn't want him back, under any circumstances, and the attorney hinted that might be for the best."

"Good Lord." She looked shocked, even upset. "Grandparents?"

"She doesn't talk to her parents, and she's adamant that they don't have any involvement in his upbringing."

"What about yours?"

"Mine died when I was young."

"Of course, I'm sorry. I think I read about that." She looked apologetic. "Just a standard background briefing."

"Did the briefing mention that I had a son?"

She laughed, then looked toward the door to the bathrooms and said, "That said, could be tricky having a child here in the next few weeks. But I'm sure you don't need me to tell you that." He poured more wine into both their glasses. "Thanks. I'm sure you also don't need me to tell you, but just in case, I understand there are people coming down from Minsk in the next day or two. They might consider you a target."

"Thanks. I did know, but I appreciate the heads up. I guess I need to find out what Rich McKenzie's plans are."

"Yes. It's perhaps getting to the point where I need to introduce myself to him, too. He's staying at the Grand."

"And are you still here as just an observer?"

"I am. I don't see that changing, but I suppose it only takes a phone call."

With that, Jay's phone buzzed. He picked it up, glanced at the simple message—*friends arrived safely*—and put it down again. She was looking expectantly at him when he raised his eyes again.

"Just a message telling me a billion dollars' worth of cocaine arrived safely in southern Italy. That'll finance Petrov's coup in Belarus."

She burst out laughing.

"You really are something, Jay. Owen's better at keeping secrets than you are."

Jay raised his hands in admission, but said, "Did you know about the shipment?"

"Yes."

"And I guess you knew it wasn't gonna be intercepted by the authorities?"

"Also yes."

"And you know Petrov is planning a coup in Belarus?"

She smiled grudgingly. "Point taken. But if those are the things you're open about, it really does make me wonder what kind of secrets you *do* keep."

Before he could answer, Owen came back and said, "The hand dryer in that bathroom is the coolest thing ever. It's like a spaceship. You put your hands in and it lights them up, like from the inside."

"Then I should go and try it," said Harry and stood. "If you'll excuse me."

Owen sat down, still excited about the hand dryer, then looked up at Jay and said, "Isn't she amazing?"

Jay had to agree with that, but said, "I've only met her two times before tonight."

"She's English. That's why she speaks the way she does."

"I did not know that."

Owen stared at him for a second, then laughed. It was such an infectious laugh that, for a moment, Jay wished Diana Clementi might be right, and that this might be the best place for Owen. But just wishing for it didn't make it true.

15

The next morning, one of Petrov's men came to collect Owen. Jay checked with Marion to see if her niece, Juliette, could stay with Owen for the next two evenings. He wanted to get the lie of the land and a feel for how things might develop over the next week or so. Above all, he needed to find out whether he had time to get Owen somewhere else, if that somewhere else even existed.

He drove toward Nice then, but turned off and headed up into the hills. Bogdanov's estate was just as sheltered from the road as Petrov's was, and had the same array of cameras on the gates. Jay didn't even stop, merely slowed as he continued past the gates and up the hill.

He'd been online and found a vacation home that was for sale, a short distance up the hill but on a small plot which was ungated. He turned into the drive and, finding the house closed up, he parked and popped the trunk. He set up the laptop, then readied the drone and set it off to scope Bogdanov's place.

Only a small fraction of roof was visible from here, a patch of terracotta, but it was enough for him to guide the drone in by sight. Once he was above the property, he turned to the laptop and looked down.

There were three vehicles parked to the front of it, two SUVs and a sedan, all BMWs by the look of them. There were tire marks in the gravel, too. Beyond that, there was no sign of occupation, no sign of life—the swimming pool was empty, so were the terraces, and the security lodge by the gates looked unoccupied.

If Bogdanov or members of his family had been there, Jay would have expected to see people about, not least security. He would have expected someone to spot the drone, too, and maybe even to bring it down.

So he guessed the cars belonged to the team that had come down from Minsk. They were here, but apparently sitting tight for the time being, waiting for their moment.

Jay did one more sweep with the drone, filming the perimeter, entry points to the building, key sections of the grounds. He doubted he'd need to come back up here, but he also couldn't be sure he'd get another chance at this kind of unimpeded surveillance.

He brought the drone back and stowed it. Then he put Petrov's address into the satnav to get an idea of the route they'd have to take from here. Sure enough, there was a back way, climbing a little farther into the hills, then dropping down again above Cotignac-sur-Mer. Jay switched on the dashcam to record the route and set off, stopping at Petrov's to update him.

When he told him, Petrov said, "What are they waiting for?"

"Orders, probably. The key question is what are they planning?"

"To kill me, of course."

"Killing you would be ideal. Prevents the coup, deters others, shows the regime has reach. But killing you is also difficult. Any direct attack on this place would be tough, unless they're sending down a lot more people. But they could target the people around you. I hope the boys enjoy their sailing today, but for the next few days, maybe even the next few weeks, I'd think about keeping Alexei within the estate."

"No." His tone was uncompromising. "Vitali Petrov shows no fear to anyone. You don't control a country like Belarus without being strong, and fearless." Petrov had won over plenty of people in the West with his talk of democracy, and Jay wondered how those people would react now to hear him talk about *controlling* Belarus. "I'll send more men with him, but Alexei will be sailing again tomorrow and the next day. I was hoping your son might also join him again?"

It was a test, of loyalty, or of belief in Petrov's power. Jay could have pointed out that Vitali himself hadn't left his estate in over a week, but in reality, there was only one acceptable answer.

"If it were anyone else in this situation, Vitali, my answer would be no. But I know you don't take your own son's safety lightly, so I know I can trust Owen to be safe, too."

"Good. Alexei has so few friends of his own age. He was very excited last night."

"So was Owen. I think they like each other a lot."

"Children," said Petrov. Jay had no idea what he meant by that, but Petrov changed track then. "What can you tell me about the CIA man?"

"I'm aiming to catch up with him today as it happens. The Americans won't want to be seen supporting you publicly, but that's why he's here, to offer support—"

"You're certain of this?"

"No question of it. He was sent down to offer any help he can. That's why I need to meet him again. I want to know exactly what he can do for us."

"What kind of status does he have?"

It was a smart question. Petrov wanted to know how much the CIA—and by association, the US Government— valued him and wanted him to succeed. If he knew that Jay wouldn't have trusted Rich McKenzie to infiltrate a troop of boy scouts, he'd be indignant.

"I'm not plugged in to the current crop of officers, but my instinct? He's top flight. They wouldn't have sent him down here on his own if they didn't think he could handle it."

Petrov looked satisfied with that. Jay only hoped McKenzie didn't prove him wrong too soon.

He called into the Grand Hotel after lunch and asked to see Rich McKenzie, but the receptionist looked at the computer screen in front of him and said, "I'm sorry, Sir, we don't have anyone staying here with that name."

Jay thought back again on how he'd talked up McKenzie to Petrov, and now he was faced with this level of amateurish behavior—he'd been all around town handing out business cards with his name on them, but had asked the hotel to register him under an alias, like some kind of celebrity, or some kind of intelligence officer.

Jay took the business card out and put it on the desk. "The yacht broker."

The receptionist lowered his eyes to look at the card, and said diplomatically, "I think I might know who you mean. But the gentleman in question is not here. He had some other business to attend to, and won't be back at the hotel until the day after tomorrow." He pointed to the bottom of the card. "Perhaps you could try his cellphone?"

"Thanks, I'll do that."

Jay walked into the bar, ordered a drink and tried the number on the card. It seemed the cellphone was switched off. He tried it again for good measure, then looked around the bar and was surprised to note he didn't recognize anyone. Maybe this what the summer season would be like, more faces but fewer familiar ones.

He sent a message to Benny, telling him that the regime in Minsk had a whole bunch of people camped out at Bogdanov's place. Five minutes later, he got a reply, saying, "Some of them—more are on the way." Jay asked him if he knew what their plans were and Benny wrote back, "I was hoping you might tell me."

Jay finished his drink and took a slow stroll back to the apartment, in plenty of time for Owen returning at four. He was relieved when Petrov's man brought him back, escorting him right to the door of the apartment. And he was surprised by how happy he was to see Owen's broad smile.

As soon as they were alone, he stood in the middle of the living room and said, "Jay, that was amazing! I loved it so much."

"Good, you know you're going again tomorrow and the next day?"

Owen punched the air and said, "Yes!" He came over, hugged him, then stepped back again and said, "Seriously, I think you'd have been really pleased. I was pretty good at it."

"I have no doubt about it. How was Alexei?"

"He was okay. I think he found it kind of hard to begin with. I thought he might lose his temper a couple of times but he just laughed it off. He's actually a good kid, just…"

"Just?"

"I don't know how to describe it. I don't think he gets to be around other kids very much."

"I think you're right. Now, you need a sleep?"

"*No*? I did tell you that I don't sleep all the time."

"I know, but you've had a long day."

"So have you."

"True." In fact, Jay was shocked by how long his day had felt. "So how about you help me prepare some dinner for later?"

"We're not eating at the Yacht Club?"

He was taken aback by the speed with which Owen was adapting to this lifestyle.

"No, we're eating at home for the next two nights, and I have to go out, but Marion's niece is coming to sit with you."

"Okay, what are we having?"

"Just some salad, pasta, ham, pretty much all the things we ate last night, but prepared by us instead of a top chef. It'll be fun."

Owen looked skeptical, but once they got started he seemed to enjoy helping Jay prepare the food, to the extent that Jay imagined it wasn't something he did with his mom back home in Denver.

That notion was confirmed by Owen when he said, "I never made food before."

"Really? Nothing at all?"

"No, nothing. Mom always says it's not good for me to be around knives." Jay wasn't sure if Megan thought that was for Owen's safety or for other people's. "But Mom doesn't cook much, either. Did you cook when you were a kid?"

"Yeah, when I was small my mom used to have me help her make cakes and cookies and things like that."

After she'd died, he'd also cooked dinner three or four times a week, depending on the housekeeper in place at the time, or how determined Jay had been to avoid his dad's overreliance on takeout. In the first couple of years, they'd eaten out once or twice a week, too, but Jay had found those meals excruciating, sensing that everyone knew who they were and what grief had befallen them, watching as his dad worked his way joylessly through a bottle of wine.

He didn't feel the need to share that history of cooking with Owen.

"That's so cool. I'd love to be able to do that, like cakes and things."

"Yeah? Maybe we can do it together sometime."

He was worried that he was starting to stack up promises he wouldn't get to keep, but Owen said, "Awesome. I'd love that. And like, Mom will be so amazed when she finds out."

"I guess that depends on how good the cakes are." He smiled at him, unsure whether or not Owen really believed he'd see his mother again—either way, it was pointless having him think about it, when in truth, neither of them knew what the future might hold. "You find out anything from Alexei today?"

"I was waiting for you to ask." He laughed to himself, at some private joke. "That's why we're sailing again tomorrow. I didn't know you'd let me, but he said they had to bring some of the lessons forward because he thinks they might go back to Minsk the Monday after next."

"Monday, he said that specific day?"

"Definitely. He said his dad's going back the day before, and Alexei and his mom are going on Monday."

"Interesting."

"Is it good information?"

If it was accurate, it was excellent information. It almost certainly meant Petrov was planning the coup for a week Sunday, which made sense—the elements of the military he was counting on for support would catch everyone else napping, unless there were demonstrations taking place, in which case the loyalist forces would be occupied with those instead.

"It's very good."

"Alexei says things could be pretty dangerous before that. He said one of his dad's men got killed last week."

"Yeah, I don't think that was connected with this, though."

"But could it be dangerous?" He looked up at Jay, curious rather than afraid.

"Possibly." Jay wasn't sure if honesty was the best policy here, but he'd prefer him to be prepared than not. "You don't have to worry about it, but you know, it's a good lesson for life, that if ever anything happens, like a terrorist attack or a crazy person with a gun, you run and hide. Run and hide, that's always the best way."

"Is that what you would do?"

Jay tried to conceal his smile—the kid was smart. "Yeah, most of the time. Sometimes you have no choice but to confront it, but if you do have the choice, it's not a computer game, you don't get three lives, so you run and hide."

Owen took that in, and looked deep in thought as he carefully sliced the tomatoes. Then he said, "Mom told me you killed people in Guatemala."

"Wow." Why would she tell him that? Why would she paint Jay the way she had and then bring Owen to live with him? "You know I worked for the government back then?"

"*Yeah.*"

"Well, it's like being in the military or the police— sometimes you have to kill people to stop then doing what they're doing. It's not something you do for fun, just a part of the job."

"Did it make you sad?"

"Honestly? No. It's hard to explain. It's like you just box it up, put it in the cellar and forget about it."

That wasn't entirely true. He did think about some of them sometimes. One of his kills in Guatemala had been a boy of about eighteen who'd looked even younger. Jay had surprised him sitting at a kitchen table, wearing little round glasses, studying a textbook. He still occasionally thought of that studious young face and wondered idly what he'd be doing now, approaching thirty, what hopes and dreams had been on the other side of that textbook. But there had also been a gun on the kitchen table that night, and the kid had gone for it and chosen his own fate in the process. So yes, he did think about it occasionally, sometimes with poignancy, but born of curiosity rather than a troubled conscience.

"When I hurt Isaac Gleick, they all asked me—like, Mom, and Principal Daniels and Mrs Singh, the counsellor—how I would have felt if he'd died."

"And what did you tell them?"

"I told them the truth. I said it was his own fault if he died and I wouldn't miss him because he wasn't my friend, and I said most of the kids in the school would have been happy anyway, even if they pretended to be sad at first, because he was just a bully."

"Yeah, I can't imagine why they threw you out."

Owen laughed and couldn't stop, and Jay laughed too, and struggled to understand how the world could turn against a kid with such a joyous and infectious laugh. Sure, he was a different drummer, and maybe there was something in Megan's claim that Owen was possessed of the same thing that was wrong with Jay, but standing here making salad together, Jay wouldn't have wanted it any other way.

16

Juliette was pretty and, like so many of the teenagers down here, emanated an air of breezy confidence. Jay thought Owen might be shy around her to begin with, but he was all open smiles and easy charm from the start and by the time Jay headed out they were sitting on the couch together laughing about things on their phones.

He headed to Zinc and had a drink with Lucien but hadn't been there long when Benny came in, once again looking more like a celebrity or high-roller than a police officer. It was unusual for him to come to Cotignac-sur-Mer, but he looked relaxed as he ordered a drink.

"I thought I might find you here. I already tried the Yacht Club."

"Am I so predictable?"

"It's a small town, and too early for the casino." He glanced around and said, "This place is perfect for you."

"How so?"

"Stylish, glamorous…" He gave him a sly smile. "And I don't understand it at all. What does *Zinc* even mean?"

"It's a metal we never think about but life would grind to a halt without it – still remind you of me?"

Benny laughed and gave Jay a mock salute.

They moved to a booth, and then Benny said, "It happens a ship arrived in Taranto this afternoon, from Algiers, and the ship was raided by the Italian authorities… after a tip-off, would you believe? I wonder who could have done that."

Jay said, "I did tell you I'd use it to my own advantage."

"Ha! So that also explains why they found nothing."

"I had the shipment brought in by plane to Brindisi, but I'll let Petrov know that the ship was intercepted. Might just sow a little more uncertainty in his camp."

"This makes what I have to tell you all the more intriguing." Jay looked expectant and Benny said, "I found out some more about the men at Bogdanov's villa. Naturally, we know their mission is to disrupt Petrov's plans. But we also believe that you might be a key target for them."

"Makes sense. I'm not in Petrov's inner circle, I'm not even sure I'm in his confidence, but they're not to know that."

"But that's what I don't understand, Jay. I've assumed for some time that you're working for the Russians—you clearly don't want Petrov to succeed—so you're on the same side as the people in Bogdanov's villa, and yet they're targeting you." Jay smiled. "What! I don't understand—that's what I'm telling you."

"Benny, I'm not working for the Russians. We share some of the same goals, that's all. And whatever happens, I'll be a target for one side or the other, so it doesn't really matter which. But I appreciate the tip."

"I hope it helps, I really do. I wouldn't like to see anything happen to you, Jay."

"Thanks."

He raised his glass and Benny followed suit, then said, "Where's your boy this evening?"

"Babysitter. I don't want him out with me so much until I know what's going down."

Benny was uncharacteristically somber in response. "That could be wise. Is your apartment secure?"

Jay said, "Secure enough to fend off a burglar, but a Belarussian hit squad? Not so sure."

"Is there nowhere else he can go, until this is all over?"

In theory, Jay could still get a call from Diana Clementi, telling him that Megan wanted Owen back or that she'd realized her parents weren't so bad after all, but it had never been highly likely and seemed less so with each passing hour.

"Looks like I'm all he's got."

"Well, as last resorts go, it's not so bad, to end up here, with you." He couldn't entirely hide his disquiet though. "For the next few weeks I'll see if I can arrange more of a police presence in the area around your building."

"Thanks. Should actually only be ten days."

"So soon?"

"Looks that way."

Benny said, "So what will you be doing until then? Anything I can know about, anything I *should* know?"

"I don't think so, Benny. I'll just be doing what I do, you know, drifting around town, picking up information, trying not to enjoy myself too much."

Benny smiled and finished his drink, but for the next day and a half, Jay drifted around without picking up any information and failed to enjoy himself at all. He needed to speak to Rich McKenzie, but he wasn't around. He wanted to see Harry again, just because, but she wasn't around either. Nor was Amandine, of course, and although he didn't much miss her, he missed her being there.

He remembered some old quote from Fitzgerald, saying no one was on the Cote d'Azur one summer before promptly reeling off a bunch of famous names of the people who actually were there. Cotignac actually felt empty suddenly, even as it visibly swelled with new arrivals day by day.

He guessed some of his sense of dislocation was centered around Owen. He'd only been there a few days, and despite Jay's assurances to the contrary, he kind of *was* in the way, and yet his arrival had inevitably made Jay reflect on the life he'd been living, and on what kind of future he might have.

The next day, when Owen was out sailing again, Jay stopped off at a café overlooking the marina and had a coffee. As he sat there at one of the outside tables, he idly watched the people walking by, then noticed a father and son on one of the moored sailing boats.

The boy looked a few years younger than Owen, but the father was showing him how to tie knots, with such patience, such reassurance, and the boy was concentrating so hard. And then after some frustration, the boy managed it and they high-fived and the father hugged him.

It made Jay forlorn, certain that he could not be that father, realizing also that he'd missed the same relationship with his own, latterly at least. In the years after his mother's death, he'd watched his dad's relentless decline into a destructive self-pity fueled by booze and pills, and he'd responded the only way he'd known how, by recoiling from it, retreating into his own world, away from that weakness.

He thought back to that lost boy, no less lost than Owen was now. He remembered being drawn constantly to every book or movie character who was a loner, who had no ties, drawn by the path out of where he'd found himself to where he'd wanted to be. Who he'd wanted to be. And now here he was, except all at once, his solitary lifestyle was gone.

The second night seemed even more desolate than the first, to the extent that Jay felt like going home and telling Juliette she could go early for the same amount of money. But Owen had been so happy to see her that Jay didn't want to ruin that simple pleasure.

Instead, he drifted to the Yacht Club and had a few drinks, chatting to a handful of people he really only knew through Amandine—two of them asked outright why he hadn't gone to Capri with her, which was his first confirmation that she'd even left. It was still before ten when he called it a night and strolled toward the apartment.

Away from the waterfront, the town was quiet, so as he turned up one narrow street he clearly saw ahead of him a young guy in black jeans and polo shirt getting out of a car and opening the back door. No one climbed out, but the guy left it open so that it was partially obstructing the sidewalk and got back into the driver seat.

It looked like the BMW sedan he'd spotted from the drone when he was scouting Bogdanov's place. The open door was no invitation, and Jay wasn't surprised when he looked behind and saw someone ten paces off, dressed the same way. He was a little closer in age to Jay, heavily built, sporting an oddly precise designer beard which looked out of place with his bulk and his shaved and scarred head.

He was also carrying a gun which he casually waved at Jay now, making sure he'd seen it. That was a relief. He was carrying a gun and hadn't used it yet, which meant they didn't plan to kill him here. They probably wanted to torture him first, get some information, but not getting shot on the street was at least something to work with.

17

As Jay reached the car, he leaned down and looked in at the driver, smiled and said hello. The guy turned—early twenties, trying not to look nervous, probably more afraid of his colleague than he was of Jay—but didn't say anything. He already had his seatbelt on, which was both conscientious and useful.

Jay stood upright again, turned to face the bigger guy behind him and said, "You want me to get in?"

"Strike a pose. Hands on the roof." His accent was convincingly American, suggesting he'd spent more than a little time there or watched a *lot* of American movies and TV.

Jay stood, filling the gap between the open door and the back seat, and splayed his hands on the roof. A brief pause and then the big guy started to pat him down, using *both* hands. Jay knew a lucky break when it presented itself—this was not a former Alpha Group member.

The guy found no shoulder holster—although this would be the last time Jay went anywhere unarmed—then checked Jay's waist, and moved down his legs all the way to the ankles. As he rose back into a standing position, Jay pounced on that brief moment of imbalance. He spun around, grabbing the guy by the head and slamming him face-first into the hard edge of the open door, once, twice…

The guy threw a punch with one arm, fumbled with the other, but he was already dazed. Jay cracked his head a third time within the space of a couple of seconds, then hurled his bulk into the backseat. The gun was still tucked into the waistband of the guy's jeans so Jay grabbed it as he scrambled in on top of him.

It had all been so quick, the young guy was only just thinking to release his seatbelt. Jay leaned across, drove the gun into the driver's side, pushing it up at an angle before pulling the trigger. The guy jolted and stopped moving but didn't cry out.

But the noise of the shot stirred the bigger guy into action. He starting bucking violently beneath him, throwing Jay against the roof of the car. He kicked out and threw wild punches with his free arm, shouting and gurgling through the bloody mess of his face.

Jay tried to regain control, but he was like a bronco beneath him. He found his moment at last, jammed the gun into the dimple on the back of the guy's neck and as soon as it touched flesh, he fired. The guy's head convulsed with the impact, once, like a final urgent attempt to throw Jay off him, and then he was still.

Jay climbed out again, catching his breath, feeling slightly pummeled, even though the struggle had only lasted seconds. He pushed the guy's legs part of the way into the car, then wedged them the rest of the way by closing the door. He took a quick look around the street. There had been two shots, one partly muffled, the other less so, but both inside a parked car—either way, no one seemed to be looking out from the closed stores or the apartments above them.

He got into the passenger seat. The driver was still alive, but he was shutting down, lost in the confusion of what was happening inside his own body, his eyes flickering as if searching for something, an image, a memory, something of the life he'd lived or the life he'd imagined. Finally he sighed and his head dropped.

Jay opened the passenger door again, released the seatbelt that the driver had never managed to free, then got out and dragged him into the passenger seat at the same time. Once he was in, Jay tipped the seat back a few notches and put the seatbelt on him.

He walked around the car, checked the street once more, got in the driver's seat and drove, up out of town, but not toward Petrov's place. He searched as he drove—there were plenty of unoccupied vacation homes but most were either gated or too close to the road.

Then he spotted a narrow track heading off the main road. He turned up it, higher up the hill, through some trees and emerging in front a slightly dated and unkempt house, shuttered, a partially collapsed trampoline on the scrappy lawn. There was an open car port to one side and Jay drove the car into it.

He set off on foot then, back down the track, onto the road, descending into town like someone who'd just decided to enjoy a stroll in the cooler air of evening. A breeze occasionally whipped up off the sea, too, and the lights twinkled below him, becoming more concentrated on the inky black edge of the waterfront.

As he rounded a bend, he noticed the terrace of the Bellevue below him and realized he'd deviated from the route he'd taken to get up here. He could see a few people sitting there, like painted figures in the lush stage-lit world of the hotel. Jay felt a stir of adrenaline as he realized even from this distance that one of those people was Harry Baverstock, sitting on her own, looking out on the dark water and the faint lights of the distant headland.

He checked the time, then walked on and into the Bellevue, through the bar and toward the terrace.

The barman said, "Good evening, Monsieur Lewis, stopping by for a nightcap?"

"Evening, Gaspard. What's Miss Baverstock drinking?"

"White wine. Puligny-Montrachet."

"Glass or bottle?"

"Bottle."

"Then I'll just take a spare glass."

"I can bring it to you."

"No need."

He stepped over to the bar, took the glass and handed Gaspard a tip, then walked out onto the terrace. He'd thought to catch her unawares, not least because he was surprised to see her sitting in a position that didn't cover the exits, but of course, she turned as he reached her and looked quite unfazed, almost as if she'd been expecting him.

He held up the empty glass. "Mind if I join you?"

She was all warmth as she gestured for him to take a seat. "Help yourself. It's terrifically expensive but just right for an evening like this." She was wearing a black dress, simple but elegant, and he briefly wondered if she'd had dinner with someone. It was none of his business, of course.

He poured some more into her glass, then his, as he said, "Your bosses are pretty generous with expenses."

"You can hardly send someone down here and expect them to do it on a budget, but as it happens, I've paid for the wine myself. I can't abide freeloading."

"Me either. Your good health." He raised his glass and they both sipped at their drinks. Jay only realized how thirsty he was as the chilled wine hit his throat.

Harry looked out across the terrace and said, "It's beautiful down here, and yet, I'm not sure the Cote d'Azur really exists anymore. You scratch the surface and underneath it's all just a little bit grubby."

"I'm not sure it ever existed outside of books and movies."

"Perhaps not."

She turned and stared at him for a moment, then an intrigued smile played across her lips. She leaned forward, took the white cloth and dipped the corner of it into the ice bucket and handed it to him.

He took it with a puzzled expression and she said, "You have a little blood on your cheek."

"Ah. Thank you." He wiped his cheek with the wet cloth, but she wagged her finger, letting him know it was the wrong side, so he moved the cloth to the other.

"All gone," she said and smiled again, to herself it seemed, finding something amusing in it. Jay draped the cloth back over the bucket. "Anything you'd like to tell us about?"

The "us" was instructive, letting him know that anything he told her would be shared with London.

"Nothing important. Two Belarussian government agents tried to pick me up off the street. Caught me sleeping as it happens—if they'd just wanted to put a bullet in me it would have been the easiest hit in the world."

"Well, you did say you've been out a long time, and we all let out guard slip every now and then."

"I haven't seen you around for a couple of days."

"I was out of town yesterday."

"Not with Rich McKenzie?"

"No, he's in Paris, although I understand he'll be back early in the morning."

"Good. You didn't ask me what happened to the two Belarussians."

"You had blood on your cheek, and it doesn't appear to be yours."

"I guess." The breeze suddenly picked up, whipping a cooler sea-laden air across the terrace. Harry put her glass on the table and pulled a shawl from the back of her chair and wrapped it around her shoulders. He already found her attractive, but something intangible in that small movement made him see all the more clearly how beautiful she was. "I… I have no idea what I was about to say. I think the coup will be a week Sunday."

She laughed. "Is that your go-to phrase when you're tongue-tied?"

He laughed too, but said, "I just thought you'd like to know."

"Thank you." She already knew, he could see it in her eyes. "How's Owen?"

"He's fine. With a babysitter, although…"

Although what? He'd toyed with vague ideas that he could solve the problem of Owen before things came to a head down here, and yet he knew now that he'd been fooling himself—Megan or her lawyer or her parents were not going to show up unannounced and spirit him away again.

Jay had known all along that an attack like the one tonight would happen, just as he knew now that it would get worse, but he'd fooled himself into thinking it wouldn't happen before he'd gotten Owen to safety, or if he were honest with himself, before he'd gotten Owen off his hands. But it had happened, and he had to figure a way of making this all work with Owen here.

Harry seemed intuitively to understand his predicament and said, "Look, I can't make any promises, because I'm doing a job down here too, but I am an observer, not a participant, and that gives me some leeway. So if there's any way I can help with Owen in the next week, just let me know. We'll swap numbers."

"I appreciate that." Yet at the same time, he was trying to work out her angle, struggling to see how it could benefit her. "I'm not sure…" He didn't know what he was unsure about.

She answered the unspoken question, saying, "You're up to your ears in a messy situation, Jay, but this boy, and what he could mean to your life, that's more important than anything. If you haven't realized that yet, you're a dummy."

"I do realize it." In reality, it was only hearing her put it into words that he knew it was the truth—Owen was more important than Jay's work, than Petrov, than whichever corrupt regime happened to be ruling Belarus. "I still don't get why you'd offer to help."

"Because I like him, Jay. He's a sweet, beautiful boy, he's fun to be around. I like him." She sipped her wine again. "I like you, too, and yes, I do mean in that way, but no, nothing's going to happen between us. I'm too professional and you're too… hmm, let me count the ways in which you would screw up my life."

He could hardly argue with that. "Busted."

She put her hand on his, and he felt the warmth of her skin, and the electricity of her thumb rubbing the back of his wrist, and he knew that she was being straight with him. She was too professional and apparently too good a judge of men, and Jay needed to change his life.

He didn't stay with her much longer, conscious of the time. Before he left, he walked into the bathroom and double-checked in the mirror that there were no other telltale signs of the earlier struggle.

He walked on through the town back to his apartment. He couldn't hear anything as he opened the door and briefly thought that Owen might be in bed. But as he walked through he saw they were both sitting out on the terrace looking over the lit town. They were chatting away quietly like they'd known each other for years.

Owen turned and saw him and said, "Hello, Jay."

"How's it going?"

Juliette jumped up with a smile and said, "We've had a great time. Will you need me tomorrow? Only, I had plans, to be out with friends."

"No, that's fine, we'll manage." He checked his watch. "I'm a little later tonight. Would you like us to walk you home?"

"No? It's really not very far."

"Okay." He didn't want to concern them, so he said, "But message me when you get there, just to be sure. I don't want Marion thinking I'm not being responsible."

"But of course, I can do that… if you like." She said it in a tone that made Jay feel a hundred years old.

Then she kissed Owen on both cheeks, casual and affectionate all at once. She said something quickly in French, too, and Owen answered her back, sounding surprisingly fluent.

"Oh, you speak French now?"

Owen gave him a wry smile as if to say, *There's a lot you don't know about me.* Jay was pretty certain that was the truth.

Juliette said, "He learns so quickly. He's *very* clever."

"Juliette's a good teacher."

"I believe you."

When Jay paid her she looked with surprise at the notes and he said, "A bonus, for the teaching. Now message me when you get home."

He tried to make it sound routine, like the old man she thought he was, but he was still uneasy, not sure how they would come after him again, or after the people around him. And he was relieved when she messaged him fifteen minutes later.

Owen had been getting ready for bed but he came into the living room now in his pajamas and said, "Oh, I forgot to mention it before. Alexei wants me to go for a sleepover—he asked his dad."

"When?"

"Not tomorrow. Sunday, I think."

Was Petrov testing him? Maybe he wasn't sure if he could trust Jay and this was a way of finding out—Jay would hardly let his own son spend time at the Petrov villa if he believed an attack was imminent. Jay thought an attack was at least possible, but he also suspected the Petrov villa would be safer than just about anywhere else at the moment. Of course, it was also possible that Petrov was simply indulging Alexei.

"Would you like to go?"

"Sure, if I can."

"Okay, I'll have to speak to Vitali, but I think it'll be fun." Owen nodded, but also stifled a yawn at the same time, and Jay had a sudden realization about the nighttime regime—or lack of it—that he'd fallen into with Owen. "Back home, does your mom normally read to you at bedtime?"

Owen looked amused by the question. "I'm kind of too old for that. But I like to read."

"Me, too. I didn't see any books when we unpacked your case."

"Too heavy. Mom said I had to travel light."

Jay had to hold off once again saying what he thought about Megan, but he was amazed at the way she'd arranged Owen's exile from his old life. He was even more amazed by how easily Owen had adapted—he seemed to be travelling light in every sense.

"There's a bookstore in town and I'm pretty sure they have English books. Unless, of course, you'd prefer French…?"

Owen shook his head, dismissing Jay's lame attempt at humor, and said, "Goodnight, Jay." He came over, hugged him. Jay reached up to pat his head, but he'd gone before he could make contact. He was not a natural to this, not like the father in the marina, or like Marion and Juliette, not even like Petrov.

"Goodnight, Owen."

He watched him traipse sleepily to his room, shoulders sagging, bare feet slapping against the floor. Jay would buy him some books tomorrow, not least because buying him stuff felt like the only thing he could do right for his son at the moment. What else did he even have to offer him?

18

After Owen left the next morning, Jay headed down to the Grand, sat in the lobby lounge and called Rich McKenzie's number. This time it rang and Rich answered.

"Good morning, Mr Lewis."

He was letting Jay know that he had his cellphone number, which was no less than Jay would have expected, but the goading tone made Jay feel like slapping him around the face.

"Call me Jay, Rich. We're on the same side, no reason why we can't be friendly."

"Fair enough," said Rich, apparently not spotting how riddled with lies that last sentence was. "What can I do for you, Jay?"

"I'm downstairs in the lobby. I thought we might meet."

There was a pause, too long.

"I'll be right down."

Jay waited long enough that he was able to order coffee for two people. He guessed Rich was probably calling his station chief to get instructions on how to best handle Jay, although that was something he should have been able to judge himself. On the other hand, it was possibly nothing more than power politics, keeping him waiting because he could.

The waiter arrived with the tray at the same time as Rich McKenzie walked in, wearing his casual and unconvincing yacht broker outfit. They shook hands.

"I ordered coffee for both of us. Is that okay, or would you prefer something else?"

The waiter hovered, and only left as Rich said, "Coffee's fine."

Jay poured two cups, then watched as Rich added cream and sugar to his.

Jay said, "Looks like things are coming to a head, so I just thought it might be an idea to touch base, see if there are any pointers I can give you on the situation with Vitali Petrov."

Rich sipped at his coffee, put it down and looked a little smug as he said, "It's good of you to offer, but with all due respect, I have the resources of the world's most powerful intelligence agency at my disposal; I'm not sure what need I would have for advice from disillusioned former employees."

"That's a pretty good point. But you have me wrong, Rich. I was never illusioned in the first place. I went in with my eyes open and I got out as soon as we stopped being useful to each other."

Rich didn't answer, but his expression suggested he now felt like slapping Jay's face, so he guessed they were even on that point.

Jay didn't fill the silence either and eventually Rich yielded grudgingly, saying, "I'm sanctioned to offer you support, but only because it's in our interests."

"As I'd expect."

"There's a group of armed men holed up in a villa not far from here, sent down by the regime in Minsk. We estimate a dozen here at present, more on the way. Their aim is to eliminate Petrov. And the people associated with him. Obviously, Petrov has a lot of people of his own, and we rate the security of his compound, but it could be a hairy two weeks."

"Why two weeks?"

"I'm sure I'm not telling you anything you don't know—you're his security adviser, after all. We think he's planning the coup for just under a fortnight from now. Friday evening, just as people are standing down for the weekend."

Jay made a show of looking impressed, even as he was actually thinking that his ten-year-old son had secured better information than "the world's most powerful intelligence agency".

"The thing is, Rich, the security relationship between me and Vitali is pretty much one-way. I find out things for him, I advise him, but he doesn't share his plans with me in exchange. So I can tell you about the situation up at the villa, who his people are, who he trusts, my general impression of the way he's thinking. I can also tell you that he's about to receive a massive cash injection from a shipment of cocaine that's arrived in Italy."

Rich's expression made it abundantly clear that the safe arrival of the drug shipment was no surprise.

"But in terms of how you might help me, given that's what you've been sanctioned to do, there's a car parked at a property above town with two bodies in it. I'm sure it's not beyond the powers of the agency to make it disappear before a civilian chances upon it."

"Whose bodies are they?"

He wasn't asking who they were but rather, who they were working for.

"Two of the Minsk agents. They tried to pick me up off the street last night."

"Were you alone?"

He sounded skeptical.

"Yeah, I was alone, and they weren't too professional—I doubt I'll be so lucky a second time."

"If you let me know the location, I'll see what I can do." He reached into his pocket and produced a USB stick which he placed on the table between them. "I can't be seen to be offering official help, for obvious reasons, but you should pass this on to Petrov. It's our assessment of which units within the Belarus military are likely to side with the coup and which will hold out, also an assessment of which officers within the loyalist units might be sympathetic to Petrov's cause. He might find it useful."

"He'll assume it's got spyware built into it."

"It's just a PDF. Open it on your own computer first, if that'll reassure him."

"I'll do that. What's the security like in the villa, the one where the regime's men are staying?"

"Beats me. We're confident Petrov has enough firepower of his own to deal with problems like that. We don't envisage anything happening down here that could impede Petrov's plans. He may take some casualties, but nothing he can't handle."

Jay made a point of looking reassured, when he was actually anything but, because he thought that assessment was probably right. The people up at Bogdanov's villa would be unlikely to stop Petrov by mounting a full-scale attack. Jay's own more subtle efforts stood a better chance of bearing fruit, but time was running short.

"Vitali's keen to know what the British involvement is in this." Rich looked confused and Jay added, "Harriet Baverstock, claims she's just down here as an observer."

"No reason to believe otherwise. The British don't want to be involved in this, no one does, certainly not publicly. But it's natural they'd have someone down here." He maintained eye contact, paused, and said, "So have the Russians."

"I'm not sure that finding Russians on the Cote d'Azur is exactly breaking news, even in the current climate."

Rich looked unamused.

"I'm gonna level with you Jay. I don't trust you. I know what everyone else's game is down here, but not yours. I don't trust you, and if it were down to me..."

He didn't finish. Jay wondered if he'd been making the case for whatever was hidden within that ellipsis while he was in Paris. And his bosses would have told him what he should have known from the start, that was there nothing they could do to stop Jay Lewis short of killing him, and there was no way anyone in the world's most powerful intelligence agency was about to sanction that.

"I'm an orphan, Rich, did you know that?"

"No, I didn't. I mean, yeah, I saw that you had no next of kin, but I didn't know it was when you were a kid."

Jay's file said he had no next of kin, which had been true, but no longer was, and he felt a strange mix of pride and discomfort at that realization.

"I wasn't really a kid. I was twelve when my mom died, eighteen when my dad died. The point I'm getting at is that it left me financially comfortable, and that gave me freedom, to quit the Agency when I wanted to, to work as a freelance security adviser without getting my hands dirty, only accepting the jobs I feel like doing. If Petrov were living in Minsk, I wouldn't have accepted the commission, but here I am, getting paid to spend time in Cotignac-sur-Mer."

"I'm not sure what your point is."

"My point, Rich, is that I have no game, I can't be bought, there's no cause I believe in more than my own. And I understand if you dislike me for being shallow and self-serving, but you're wasting your time if you go looking for things that aren't there."

"So why are you meeting regularly with Georgy Gumilev?"

"Seriously? Were you off sick the day they taught Asset Handling 101?" Rich looked stung by the note of derision in Jay's voice, and even looked as if he suspected that was the name of a real course. "Gumilev thinks I'm handing him information on Petrov. I'm playing him. Vitali knows about the meetings and I report back to him."

Rich looked into his coffee cup as if expecting to see something there, then put it down on the table.

"I don't believe you."

"Isn't that the nature of our line of work? We're believed when we're lying, but not when we're telling the truth."

Jay smiled, picked up the USB stick and slipped it into his pocket. Rich McKenzie didn't believe him. It was quite possible he mistrusted Jay for all the wrong reasons, but it was how people called a situation that mattered, not why. So maybe Rich wasn't such a bad intelligence officer after all.

19

Jay stopped at the bookstore on the way home and picked up a handful of the English titles they had for Owen's age group. When he got home, he left the books in Owen's room, then went and plugged in the USB stick and printed two copies of the PDF.

He called Petrov's place and told them he'd pick Owen up from there, that he had something Vitali needed to see. Then he called Georgy and told him he had something for him too, and they arranged for Georgy's contact to pick it up in the usual place.

He knew Juliette wasn't free this evening, so he called Harry, and when she answered, he said, "I know it's pretty soon to be calling in that favor, but would you be able to watch Owen for me this evening—an hour at the most? I have to be in the casino—"

"Oh, well as long as it's for something urgent! Blackjack or roulette?"

"Probably blackjack, but I guess you know I'm not going to play the tables."

"No. But of course I'll take him off your hands for a while. I was planning to eat alone at the Yacht Club, so why don't I pick him up just before eight and he can be my date for the night?"

Despite her assurances—which he believed—that nothing would ever happen between the two of them, he liked the idea of being Harriet Baverstock's date himself for the evening.

"He'd enjoy that, and I'll be there by nine-thirty. Do you need my address?"

She said pointedly, "I'll see you this evening."

She ended the call and then Jay leafed through the printed document. There wasn't much in the report to interest him, just a whole bunch of military units and names that meant nothing to him.

He drove up to Petrov's around four and was shown out onto the terrace. Petrov was sitting there at a table, and so was Stas, the latter dressed as if he were about to go on stage in a nightclub, despite the heat of the afternoon. Petrov was wearing shorts and a short-sleeved shirt that was stretched to breaking point over his belly.

As Jay sat, he noticed the glasses on the table. One was empty and clearly showed a lipstick mark on the glass— Jay had still never seen Mrs Petrov and found himself fascinated by this potential evidence of her existence.

A girl came out with a tray and cleared away the glasses, and Vitali said, "What can I get for you, Jay? Too early for vodka tonic?"

The girl looked expectantly, and Jay held his finger and thumb close together and said, "Very small—I'm driving."

Vitali asked for the same for him and Stas, speaking in Russian.

She left and Jay put the document on the table and said, "A gift from our CIA friend. He gave it to me on a USB stick but… look, I'm sure we can trust them, that they're genuinely on our side, but just in case they loaded it with spyware. They can't do that with paper." Vitali looked pleased with his logic. Stas looked theatrically bored. "It's the CIA assessment of all the units that you can expect to support you and those likely to remain loyal to the government. But it also includes the senior officers in the loyalist units who they think would be on your side."

Vitali could barely conceal his satisfaction, probably not so much at the contents of the report, but at what it suggested about the tacit support of the US Government. He picked up the document and handed it to Stas who simultaneously made a show of studying it at the same time as being underwhelmed by everything he saw there.

Then Vitali said, "I heard you had a problem, people from Bogdanov's place."

It was good that he'd been told, but Jay still wondered who'd told him. It seemed highly unlikely that it could have come via Rich McKenzie or Harry, and no one else knew about it, apart from the people at Bogdanov's villa who would have known that two people were sent out to pick up Jay and that neither of them had returned.

"Two of them tried to pick me up off the street."

"And?"

"They didn't send their best people."

Vitali appeared to take some pleasure from that.

"And the bodies?"

"Our CIA friend dealt with it for us."

"This is very good to hear. I like this CIA man."

He turned to Stas then who looked up from the document and offered a grudging acceptance that it might be helpful.

"Mostly things we already knew, but one or two surprises. It could be useful."

"Good." As if he had no further interest in the forthcoming coup, he smiled and said to Jay, "Owen comes for a sleepover tomorrow. That's okay with you?"

"Of course. He asked me last night. He and Alexei seem to get on well."

"Yes, I think this is true. And the sleepover, it's an American thing, I think."

"Sure, I had them when I was a kid. I didn't know it started in America." Sleepovers had finished for Jay when he was around eleven, and he didn't know if it was the same for most boys, or if once again, his particular circumstances had curtailed that aspect of his life, pushing him on into a twilight adult world before his time. "But it's good for them to hang out together, you know, just being regular kids."

"I agree," said Vitali, with the tone of someone who believed his own son was a prince who might benefit from exposure to a regular American boy. "Maybe Owen can visit us in Minsk, too. We go next weekend."

It was the first time Vitali had entrusted Jay with the date for the planned coup, and Jay suspected he knew why.

He said, "Interesting. The CIA thinks the coup will be the following Friday."

Vitali offered a satisfied smile. "That is what I want them to believe. Even if they support me as you say they do— and I believe it—it's still better they don't know the full details until all is done."

The girl came back with the drinks, and Jay raised his glass and said, "To next weekend."

"To Belarus," said Vitali, and they drank.

Jay's glass was only half empty by the time a commotion emerged from the house and Owen and Alexei spilled out onto the terrace. Alexei ran up to his father and spoke rapidly in excitable Russian—Jay only picked up stray words here and there but there was no question that he was talking about the thrills of the sailing lesson. Jay also couldn't help but note the difference between Alexei's immaturity and Owen's slightly more chilled demeanor. Owen actually looked at Jay and raised an eyebrow as Alexei smothered his father.

Jay noticed Owen staring at Stas, too, and so when they left Jay said, "Did you know that other man who was sitting with us?"

"I haven't spoken to him, but I know who he is. Stas, right? He's really important."

"How do you mean?"

"Alexei says his dad always likes to keep Stas close, like a righthand man."

That wasn't exactly news, but it was a confirmation of what Jay had suspected, that he really needed to kill Stas, preferably in the very near future.

But then Owen said, "Alexei's mom doesn't like him."

"Why not?"

"I don't really know. I don't think Alexei really knows, either. But he said she doesn't trust him. And he gives her the creeps."

"Interesting." He glanced across and noticed Owen smiling to himself, pleased to have come up with something useful. "Have you met Alexei's mom?"

"Sure, couple times. She's nice, but she's really quiet, and she's not around much."

"No kidding. I've been going up there six months and I've never even seen her."

"No way."

"Yes way. I was beginning to think she didn't exist."

"I think she's a lot younger than Alexei's dad, like someone on TV."

"What do you mean?"

"I mean like she has her hair all up, like… and she has a lot of make-up, and nails and jewels. She's pretty, I guess, but not like Mom or Harry."

Jay guessed he meant that she was highly-maintained.

"Speaking of which, I have to go out tonight—"

He interrupted, his face lighting up as he said, "Is Juliette coming?"

"No, it's Saturday. I guess she's out with friends."

"She just broke up with her boyfriend, but there's another boy she likes. She worries about her friend, too, because she doesn't eat."

Jay glanced at him and saw the pleasure Owen took from impressing him with his intelligence gathering.

"Anyway, Harry's coming to pick you up just before eight. She's taking you out for dinner at the Yacht Club."

Owen punched the air. "Awesome! Actually, double-awesome, because she's really cool and I love the food there."

Jay grinned, loving how enthusiastic this boy was for life. Had he been like that himself, he wondered, before his mother's cancer. He couldn't remember.

"Why are you smiling?"

"Just smiling because we both think the same way. I love the food there, too, and I also think she's really cool."

"Is she a spy? Like MI6?"

"You know about MI6?"

"Duh! It's in *so* many movies, and it's British, like Harry."

"There are a lot of British people. What makes you think she's in MI6?"

"I don't know. Just a feeling, I guess. Like, I can't explain it, but I just think there's something about her, like hidden."

Jay was fascinated by the way the boy's mind worked.

"That's good, because yeah, she's in MI6."

Owen looked like he might punch the air again, thrilled at having guessed right. And Jay was once more left thinking maybe Megan's rambling hadn't been entirely crazy, because for good or ill, it seemed the poor boy was entirely his father's son.

20

Owen chose a shirt to put on and wet his hair, so that he really did look like he was going on a date. Harry arrived just before eight wearing a red dress and white sneakers, and Jay was glad he hadn't already put on his tux because Harry and Owen looked unbearably cool and relaxed together.

Jay was in no real rush but he headed down to the casino just before nine. It was busy enough already, and a few of the regulars said hello to him, as well as most of the staff. He sat for a little while at blackjack, then left the table and walked across to the bar where the only patrons at the moment were a middle-aged couple engaged in what seemed to be a whispered argument.

Sasha, the young Russian barman, paid no attention to the couple and their domestic dramas, gliding over instead as Jay sat on one of the stools.

"Good evening, Mr Lewis."

"How are you, Sasha?"

"Very well, thank you. A gimlet?"

"Thanks."

As Sasha set about making the drink, Jay took the envelope from his inside pocket and placed it on the bar, then took out his wallet and put a couple of notes down in front of him.

Sasha came back with the drink, and looked at the notes, and Jay said, "I have to be somewhere, so just one tonight. Keep the change."

He would have used the excuse that his luck was out, but he'd won seven out of the ten hands he'd played at the table. Sasha took the notes with an appreciative nod of the head.

"*Non!*" Both Sasha and Jay looked along the bar where the woman had briefly raised her voice. The man was trying to appease her now, his hands up in surrender. She whispered something urgently and angrily, close to his face, and his head sank, his shoulders heaving. Some agreement had been reached and the two of them slid from their stools and made for the exit.

Jay faced forward again, sipped at his drink, and watched as Sasha walked over and cleared the bar where the arguing couple had been sitting. Jay had finished by the time he came back.

"Sure I can't tempt you with another, Mr Lewis?"

"I'm sure you could, Sasha, but you're not going to." He stood, looked around the casino as if in two minds, then said, "Another time. Goodnight, Sasha."

"Goodnight, Mr Lewis."

Jay walked away, knowing that Sasha would be sweeping away the empty glass and the abandoned envelope in one seamless movement. And the contents *would* mean something to Georgy, and give Moscow something they could share with Minsk. In Jay's experience, a coup needed everything to be lined up perfectly, so he just had to make sure those lines kept breaking down.

He walked the short distance to the Yacht Club and found Owen and Harry just embarking on their dessert. He couldn't help but see how natural they looked with each other, to the extent that people would have just assumed they were a mother and son out for dinner together.

Owen looked up, spoon suspended halfway between bowl and mouth, and said, "Wow, Jay, you look like James Bond."

Harry sounded playfully mocking as she said, "Was that the look you were going for?"

Jay raised one eyebrow and she laughed.

He pulled a chair and sat down. "How was dinner?"

"Amazing! Seriously, Jay, I love the food here."

"So do I." He turned to face Harry. "Thanks for stepping in."

"Not at all. We've had a lovely time."

"Well, Owen's at a sleepover tomorrow, so maybe I could return the favor."

"Two gallant gentlemen two nights in a row. Why not?"

"Great. There's a beautiful place up in Èze, stunning views."

"Sounds romantic. How about the rooftop restaurant at the Grand instead. I'll book. Meet you there at 8.30?"

"Sounds businesslike, but sure."

He noticed the whole time they were talking, Owen was looking from one to the other like someone watching a tennis match. He had a kid's idea of the world they were both involved in and for the time being seemed completely fascinated by it.

Harry parted from them outside the Yacht Club and Jay and Owen walked up toward their apartment.

As soon as he was certain they were out of earshot, Jay said, "So what did you talk about?"

"All kinds of things. She knows a lot, about everything."

"I'm sure she does. Did she ask many questions?"

Owen looked up at him, seeking clarification. "You mean, about you and Alexei's dad?"

"That kind of thing."

"No, not really, but… it's hard to explain. She didn't ask questions but I could kind of tell she wanted me to talk about them."

"Actually, that's a really good explanation."

"But I didn't tell her anything, Jay. I mean, I like Harry, but I didn't tell her anything about Alexei's dad, or Stas or moving back to Minsk. I know you want me to keep all that secret."

It troubled Jay to hear him talk like that.

"That's good, but I don't want you to feel you have to keep secrets. I mean, sure, most of the time it's the smart play, but it's no big deal if…" He paused, knowing that he didn't believe that, and that secrets *were* a big deal. Then he noticed Owen had found some humor in what he'd said. "What are you laughing about?"

"Just that, it's like you just said two opposite things all in one sentence."

"I guess I did." He laughed too and ruffled Owen's hair. "All I'm saying is, if you can keep some things secret, that's better, but I won't be angry if you let something slip."

"I won't, Jay, you can trust me."

"I believe it."

And he did believe it in some way, as short a time as he'd known him. There was something about the boy, something contained, a trait Jay was acutely conscious of within himself.

A car turned into the street up ahead and cruised toward them. Jay caught the make first, a BMW SUV, then the two guys inside, then the crawling pace. The windows were shut, and if they stayed that way, there wouldn't be a problem, but he was ready, suddenly conscious of the weight of the gun in its holster against his chest, conscious of the angle and where Owen was and how quickly he could get him on the ground.

The car didn't stop, but the two guys both stared at Jay as they cruised past. They looked to be in their thirties, one with short hair, the other almost shaved. Jay kept walking, but glanced back to make sure they weren't turning around at the bottom of the street.

"Did you know those men?"

He looked down at Owen.

"No."

"They didn't look very friendly."

"No."

"Are you gonna kill them?"

"No." Jay laughed. "I don't know what your mom told you, but no. Those men work for the other side, against Alexei's dad, but I don't kill people just because they're on the other side."

"But you're wearing a gun, right?"

"You noticed, huh?" Owen nodded. "Even so, a gun is always a last resort. And let me tell you right now, one serious rule, don't ever play with guns. If I ever accidentally leave a gun lying around, which I won't, I don't want you to touch it. Okay?"

"I won't, I promise."

Jay smiled, but he was uneasy, because that car had driven past while he was with Owen, which meant this was no longer just about him. He was relieved, too, when they turned the corner into his street and he spotted a patrol car parked a little way up from the apartment block—Benny had kept his word, but Jay knew it was unlikely to be a permanent presence, and nowhere near a permanent solution.

Briefly, when they got inside the apartment, he forgot about the SUV and the threat from the people up at Bogdanov's place. He concentrated instead on overseeing Owen's bedtime routine and helping him choose one of his new books to read. Then he left him and went through and poured himself a drink.

He sat on the balcony to begin with, but didn't like not being able to hear everything from the other side of the building. He walked in and sat in the living room. But the uneasiness was growing once more. He took his gun from the holster, attached the silencer and put it on the coffee table. Then he remembered what he'd said to Owen about accidentally leaving it around, and placed it instead up on one of the shelves where Marion maintained a handful of houseplants.

He sat again, nursed his drink but didn't drink. His senses seemed finely tuned now, to the extent that he could hear Owen turning a page every few minutes, even heard him mumble some commentary to himself. Still, Jay could not relax. It would be tonight. The patrol car wouldn't stay there forever, and they would come tonight.

He'd been in positions like this before, plenty of times, but it had never put him in such a heightened state before, and knowing the reason for that change hardly helped. A page turned. A scooter engine strained the night air several streets away. A plane high above sounded like it was beginning the descent into Nice Airport. A small dog yapped somewhere in a neighboring building. A page turned…

21

The drink was still untouched a half hour later so he threw it away and went through to check on Owen. He was asleep, the book splayed open on his chest. Jay was about to pick it up, but he heard a car door close out in the street, then another.

He moved over to the window and eased the blind back a little. The SUV was parked across from his building and the two guys he'd seen earlier were standing either side of it looking up the street. He followed their gaze, saw that the patrol car had gone and another SUV was in its place. Three more men were getting out, a fourth remaining behind the wheel.

They started walking toward the other two below. Five in total. Jay didn't risk looking at Owen again, fearing it would cloud his judgement, even though it was the thought of protecting the boy that was driving his heart rate higher. Instead, he moved swiftly out of the room, closing the door gently behind him.

He stepped out of the apartment, pressed the elevator button and waited to hear the mechanism jolting into life. In automatic survival mode now, he walked into the kitchen, grabbed a towel, a knife from the block, his gun from the shelf.

The elevator door was just opening as he got back to it. He lay the towel on the floor to prevent the door closing again, then moved to the top of the stairs and listened. This was a quiet building, half empty most of the time, and he was thankful for that now.

He could hear the faintest steps down below—two men, he thought, so maybe the other three would be split between the lobby and the parking garage. He set off down the stairs, suddenly remembering Owen's heroic struggle with Isaac Gleick on the stairs of his school back in Colorado.

He turned the corner after the first half-flight and ran right into them. They were surprised too—a crucial moment of indecision. Jay threw himself forward on the back of the adrenaline shot, pummeling into the first guy before he could even react, punching the knife into him even as all three of them crashed down onto the lower landing.

With the crunching impact, Jay heard something crack violently—bone—not his. Jay was moving quicker than he knew. Stabbing the first guy under the jaw, he rammed the blade home so hard that it snapped and he was left holding the handle. He pulled the guy by the shoulder to get to the other beneath him, but could see right away that the second guy's neck was broken, that the cracking bones had been his.

It had lasted only seconds, the whole act played out in silence, as if they'd still been hoping to maintain the element of surprise. He took each of them by the collar and dragged them along to the elevator door, then pulled free a dagger that one of them had strapped to his thigh.

Jay leapt back up the stairs, pulled the towel free and rode down to the next floor. He pulled them both inside, then pressed for the lobby and stepped out. He went back to the stairs, moving down them lightly, noiselessly, all the better to hear.

Someone was whispering, no replies, which probably meant there was only one in the lobby and he was telling the other two about the elevator coming down. Jay reached the lobby at the same time as the elevator door started to open.

Again, there was no time or room for strategy—he just had to rely on the guy's attention being elsewhere for a second or two. He slipped his gun into the back of his pants and stepped up behind the guy as he started to take in the scene in front of him. With one swift movement, Jay grabbed his face with one hand and thrust the dagger hard into the back of his neck and up under his skull with the other.

The guy twitched as Jay held him, like a spider and its prey locked together, and he pushed him forward even as his legs began to buckle, into the elevator. Once the door had closed, Jay wedged the guy against it, holding him upright even now that he'd stopped twitching. He pressed for the parking garage and pulled his gun free.

They were all wearing Kevlar, so he'd have to go for headshots and would have to be quick about it. For the first time, he felt a moment of unease at his own capabilities. It had been a while since he'd been in a position quite like this, and he didn't know how fast his reactions were. At least, he thought, if they killed him here, they wouldn't go up to the apartment.

The elevator arrived and a long second passed with nothing happening, with Jay holding the gun in one hand, and the muscles of his other arm straining to hold the dead guy against the door.

At last it opened, and he pushed the guy forward, but was surprised by how quickly silenced shots—still amazingly loud down here in the parking garage—tore through the air, one hitting the dead guy as he fell, another couple clipping the wall to the right of the elevator.

A split second followed, a split second in which they regrouped between those reactive first shots and their next, more considered moves, and in that half moment, Jay stepped out, aimed, fired, three times. Two shots found their targets, the middle one finding the far wall instead.

They fell with a clatter of guns, and Jay ran the few steps to where they'd fallen and looked down. He'd managed to hit one right in the eye. The other had been hit to the side of the mouth and his face was a mess but he wasn't dead yet. He lay there, his broken and bloodied jaw moving involuntarily, his eyes flitting about and looking for something that wouldn't be found.

Jay didn't need to do anything else—he'd be dead by the time he got back. Instead, he ran up the ramp and slowed as he reached the street, then ran in a crouch alongside the parked cars until he was directly across from the second SUV.

The driver looked to be about Jay's age, and amazingly, his face was illuminated because he was studying his phone. Jay crossed the street and opened the door. The driver jumped in surprise, but more as if he'd been caught being unprofessional by his colleagues rather than fearing for his life. By the time he'd realized his mistake, Jay had jammed the silencer under his armpit, above the Kevlar vest, and fired a single shot.

The driver jerked upright in his seat, dropped the phone, reached blindly for a gun he'd never fire. Jay opened the back door and lowered the seats. He pulled the driver out then, and was surprised to find him still trying to struggle, to resist, although that made him easier to move than if he'd been a deadweight. Jay heaved him in the through the open tailgate onto the flat trunk space and now that the guy was down, he allowed himself to be moved and settled into surrender or death.

Jay looked quickly around the street—deserted—then drove the SUV down into the garage. He opened up the back and piled the remaining five bodies into the trunk space, but it was hard work now, and even though most of the wounds weren't bloody, his white shirt was smeared and stained with it by the time he'd finished.

Six dead bodies was also pushing the boundaries of the BMW's cargo capacity. Across the garage was what looked like a Range Rover sitting under a tarp. He went and pulled the cover free and arranged it over the bodies, then closed the trunk.

He took the elevator back to the apartment, checked on Owen—still sleeping exactly as he had been—changed his clothes and threw the white shirt in the trash. On the way out, he picked up a kitchen sponge, and a bottle of cleaning spray, then retraced his route, cleaning a few spots from the landing one flight down, a little more from the elevator, none from the lobby.

In the basement he found a bucket that he filled with water, using it to sluice the floor of the garage, particularly where the two had fallen with gunshots. He stood for a moment and took in the scene then. There wasn't anything to catch the eye. A forensic team would find evidence easily enough, but it wasn't as if anyone was likely to report a hit squad missing, last seen heading to Jay's apartment building.

He drove the SUV to the edge of town. He considered driving it up to the same place in the hills where he'd left the other, but even though this whole operation had taken little more than half an hour, he didn't like the idea of leaving Owen unattended any longer than he had to.

He settled instead on one of the public parking garages, probably the oldest, and the only one with no CCTV. He parked the car in a corner near the back, pulled the cover from the bodies and put it over the car itself. That would do for a day or two, until Jay could ask Rich McKenzie to do his magic and make it disappear.

He had to call Georgy, too. It was a risk, but he needed the Russian to let the people in Minsk know to leave Jay alone. The risk was to Jay's cover, because if Petrov had people inside the regime in Belarus—which he most likely did—then word could get back that Jay was actually working against him. But that was the chance he'd have to take, because tonight had been too close.

And only now that it was done did his nerves get the better of him in a way he'd never experienced before. What if he hadn't been forewarned by seeing that first car pass in the street? What if he hadn't heard them outside his building? Or if they'd been more professional? What, above all, if he had let anything happen to this child?

22

Jay walked back through calm streets, even though he could hear plenty of activity in the heart of town, sports car engines and scooters, snatches of music, occasional shrieks of delight coming from some outdoor venue or other.

He guessed Juliette was somewhere in that easy night and felt a sudden pang of loss or longing, not for his own youth, but for the youth he hadn't had. He packed it away instantly, repulsed as ever by any hint of self-pity. And besides, he'd seen enough in his adult life to know that his teenage years had still been happier and more secure than those of a lot of other kids in the world.

When he got back to the building he saw a plump and moneyed middle-aged couple coming in the other direction, a couple he vaguely remembered seeing before. All three reached the building at the same time, said hello to each other and shared the elevator, even though the couple were only going up one floor.

They smelt of booze and cigar smoke, and he doubted they'd have noticed even if the elevator door had still been smeared with blood. As it was, they were oblivious to what had happened here just a short time before. They bid each other goodnight and as Jay rode the elevator to the top, he looked around again, making sure he hadn't missed anything a more sober observer might see.

Inside the apartment, it was as if he hadn't been away. Owen was lost in a contented sleep, the splayed book barely moving with the shallow rise and fall of his chest.

Jay stared at him for a moment in wonder, at the lack of strangeness. Here was a boy living in his apartment, a part of his life, a boy who had not existed as far as Jay was concerned until a few days ago, and yet it felt so natural for him to be sleeping there.

Jay gently lifted the book from his chest and bookmarked the page, reading a few lines as he did so. And then a half-memory crept from the recesses of his mind before slipping out of reach again, of being drowsily aware of his own father taking a book from Jay in almost identical circumstances.

It must have been after she'd died, or at least when she'd already been sick, but he remembered that feeling, that vague sense of security, that his dad was there for him, that everything would be okay. And tears pricked his eyes, because he saw now, as he'd never really seen before, that his dad had been so alone, so adrift in grief, and yet had tried so hard to make it right for him.

Jay had always been able to express in words how much he'd known his father had cared for him, but for the first time standing there he actually *felt* it, maybe because he'd been unexpectedly landed with a son of his own to care for. It made him emotional and grateful simultaneously, emotional because he'd never had the chance to talk to him, not as an adult, grateful because he'd been given the opportunity to have those conversations with Owen.

That thought galvanized him. He put the book on the nightstand, turned out the lamp and left, closing the bedroom door behind him. He walked into the living room and brought up Georgy's number on his phone, but then realized how late it was.

Anyway, he wouldn't need to call Georgy until Monday. The people up at Bogdanov's villa would take a little while to regroup after six men had gone out and failed to return, and tomorrow night Owen would be sleeping at Petrov's place—even that now made Jay uneasy, and yet he knew the boy was almost certainly safer there than anywhere else in town.

He called Rich McKenzie who answered immediately. He sounded fresh, like someone working, like someone still on Eastern Standard Time.

"What can I do for you, Jay?"

"Did you manage to remove the car from the place up the hill?"

"It's taken care of."

"There's another, an SUV in a parking garage on the edge of town, under a tarp. I'll send you the address."

There was a pause, as if Rich were about to say one thing—maybe some smart line about how he wasn't Jay's one-man cleaning outfit—but then changed his mind.

"Is it… is it occupied?"

"Yeah. Six of them."

"*Six?*"

"Six."

"And they all came in one car?"

Jay actually looked at his phone in disbelief. That was his takeaway, not that Jay had managed to kill all six, but what their transport arrangements had been?

"No, the other SUV is on the street outside my building. I doubt anyone's coming back for it."

"Okay, send me the address and I'll see what we can do."

"Thanks."

"You're welcome. But you know, I still don't get why they're trying to kill you. No offence, but your death won't derail anything. You'd think they'd be concentrating all their fire on Petrov himself or his man, Stas."

Petrov was self-explanatory, and Jay had no doubt the regime would love nothing more than to kill him. But he couldn't imagine Stas being so important, despite what Alexei had told Owen about his dad always wanting to have Stas by his side.

"I don't get it. Why Stas?"

"You don't get it?" He sounded contemptuous. "Well, I guess at least you're aware of your limitations. Stas is ex-Belarussian KGB. They're on side because of him, and without him, Petrov's chance of succeeding… Well, it all becomes a lot less certain."

"Interesting." It explained, for one thing, why Vitali was so eager to ask if there were any current Alpha Group members up at Bogdanov's villa, because it would suggest Stas held less sway with his old colleagues than he was claiming. It also made targeting Stas even more of a priority for Jay. "Then I think you're right—Stas is the man they should be gunning for."

Rich didn't respond for a second, then, as if fearing he'd told Jay too much, he said, "What did you hand to the Russian barman in the casino tonight?"

"Were you there? You should have come and said hello." He was actually trying to think how Rich had found out. That end of the bar was a blind spot for the casino's cameras, and he couldn't remember anyone who'd looked out of place. Had Rich managed to get his own cameras in there? That seemed like too much effort and risk for highly uncertain rewards. So Jay must have been tailed and had missed it, a failure that troubled him. "I was giving him a printed copy of your PDF."

"Excuse me?" He sounded outraged.

"Relax, Rich. That's why it was printed, so they can't tell that it was a doctored version of it. Like I told you, I've been handing them phony intelligence for the last six months."

There was another pause, but Jay could almost hear Rich seething on the other end of the line.

Finally, he said, "I'll take your word for it, this time, and I'll give the benefit of the doubt that you know what you're doing, but I'm warning you, Lewis, if you do anything to jeopardize the interests of the United States in this matter, we'll make absolutely sure that you pay the severest penalty. I am *not* sharing intelligence with you so that you can pass it around town to whomever you so choose."

Jay couldn't help but smile. Every now and then, there was something about the way Rich McKenzie spoke that made him sound like a teacher at some fusty New England prep. He should have been inspiring boys with Whitman and Thoreau, not floundering in a line of work he wasn't cut out for.

"Rich, I know you don't like what I do, and I know you don't trust me. I'd be the same if I were in your position. But I give you my word, I would never jeopardize the interests of the United States. Never."

The reluctance was there in his voice as he said, "Noted. Not that I'm entirely sure how much your word is worth."

"There are six bodies in the back of a BMW—you can take that as my guarantee."

"I guess I'll have to."

"Who tailed me to the casino, Rich?"

"No one tailed you. I have a contact in the casino, and your movements around this town are not exactly inconspicuous."

That was rich coming from the least convincing yacht broker on the Cote d'Azur, but Jay was happy to take the hit. It meant Rich was still on his own down here, and relying on sources in all the most obvious places to keep him abreast of Jay's movements.

In turn, that reassured Jay that Rich was even less of a threat than he'd believed him to be. He wasn't fully resourced and would make no impact on his own. Jay knew it, Rich's superiors knew it, probably so did Georgy and Harry. Quite possibly the only people who believed Rich's presence here would make a difference were Vitali Petrov and Rich McKenzie himself.

23

Owen emerged fully dressed from his room the next morning and it was immediately apparent that he was in good spirits. Jay wasn't sure if that was because of going to dinner with Harry the night before or the fact he was looking forward to his sleepover—Jay was taking him up there early in the afternoon.

He made his own breakfast and as he sat down, said to Jay, "That book is so good. I mean, really!"

"I'm glad. They didn't have a massive selection." Jay was still on his first cup of coffee and hadn't eaten anything yet. "Maybe when you get through those we can order some online."

Owen nodded, his mouth full of cereal, then once he'd swallowed, he said, "There's a knife missing."

Jay made a show of looking puzzled.

"In the knife block. There's a knife missing. Marion won't be happy."

It was Sunday, so Marion wasn't in.

"It's probably just been put back in the wrong place. Who knows, maybe Marion lost it."

"I don't think so. It was there last night."

Jay liked his attention to detail, for certain things at least, and as if to back that up, Owen said with uncanny coincidence, "What's the best way to kill someone with a knife?"

"Is this the kind of thing you discuss with Harry over dinner?"

Owen looked askance.

"*No!* Me and Walden used to talk about things like this all the time. He always said it was best to stab them through the top of the head, but that's kind of silly because your skull is really hard."

"True. What did you say?" Owen mimed stabbing himself in the heart. Jay said, "Good thinking. Of course, it needs a lot of force, and it's not immediate, but it's also not so messy. That's the thing with knives—messy, unpredictable, high-risk. Nine times out of ten, a gun is a far better option."

"That's what I think!"

"Well, great minds think alike." Of course, the previous night had been the one out of ten times where a knife was by far the best way to go. "But less talk of killing people. It's another beautiful day in Cotignac-sur-Mer and you're going on a sleepover."

Owen punched the air, as if he'd completely forgotten about it until that moment.

"Will someone come collect me?"

"No, I'll drive you up there. I need to speak to Vitali." He thought about Owen staying the night, thought about the way he'd been prodding Alexei for information, and about how unwise that might be now that things were coming to a head. "By the way, you've managed to get some really good information out of Alexei for me, but don't ask any questions today. Just enjoy yourself, have fun."

"I do have fun, but I can still ask questions. I don't make it obvious or anything."

"I know. One day you'll make a really good intelligence officer." Owen smiled, trying not to show how much that compliment meant to him. "But big things are happening this week and people are getting nervous, touchy. Sometimes, being an intelligence officer is about knowing when *not* to ask questions. Now's one of those times."

Owen's face grew serious as he tried to assimilate this new concept, then he gave what seemed to be becoming his stock response.

"Don't worry, Jay, you can trust me."

"I know it. You're a smart boy."

He offered a modest smile in response.

After breakfast, Jay helped Owen load up his little backpack with overnight things. The boy seemed so self-reliant that Jay was surprised by the parental responsibility of having to remind him to pack his toothbrush.

They drove up there in the early afternoon. Alexei rushed out to meet them in the entrance hall, and Owen threw out a casual "Bye, Jay, see you tomorrow" before being dragged off upstairs.

It was a glorious day, and Jay expected to be shown out again to the terrace, but instead he was taken by the polite young flunky into the dining room where he found Vitali, Stas and a third guy whose name Jay had never known. They were standing around the table which had a map spread out, held down at the corners with various gawdy ornaments. Getting closer, he saw it was a detailed map of Minsk.

Stas was holding a sheet of paper, but as Jay approached, he deliberately placed it face down on the map. From the manner of the placing, Jay guessed there was something written on the map that Stas thought it better to conceal.

Vitali smiled at Jay and held out his hands to encompass the city before him, as if it were already his.

"One week!"

Jay looked suitably impressed and said, "And I bring good news, good for two reasons."

Vitali responded by saying, "A drink?"

"No, I won't keep you, I know you have a lot of work." He was also conscious of Stas staring hard at him—he trusted Jay even less than Rich McKenzie did. "The people in Bogdanov's villa, they came after me again last night. Six of them came to my apartment."

The third guy apparently didn't speak English because he was looking at Vitali to gauge his reaction rather than listening to Jay. Stas looked suspicious of a sleight of hand. Vitali looked concerned.

"Why is this good news?"

"Firstly, they're coming after me. That means they're not confident enough to come after you. They don't have the numbers to man an assault on this place."

Vitali smiled. "And?"

"And I killed them all. I spoke to the CIA guy last night and he's gonna make the bodies disappear. Like I told you, they're on our side. They want this to happen."

Vitali appeared satisfied with that, and looked down at the map again, as if he could see something on those two dimensional city streets—probably a victory parade.

Jay made his excuses shortly afterwards. As he was driving back into town, his phone rang and he saw who it was and pulled to the side of the road and answered.

"Can you talk?"

"Sure." Jay stepped out of the car, even though he was pretty confident it wasn't bugged. He looked around, walled gardens and glimpses of roofs, Mediterranean pines, no sign of actual life. "I was planning to call you anyway."

Georgy chuckled. "Great minds, Jay, great minds." And Jay smiled to himself, remembering that he'd used the same phrase with Owen just this morning. "This document is *very* interesting. Most of it we knew about, but we've shared it with our friends, and they'll use it."

"In a messy way?"

Another chuckle. Georgy was in a surprisingly upbeat mood, which made Jay wonder if the intelligence in Rich's document was even better than Georgy was saying.

"Those days are long behind us, Jay. No, but some units will unexpectedly find themselves on exercises this week, far from the capital. And yes, one or two people might get sick. You know. But it's also helped ease any remaining suspicions between Minsk and Moscow."

"That's good." Jay began to feel Georgy's upbeat mood himself. This looked like it might all be heading in the right direction. "It's good for another reason. I need you to alert Minsk that they should stop their people from targeting me."

There was a pause, and Georgy's tone was much flatter when he replied. "Are you sure about this? You know, if Petrov were to have the right person in the right place inside the regime, word could get back."

"It's a risk, I know, and I'll be relying on you to let me know if that happens. But six of them came after me last night, came to my apartment. I can't allow that risk."

"Of course." Another pause, but Georgy needed no more explanations. "The boy changes everything. I know this."

"Exactly. If you can come up with some other reason for why they should leave me alone, great, but if you have to, just tell them the truth. It's only for a week, at the most."

"Okay, I'll do it. You killed the six?"

"Yeah."

"Good. So, they won't send anyone else today. I'll make the call in the morning. That makes one day less in which you might be compromised."

"Thanks, Georgy."

"No, thank *you*, Jay. I think we can do this. Between us, we'll avert a catastrophe."

They finished the call and Jay looked around again and noticed for the first time that a Doberman was staring at him from just a few feet away, it's face pressed between the bars of an electric gate. He walked over and the dog growled, the sound like the outboard motor of a distant boat, but when he reached out his hand the dog whined a little and licked him, and Jay stroked it under the chin. Maybe it was just professional courtesy.

24

Jay arrived first at the rooftop restaurant at the Grand Hotel. He hadn't been up there before. In fact, it had only opened for the season in the last few weeks and the night air was still cool enough that the entire space was dotted with heaters. Every table was occupied, but the chatter and clatter of all those people seemed to float away on the evening air.

Dusk was falling, and Cotignac-sur-Mer looked beautiful from up there, a patchwork of rooftops and trees and the soft yellow glow of lit streets. He turned and looked out at the growing dark of the bay behind him, and when he turned back, Harry was walking toward him.

It took Jay a moment to realize it was the same black dress she'd been wearing on the terrace at her own hotel. It took him a moment because of the way she simply owned that restaurant as she walked across it, poised and relaxed all at once, a slight smile playing on her lips, a few wisps of her hair catching in an almost unnoticeable breeze. He couldn't remember the last time he'd been this attracted to anyone, and wondered if that might be in part because she'd ruled out any romance.

As if to reinforce that point, as she reached the table she said, "It's rude to stare."

A waiter rushed over and pulled the chair for her. She looked up at him and smiled her thanks.

Jay said by way of explanation, "It's hard not to. You're incredibly attractive."

"Not so bad yourself. It's still a no." And with that settled, she took the menu another waiter proffered and gave it her full interest. "What looks good? I rather feel like eating meat."

"How do you like it?"

"Without inuendo."

Jay laughed.

"I don't think you gave Owen this much of a hard time."

Harry laughed a little herself and said, "I won't lie, Jay, when I was younger, I enjoyed… all of this, and yes, I played the field a little, but I realized that ultimately it wasn't very satisfying, and I insist nowadays on only getting involved with people with whom there might be some future. I don't do one-nighters and I don't do flings. And before you say another word, neither you nor I know where we're going to be after next weekend, let alone next year."

He was about to respond, but he knew she was right, at every level, and in the end, he said only, "True."

The waiter came back with a questioning expression and she smiled at him and said, "Don't give us any more time—we'll only waste it. I'll have the veal tartare and the duck."

She wasn't joking about wanting to eat meat. Jay ordered too and they chose a bottle of wine and handed the menus back to the waiter. Just as he was about to head off again, Harry raised her hand to stop him.

"And perhaps we might both start with a glass of champagne."

Whatever quality it was that she possessed, the middle-aged waiter almost blushed as he said, "Of course, mademoiselle."

She turned and looked at the view then, as if she hadn't seen it before, and said, "Isn't it spectacular up here?"

"Have you been here before?" He thought of seeing her in that black dress some days before and felt an odd pang of jealousy, wondering who she'd been with and where they'd gone.

"Only once. A professional meeting of sorts."

"So this *isn't* a professional meeting?"

She smiled, teasing. "I'm not sure how much you might have to tell me that I couldn't find out anywhere else."

"Ah, so you've met Rich McKenzie."

She sighed and said, "He's quite sweet, actually, beneath all the company bluff and bluster. I kept thinking of Graham Greene the whole time I was with him."

Jay didn't get the reference.

"I don't follow."

"I mean, I think he'll end up dead, sooner rather than later."

"Oh."

Jay couldn't argue with that, but before he could respond at any greater length, the waiter came back with the champagne and they drank an unspoken toast.

"Speaking of which, I heard a BMW X5 was left in a multistory car park with six bodies in the back. Minsk regime loyalists. Who came after you."

"Yeah, that's about right. After we left you last night, two of them drove past in an SUV. Then later, when Owen was asleep, another car arrived, and five of them came into my building. I heard some of the guys up at Bogdanov's place are ex-Alpha Group, but the ones I've encountered so far have all been strictly amateur hour."

"So you killed all five?"

"And the driver." She looked puzzled and he said, "What is it?"

Harry shook her head. "I was just thinking, even with the seats down, six bodies in the back of an X5 is a big ask."

"I don't think it's something they highlight in the brochure." She laughed. "Truth is, it wasn't so tough. And I guess I was more determined than usual, because of Owen. I didn't want them reaching the apartment, didn't want them threatening him, didn't want him exposed to any of that. I've never been in that position before, where I felt like I had to protect someone else."

She was all warmth as she said, "I can understand that. He's adorable." A waiter arrived with an amuse bouche and once they'd finished it she returned to her point. "It's not for me to criticize, but I'm completely dumbfounded by his mother's decision to give up on him. I'm sorry if that's overstepping the mark."

"Not at all. I didn't really know his mom that well." Harry raised her eyebrows and Jay put a hand up in admission, realizing that sounded like an affirmation of Harry's decision not to get involved with him. "What I mean is, we were together for months, but it was an intense time, and there was a physical attraction, but I don't think either of us made much of an effort to think about who the other really was. I knew she suffered from depression, maybe some other issues, but I guess I was too young and too shallow to take it seriously."

"I'm not judging you. She was a charity worker, right?"

The question seemed loaded. In their line of work, they were often in places where, apart from an occasional journalist, the only other English-speaking people were charity workers or mercenaries. In other words, they split into two groups of people whose aims and interests and methods were simultaneously intertwined and diametrically opposed. In Guatemala, Jay's outfit had even been involved in funding some of the charities whose work they were undermining with their own operations.

"Yeah, helping street kids. She knew who I worked for, but she found out a little too much and that was why we broke up. Well, I left a few weeks later anyway, but… She became convinced I'm a monster, and now she thinks Owen is, too. She thinks that what's wrong with me is also wrong with him."

"I don't see anything wrong with Owen at all." Jay made a show of mock offence. "We'll come back to you. But Owen's just a regular little boy."

"You think? I mean, I think the whole monster thing is more about Megan than it is about Owen, but you have to admit, the way he talks sometimes isn't like a regular kid, nor some of the things he's done."

"*Really*? That's not innate, it's about who he wants to be. All that business with Isaac Gleick, getting his friend to track you down, the way he speaks sometimes, he's trying to be like you, Jay."

"Harry, we've known each other a week."

"No, you've known him a week. But he knew about you, heard about you, probably had it thrown in his face every time he did something wrong, that he was just like his father, and so he wanted to be like he imagined you. And yes, naturally you're both alike, and he does have some qualities that… that seem to be quite common in our line of work. It doesn't change the fact that he's just a little boy trying to figure out his place in the world, looking for role models." She smiled mischievously. "And now he has you."

"He has you, too. He made you for a spook right from the start."

"Really?" She looked intrigued. "How extraordinary. He didn't mention it to me."

"He's discreet."

"Oh, I know that." Was that an admission that she had tried to prise information out of Owen but had failed? She added, "Did he say why he thought that about me?"

"To be fair, I think the cut-glass English accent was his most compelling evidence."

She laughed, but also put her hands over her heart, looking smitten, and then the first courses arrived. They talked through the meal then about their backgrounds, early childhoods, college years, and as much as they could about their early careers—it came as little surprise to Jay that Harry's father and uncle had both been in "the same line of work" and that her grandfather had been a baronet.

It was only when they'd finished eating that Harry said, "You don't have to tell me, of course, but I can't help but notice that you've avoided mention of a sizeable part of your childhood, and indeed, almost any mention of your parents."

"That obvious, huh?"

"I'm sorry, I'm being rude. I didn't mean to pry."

"It's okay, it's fine. I don't talk about it because… I mean, I don't meet that many people with whom I'd share as much as I already have tonight, but certainly about that. It's not exactly lighthearted conversation."

"I'd still like to hear about it, if you wanted to talk about it."

"As an observer?"

She dismissed the joke. "As a friend."

"Okay, as a friend."

He wasn't sure it meant so much anyway, or why he avoided discussing it with people. It was true what he'd said—most of his interactions were too shallow for sharing details of how he'd become an orphan, but maybe in the past he'd also feared exposing some vulnerable part of himself. And now that fear had been reduced to insignificance by the more primal vulnerability that had suddenly entered his life.

"My mom got sick and died of an aggressive form of breast cancer when I was twelve. It happened too fast, as these things do, and simultaneously seemed to go on forever, you know, to consume us as a family. My dad blamed himself."

"Why?"

"He was a cardio-vascular surgeon so he thought… I don't know what he thought, or nothing that made sense."

"I suppose grief will do that, and being in the medical profession… I can understand him feeling like that."

"I guess. Anyway, he drank and medicated himself to death over the next six years. Somehow he kept working for most of it, which is scary in retrospect. The last two years, though, he quit. He had the good grace to die on the night of what would have been my senior prom, not that I'd planned on going anyway."

He'd long become a distant or at least semi-detached figure in high school by that stage, but he remembered driving to the hospital that night and passing Chloe David's house, seeing Zac Harkness picking her up, both of them dressed in their prom finery. He'd known at that point about his father—that he'd deteriorated unexpectedly during the afternoon and had died forty minutes earlier without regaining consciousness—and he remembered seeing Chloe and Zac and feeling like a ghost, like he could no longer have a presence in that world even if he wanted to.

"What do you mean by that, good grace?"

"Oh, only that I was old enough to look after myself. I mean legally; I'd been more or less looking after myself for years."

"I see." She thought about it, studied the wine in her glass. "And you think that's why you ended up doing what you did?"

"Is it that transparent?" He smiled. "I've thought about it a lot the last few days. Every book I read in those years, every movie I saw, I always gravitated toward the lone hero, the man with no connections, no liabilities. It's almost laughable, but it's obvious I was trying to find some model of how to be, something as little like my dad as it was possible to find. And clearly, that part of me was there already or else it wouldn't have taken the way it did."

"Maybe it was in your dad too." Jay looked puzzled and she said, "It sounds like he was totally grief stricken, and yet for the first four years after your mother died he was able to continue his career as a surgeon—to me, that sounds like exactly the same level of detachment as you're talking about."

Jay could see that and yet he struggled to think of his dad as that person, a surgeon—"completely calm in the middle of the storm", one of his friends had said at the funeral—only as the self-pitying drunk fading away before his eyes, sinking a little lower each night into his armchair, oblivious to everything outside of his own private torment. Maybe Jay had just been too young to see the entirety of his father's personality.

"Do you think it's in Owen, too?"

"Possibly. He's remarkably composed for a child of his age, but… Look, I'm not the best judge, because I find most children tiresome, but I like being around your son. At the risk of sounding like some new-age flake, he has a good energy."

"I think so too. But it's true, we're probably not the best judges. And on that subject, what about you?"

She dismissed the question easily and lightly. "No trauma, I'm afraid. I had an idyllic childhood. Loving parents, didn't board until sixth form and was never drawn to drugs, so all the classic middle-class English tropes don't apply. Truth be told, I just think it's in our national character—we're all born with a little ice in our veins."

He smiled but before he could respond, a waiter came and offered them coffee.

Harry said, "Not for me, thank you."

Jay looked at the waiter and said, "Maybe we could just get the check."

The waiter appeared confused in response, looking at Harry, then back to Jay. "But… Mademoiselle Baverstock has already paid."

She looked at him, teasing. "Presumably it doesn't offend you to be the guest of Her Majesty's Government for the evening?"

"Not at all. As long as you allow me to return the favor sometime, not on behalf of my government, of course. I have no choice but to entertain on my own dime."

Her eyes fixed on his, almost as if she might be considering saying something pointed in reply to that. It felt like a dangerous moment to Jay, a hint that she knew or suspected the true nature of his work and who he worked for.

But she chose not to say whatever was on her mind and the moment passed. The conversation moved on, but it left Jay wondering, did she know, or had she guessed, who he really was and what he was really doing down here?

25

Harry decided to take "a leisurely stroll" back to the Bellevue and Jay walked with her. She made clear once again that if he was doing it for the exercise it was fine, but if he was expecting to be invited up for coffee, he was in for a disappointment. The irony was, he didn't want anything from her—he simply enjoyed her company, and liked the thought of walking through the town with her more than that of being anywhere else or with anyone else—Amandine already felt like a distant memory.

When they got to the hotel, she did invite him to have a drink on the terrace and while Harry went up to her room, Jay chose almost the same spot as last time and ordered the drinks. There were a few more people about tonight, most of them looking like people who'd eaten in the Bellevue's Michelin-Starred restaurant and were topping off their night here with the lights of the coast and the dark water below them.

Harry came back with her shawl and put it over her shoulders now as she sat down.

Then, as if she'd been thinking about it, she said, "Will you ever settle down, do you think?"

He raised his glass to her, they both drank, and he said, "I don't know. I'd never really thought about it. Even now, I'm kind of getting my head around the fact that Owen might be a permanent fixture, but I can't see us settling in some small town like the one I grew up in. I just don't know."

He hadn't given it any thought. In his defense, he'd barely had time to do so. Owen would need some kind of stability, but what precisely did that mean? He guessed the boy's first ten years had been stable, but that hadn't exactly worked out either.

As if reading his thoughts, Harry said, "I think children are incredibly resilient. As long as he has some certainty—you, for example—he won't mind moving from place to place as your job dictates. And of course, as a freelancer, you can work as much or as little as you like."

It felt once again as if she were subtly probing at the real nature of his business here in Cotignac-sur-Mer.

"What about you, Harry? Likely to settle down?"

"If I met someone worth settling for."

"Maybe you already have."

She laughed, but there was warmth in it. "You really are quite feral, aren't you? But no, it will be someone much more dependable. You'll have to settle for staring at the green light across the water and wondering what might have been."

"Even I get that literary reference. My mom named me after him."

"Your mother named you after Jay Gatsby?"

"It was her favorite book."

"It's one of mine, too. I'm more amused that she named you after a character who's not at all what he seems."

"Says Harriet the Spy."

"Touché," she said, and raised her glass again. Then she looked around at the other people on the terrace. "You know, something I often think about—when you travel as much as we do—all these people, like the people here tonight, seen so briefly, and the chances are, we'll never see them again, never learn anything more about them. They all have their own stories, their own tragedies and triumphs, and yet they mean nothing to us, just faces in the crowd. And how many of those people, if given just a moment, could end up becoming a really important parts of our lives?"

Strangely, Jay thought again of the studious teenager he'd killed all those years ago in Guatemala, even though there could have been no other outcome to that encounter on that particular night.

"I guess I try not to think too much about things like that. Maybe it's what you do with the connections you have that's important, not all the people who might have been."

She looked quietly triumphant, as if she'd been playing chess with him and had just lured him into checkmate.

"That's interesting. I mentioned it because I so very nearly didn't engineer a meeting with you. I studied your file and didn't think I'd get much from you. If I'd stuck to my instincts, you and Owen would have been reduced to part of that human scenery, faces without stories."

"Maybe that's fate telling you something."

She burst out laughing, and he couldn't help but laugh himself. At least she couldn't accuse him of not trying.

It was a little after midnight when Jay left. He walked back through quieter streets, feeling a little like the teenager he'd never been, or almost never. His adolescence had been pretty solitary, but in his freshman year at college he'd met a girl who he ended up staying with for over a year. The night they'd first met, they'd stayed up until three in the morning, just talking, bonding, and the way he'd felt walking back across campus in the small hours—lightheaded and light of step and suffused with endorphins—that was kind of how he felt now, probably for the first time since.

It made no sense. Of course it didn't. They'd known each other ten minutes, she was probably being as evasive with him as he was with her, and as she'd said, they would be going their separate ways within a week, inevitably slipping back into that "human scenery" she'd talked about.

Added to that, Jay's brain had been scrambled by the sudden arrival of an unexpected child. But he couldn't help the way he felt, and maybe her insistence that nothing would happen between them only intensified those feelings.

He turned a corner just as someone had come out of an apartment building up ahead. The man was walking away from Jay, crossing the empty street at the same time, diagonally, making for the far corner.

Jay glanced at the apartment building, wondering who lived there, and what Stas had been doing there, because that's who it was walking away from him. More to the point, Stas surely knew he was a target of the people up at Bogdanov's villa, so what was he doing creeping around town on his own after midnight?

Whatever the story, Jay knew this was a perfect opportunity falling at his feet. With the intelligence he'd already handed to Minsk via Georgy, killing Stas might be enough to undermine Petrov's coup altogether. Kill Stas and it could well be job done.

He reached into his jacket and pulled the gun, then attached the silencer. He picked up his pace at the same time, crossing the street and keeping close to the buildings, running toward the corner as soon as Stas had disappeared around it.

When he reached the corner himself, he was surprised to find Stas hadn't made it very far. He was still walking, but slowly, his usually upright frame sagging, looking almost like he might run out of energy entirely. Jay wondered if he might be drunk.

Somewhere a few streets away, a motorbike started to rev loudly and Stas looked vaguely to his left, up into the sky, then took another couple of steps, stopped and turned to look to his right, into a back alley between the buildings. He looked lost, as if he didn't know where he was headed or why.

Jay picked up his pace and was only a few steps away when Stas heard him approaching and slowly turned to face him. It was a shock to see him. Stas was crying, his eyes red as if it had been going on for some time, and although he was still wearing his nightclub crooner look of shiny suit and dark shirt, the collar was open and for the first time ever in Jay's experience, he wasn't wearing a tie.

Jay slammed into him, pushing him into the back alley and off his feet, just as the motorbike roared into life, its engine tearing a scar across the night's calm. The shock of hitting the ground seemed to bring Stas back to himself, but Jay had shot him in the chest before he had the chance to speak or react in any meaningful way.

The motorbike was already growing distant. It had swallowed up the first shot, but wouldn't cover a second. There wouldn't be a need anyway. Even in the dark of the alley, Jay could see that Stas was dying. It shouldn't have been that easy, not for a former KGB man, but it was the results that counted, and Jay couldn't resist a brief moment of satisfaction.

This would be enough, for the time being at least. If he had any sense, Vitali would delay, which meant Jay might be staying down here a while longer. If he didn't delay, there was a much higher likelihood of the coup failing. Either way, Jay would have achieved what he'd set out to do.

Stas made a noise—a groan, maybe even an attempt at speech. Jay stepped to one side so that the light from the street illuminated the prone man's face. But his eyes were blank now. Jay crouched down, felt for a pulse, then stood again and looked down at the corpse.

This had been a piece of good fortune, he knew it, and yet… The man below him in the shadows was not the man he'd known, as superficial as their acquaintance had been.

He had looked so beaten, heartbroken even, almost as if he had welcomed the bullet.

And although Stas's hidden personal life bore no relation to the professional consequences of his death, that tear-soaked face somehow seemed to take the edge off Jay's moment of triumph. He'd killed Stas, Vitali's right-hand man. It should have left Jay feeling victorious, so why didn't it?

26

Jay arrived at Petrov's place just after lunch the next day. He was met by the young suited flunky who seemed buoyant, as if he sensed he might be close to some kind of career advancement, now that his boss was soon to be President of Belarus.

"A very good afternoon to you, Mr Lewis. Mr Petrov would like to see you in the study."

He led the way and knocked, opening the door for Jay and announcing his name.

Vitali was standing looking out of the window, but he turned briefly to say, "Jay, come on in. Come and see."

He too seemed in remarkably high spirits.

Jay walked over and stood next to him, looking out of the window which offered a view over the pool. The two boys were out there, lolling about in inflatables, idling, but giggling together almost constantly.

Jay smiled as Owen's infectious laugh reached him even from there. Then he noticed a woman sitting nearby and wondered for a moment if it might be the elusive Mrs Petrov, but he guessed it was actually a nanny.

Vitali said, "It's very pleasing for me to see this. Come, let's sit down. Would you like something to drink?"

"I'm good, thanks."

They sat in the armchairs. Vitali had an unmistakable air of satisfaction about him. He was so upbeat that Jay began to suspect he didn't yet know why his right-hand man had failed to show up this morning.

But then Vitali said, "You might not have heard the news, but Stas went into town on his own last night. I don't know where he went or why. But it seems somebody else did know. His body was found this morning, shot once, straight through the heart."

"I'm sorry to hear that. I can't lie, I don't think we liked each other very much, but I can imagine it's problematic for you, and that concerns me."

"On the contrary, for me, this is a solution to a problem. You see, I've known for some time that Stas was working for the regime. I always planned to kill him, sooner or later—it was just the delicate question of deciding when, and now that decision has been made for me, and all is good."

So that was why he was so upbeat, and also why he'd liked to keep Stas close, not because he was indispensable, but because he was a threat. It also meant Jay's vague misgivings of the night before had been well-placed—far from eliminating one of Vitali's key allies, Jay had inadvertently eliminated one of his own.

"Are you sure? I mean, about Stas."

"About Stas, yes." He stared at Jay for a second, the hint of a smile. By the end of this week, if Vitali's plans came to fruition, he would be in the presidential palace in Minsk, and looking at him now, it seemed he could feel it was within reach. His sense of his own power and invincibility appeared to be growing even as they sat there. "About Stas, I am sure. But about you, Jay, I am less certain. I hear rumors, and I discount them, because it makes no sense. But still these rumors persist."

Jay smiled, and felt relaxed enough for the smile to be genuine. He was surprised that they'd been working together for six months and yet the question of Jay's trustworthiness was only just being raised.

"If he weren't dead, I'd have assumed Stas was responsible for those rumors." Vitali's eyes flickered, a small tell that suggested Stas might have indeed been responsible for some of them. "But *you're* my client, Vitali, only you, and anyone who tells you otherwise is playing a game of their own. I think I've killed enough of your government's agents in the last week to prove my loyalty on that score."

"This is true." His expression was hard to read, but Jay didn't like it, and less so as Petrov said, "And I hope you do tell the truth. Alexei, as you see… is very fond of Owen."

Two paces. Jay could get up, walk two paces, and break his neck before he had chance to call out.

"Would you put your son in harm's way, Vitali?"

"Never!" A sudden hint of anger crossed his face. "My son is everything to me."

"As is mine to me. And if I were betraying you, I wouldn't be entrusting my son to your safety."

The anger passed as Vitali took in his meaning, and then finally he yielded.

"My apologies, Jay, as one father to another. You know, this is quite a tense time."

"I understand, of course."

Vitali waved his hand dismissively, the whole matter apparently forgotten, along with the unfortunate Stas and his mysteriously tear-soaked face.

"And speaking of which, I've arranged one final day of sailing for the boys, if you don't mind, tomorrow. I'll have someone come for Owen at eleven in the morning."

Jay could hardly object, given that he'd just linked his own loyalty to the trust he had in Owen spending time within the Petrov bubble.

"I'm sure he'd love to. We'll be there."

"Good. It's important, for Alexei." He looked lost in thought for a moment, perhaps thinking about his son, then said, "I played chess as a boy, did you know that?"

"I didn't." Jay couldn't imagine Vitali's huge hands deftly moving pieces about a chessboard.

"I was very good. But if I lost a match, my father would make me sleep in the corridor outside our apartment, even in winter. He also played against me every day, from when I was this big." He held a hand out, suggesting a very young child. "And if he won, he would slap my face, hard. By the time I was nine, he rarely won. Last time ever was when I was twelve. When I was seventeen, I set fire to the chess set, right there on the kitchen table, right in front of him. I walked out of that apartment and I never saw him or my mother again, and I never played chess again. That's the old Belarus."

"You never saw your mother again, either?"

"No. Because she could have stopped him and she didn't. I have no regrets."

"Then you're a lucky man."

It was probably the first ever glimpse he'd had of Vitali Petrov himself, the man beneath all the power and wealth, and it made Jay uneasy in some way.

"They're both dead anyway," said Vitali, dismissing the subject.

He reached over and picked up a phone, speaking briefly into it in Russian. Jay understood enough to know that he was telling someone that Owen's father was here to collect him.

He put the phone down again and Jay took the opportunity to move away from Petrov's strange childhood, saying, "There's one thing that troubles me, from a security perspective. Who killed Stas? If he was working for the regime, the guys up at Bogdanov's place wouldn't have killed him. I'm guessing no one here knew he was working for the other side. It doesn't leave many people."

Vitali responded with a nonchalance that gave a flavor of the kind of president he'd be if the coup succeeded.

"Maybe the American killed him. The CIA. You said they're on our side. Maybe they knew that Stas was a traitor and they were worried he would make trouble for me. But these are things we don't need to concern ourselves with. In six days, I will be the President of Belarus. And America will be remembered for the assistance it's given me, as will you."

"I appreciate that, Vitali."

Above all, he appreciated that killing Stas had done nothing to undermine Vitali's prediction for the next six days, and might have gone some way toward helping it happen. He was left relying on the disruptive potential of the documents he'd handed to Georgy, and right now, he was no longer sure that would be enough.

Owen came in a short while later, his hair still wet from the pool. He thanked Vitali in Russian, earning a pat on the head in response. The boy had a facility with languages, and a charm that left Jay's in the shade.

As they drove away, Jay said, "So how was that?"

"It was pretty cool. Alexei's kind of lame, but I don't think that's his fault. It's because he never gets to hang out with other kids. Once you get to know him, he's really not too bad."

"I'm glad. You know you're going sailing again tomorrow?"

"Yes!" He punched the air, a little habit Jay was becoming familiar with. "I knew you'd say yes."

"Why would I say no?"

"Well…" He hesitated, looked sad for a fleeting second, then brushed it away. "Mom would have said no. She said no a lot, but I think that was just because…"

He clearly had no idea why his mom had said "no" so much, why she'd so disliked the person she thought he was becoming. At least, he had no idea that would make sense to his ten year old mind.

"You know, Owen, it's difficult to see it sometimes, but even when people act in a way you don't like or that makes you mad, they're still usually trying their best." Even as he spoke, he realized he could be speaking about his own dad as much as he was talking about Owen's mother. "Your mom is obviously someone who cares a lot, about a lot of things, but I guess sometimes that just leaves her overwhelmed, and maybe that's why she doesn't always act in a way that makes sense."

Owen nodded, although Jay wasn't sure he'd understood, and then the boy caught him unawares by saying, "You're not gonna make me go back, are you, Jay?"

"No. No, not at all." He glanced over to see Owen looking visibly relieved. Jay was about to point out the obvious, that Megan didn't want him back and had gone to considerable lengths to ensure that didn't happen, but Owen hardly needed to be reminded of that brutal fact. "I don't have all the answers. I don't know what's gonna happen, but as long as you want to stay with me, you'll stay with me. You're a good kid. Don't ever forget that."

"Thanks, Jay." The gratitude sounded genuine.

"You're welcome. Anyway, everyone seemed very happy at the Petrov place this morning."

"Oh, yeah, I forgot to tell you! Wait till you hear." They were back on familiar ground. "That guy Stas, he got killed last night. And everyone was really happy about it. Like, Alexei's mom was happy because, like I told you, she didn't like him at all. But Alexei's dad was really happy too. Alexei said it was because his dad had found out Stas was a rat. What's a rat?"

"You don't know what a rat is?"

"Duh? I don't mean *a rat*, like a rodent. I mean when they called Stas a rat, what do they mean?"

"I wouldn't say he was a rat. A rat is someone in a criminal gang who's giving information to the police. Stas was working for the government in Minsk, so, the opposite side to Alexei's dad, even though he pretended to be on the same side."

Owen thought about that and said, "So it is kind of like being a rat then."

"I guess so, now that I think about it."

"Anyway, they're all really happy he's dead."

"That's good to know," said Jay, even as he cursed himself—for the first time in six months, he'd accidentally done what he was being paid to do and advanced Vitali Petrov's interests.

He felt his phone buzz in his pocket as they were turning down into the parking garage and he looked at it as they went up in the elevator. It was a message from Rich McKenzie.

"We need to talk. Urgently! Tonight at 9, in Zinc."

That was puzzling on any number of levels. Six hours from now didn't feel particularly urgent. And why in Zinc if it was—presumably—something sensitive? Even on a Monday evening, there were usually enough people in Zinc to make being overheard a distinct possibility.

Only the reason for the meeting was easy to guess. Rich had heard about Stas. He'd assumed Jay had acted on the intelligence Rich had himself shared with him, that Jay was indeed in league with the Russians, had maybe even killed Stas himself. All of that was true, but even so, right now Rich was the least of his problems.

27

Juliette arrived at eight, casually said hello to Jay, then greeted Owen in French like an old friend.

He responded in French, but then slipped into English to say, "You want me to teach you some Russian?"

"You know Russian?"

"Only a little."

Juliette glanced at Jay who said, "C'est une éponge."

She nodded, like that was an understatement, and then Owen looked suspicious and said, "What did you just call me?"

"A sponge. It's a compliment. I mean you soak up information."

"*Oui*," said Juliette. "You're très intelligent!"

He looked momentarily bashful before regaining his cool, and Jay took that as his cue to leave them to it.

The evening was warm, lacking the chill that had come with dusk until now, but he wore a jacket, because he was still holstered—he was confident Georgy would have sent word to the right people in Minsk, but he couldn't be sure that word had since reached the people up at Bogdanov's place. Even if it had, some of them might still want to take a shot at the American who'd killed so many of their colleagues.

He walked to the Yacht Club first. He'd already eaten, so he only sat at the bar and had a drink. He'd gone mainly in the hope that Harry might be there. She wasn't, his disappointment out of all proportion.

Then as he was leaving, he almost bumped into someone as she came in, and despite the complete lack of physical similarity, it took him a moment to see that it wasn't Harry.

"Amandine. When did you get back?"

She kissed him on both cheeks, her hands on his shoulders, a strangely formal greeting.

"Hello, Jay. Just this morning, and I'm only staying a day or two. I was hoping we'd have the opportunity to chat."

"Sure. Um, I'm kind of busy—"

"With your son?" She looked over his shoulder, as if half expecting to see a boy standing behind him.

"No. I mean, yeah, he's with a babysitter tonight. But work. I'm on my way to a meeting right now."

"Of course." She was still no less beautiful, and yet looking at her, he no longer felt anything at all, and wasn't sure he'd ever felt much more than a mixture of lust and convenience. He imagined it had been much the same for her, but how had that ever been enough? She frowned. "I know it's only been a week or… It feels longer."

"It does."

She looked around. They were standing near the entrance and she apparently wanted to make sure no one would overhear.

"This was not my intention and I don't know how it happened. But I met someone, a friend of my sister, and he… We actually knew each other years ago. I just, I'm not sure what to say."

He was surprised by how genuinely pleased he was for her.

"You don't have to say a word. We had some fun, Amandine, but you always deserved more than I could give you."

"It's true."

She didn't mean to sound as brutal as she did, but it still stung, for all his feelings of generosity toward her. Then she hugged him, but as she backed away she looked at the spot where his gun rested below his shoulder, then with concern at him.

"Since when was the Yacht Club so dangerous?"

"It's not. So long, Amandine."

She brushed his cheek with her fingers, the concern lingering, and he left her. It was true what she'd said, that the last week or so had felt so much longer. Amandine already seemed like a relic of a distant age, maybe of a distant person, even though he knew at heart that he hadn't changed that much.

When he reached Zinc he found it busy enough, although no one was at the bar. Lucien was mixing a drink, just adding the garnish. He slid it across the bar.

"I have a feeling you might not be in town for too much longer, and you've never tried my Martini."

Jay acknowledged the gesture, took the drink and sipped it, immediately won over by its crystalline smoothness.

"Very good, Lucien. I wish I'd known how good it was sooner."

"Such a simple cocktail, but so many minute variations. You'll never have one as good as this."

"I believe it."

Lucien gave a tip of the head across the room. "He's in the back corner."

Jay turned and saw that Rich was already there, in the same seat where Harry had been with her laptop on their second meeting. Jay walked over and sat down. Rich had a Negroni, and once again seemed to have barely touched it.

"Hello, Rich."

"Jay."

"What's so urgent?"

He was about to add "that it could wait six hours", but stopped himself, realizing that Rich had probably been in touch with his superiors in that time, checking on his rules of engagement, maybe even on what kind of protection or immunity Jay still had.

"I think you know the answer to that. I've suspected all along that you're working as a triple agent. You say you're bluffing the Russians, but you're not, you're helping them, and by association, you're helping the regime in Minsk." Jay didn't have any response to that, so he sipped his drink. Lucien was right, Jay wouldn't be here for many more days, and he regretted already that he hadn't discovered the Zinc Martini sooner. Rich bit his bottom lip, apparently furious, and said, "I told you Stas was a key player in securing the success of the coup, and then he gets killed almost immediately afterwards. I dare you to deny that it was you who killed him."

"You could keep your voice down there, Rich. No one else knows and I'd prefer it to stay that way."

Lowering his voice, but incredulous, Rich said, "So it *was* you?"

"Yeah, it was me. I didn't want to tell you at the time, because I don't work for you or your agency anymore, but Stas was a trojan horse. He was working for the regime in Minsk. Vitali always planned to kill him, but I thought he was leaving it too late, so I took matters into my own hands."

"No, our intelligence—"

"Your intelligence was wrong, Rich, on that at least. The worst of it is that the other intelligence you gave me, on the loyalty or otherwise of the military in Belarus, that was sound, but Stas would have had access to it."

"Damn it." It was almost a whisper. Finally, he took a gulp of his Negroni.

Silently, Jay echoed his curse, too, because he realized that document couldn't be as crucial to undermining Vitali's cause as Jay had hoped it might be. Vitali had known Stas was working for the regime, and yet he'd handed it to him directly, asked his opinion of it. It was either massive hubris on Vitali's part, or he knew more than anyone else about how the military would act this coming Sunday.

"Can Petrov delay?"

"It's not that he can't. He won't. But I hope I can offer you some reassurance. Vitali knew that Stas was working against him, but he was completely relaxed about him seeing that document."

Rich began to look hopeful. "Meaning?"

"Meaning that Vitali Petrov needs your help and my help less than we imagine. He's a formidable player, and if anyone can topple the regime in Minsk, I'd put my money on it being him."

He took that in, thought about it.

"Okay." He took another gulp of his drink, but then pushed the glass aside, still half full. "I need to call in on some of this."

Jay finished his own drink. "I'll walk back with you as far as the Grand, if that's where you're headed."

"Of course." Rich seemed distracted, even as he got out of his seat.

This meeting had gone better, and been shorter, than Jay had imagined it would be. But he was also heading to the Grand for the same reason he'd gone to the Yacht Club, and even felt embarrassed that he was drifting around town in the hope of bumping into a woman who was undoubtedly immune to everything about him apart from his child.

Jay reached for his wallet but Lucien waved it away. "That one was on the house."

"Then I'll be back," said Jay, and they stepped out and walked toward the Grand.

After a few paces in silence, Rich said, "I apologize if I... Look, I'll be straight, I'm still not convinced I can trust you, but I apologize if I *have* read you wrong."

"I appreciate that Rich. I know it can't be easy."

"It isn't. Or wasn't. There are people higher up the food chain who still rate you."

"It's good that they even remember me."

"Remember you?" Rich almost seemed in good humor now. "I had a phone conversation today with someone very high up who sang your praises so much I was beginning to think *he* might be a traitor."

"Yeah, I think I can guess who that—"

Jay heard footsteps behind them and turned. After a half pace extra, Rich registered and turned too. There were two men there, both dressed in black like it was their uniform.

Jay had scoped the street as he'd left Zinc—Rich had no doubt done the same—but these two had seemingly appeared out of nowhere. Jay made a movement toward his gun, but the one facing him had beat him to it, and was already pointing his own gun right at Jay's stomach.

He didn't even have time to react, didn't even have time to castigate himself for being caught off guard. He glimpsed a knife in the other guy's hand only as he stepped forward and thrust himself into a violent embrace with Rich McKenzie, his arm jabbing back and forward in three swift brutal strikes.

The knifeman backed away then. The gunman started to do the same, moving backwards, keeping the gun on Jay and shaking his head at the same time, making clear he'd been spared. Jay knew that to be the truth.

He glanced to the side to see Rich crumple, stunned as he fell to his knees, then over on his side, the blood spreading glossily across his shirt. The two men were running now, a little way up the street before jumping into a car that sped off.

And now somebody screamed. There were people about, maybe a couple dozen within fifty yards, and some were running away, but most were converging on the screaming woman who stood a short distance away.

Jay looked at another young woman who was approaching with an appearance of curiosity and composure, and yelled, "Call an ambulance!"

He knelt down then, eased Rich onto his back, pulled the shirt free. The three wounds were lost in a sea of blood, pumping out still. He slipped off his jacket, balled it up and pushed it against the three inch-long puncture points.

People were gathering around now and he looked up at a young guy who'd arrived and said, "Hold this! Press it. There. And there."

The guy dropped to his knees, almost as Rich had, and put his hands on top of the jacket. Jay moved up to Rich's face, tapping him lightly on the cheek. He was still there, but Jay could already see that the external pressure would never be enough, that those three punching stabs had done their job.

"Stay with me, Rich! Stay with me."

Rich's eyes found his but appeared not to recognize Jay or anything else.

Jay looked up at the gathering crowd. "Is anyone here a doctor or a nurse?"

But they all looked helpless, and when Jay looked again at Rich's eyes he knew it wouldn't have made a difference anyway. He turned to the young guy who was sobbing as he concentrated on holding the jacket against Rich's lifeless body.

"It's okay, you can let go." The guy didn't react, so Jay put his hands on top of his and gently prized them away. "It's okay. You did your best."

The young guy glanced to the side, but not enough, as if he wanted to look at Rich's face but didn't dare, and his voice was full of dread as he said, "He's dead?"

"Yeah, he's dead. I'm sorry."

The young guy accepted the condolences as if it had been his friend who'd been attacked and Jay was just a random stranger. Possibly there was some truth in that, too, because Jay could imagine that it would trouble this good Samaritan's dreams and waking hours for months and years to come, maybe even for the rest of his life.

Jay heard a siren in the distance, and he sank down so that he was sitting on the ground now, alongside Rich's body. He looked at his face, the yacht broker's face, and the little white scar on his chin.

He hadn't found much to like about Rich McKenzie, and didn't know the first thing about him, not least where or when he'd managed to get that scar. But somehow looking at it now, Jay was reminded that this too was someone's son lying here next to him, someone who'd also had hopes and fears and formative experiences, and a childhood in some suburb or small town.

It was a waste, of course, as so much of this work was. Rich McKenzie had been sent down here, and the people who'd sent him would have known that his role was illusory, that he was completely redundant. They might not have intended to sacrifice him, only to waste his time and give him a false sense of purpose, but sacrifice him they had.

28

Jay stayed until the ambulance and the police arrived. He had little choice when there were so many bystanders, members of the public who'd also seen that he was wearing a shoulder holster.

He gave the police Benny's details and after a few calls, Jay was sent on his way without needing to give a formal statement. One of the officers asked if he needed a car to take him home, but he refused the offer and started along the street, the remaining crowd parting in silence for him to pass.

He was carrying the jacket, but he turned and saw himself in a store window, his clothes blood-stained, and realized he couldn't go back to the apartment looking like that. It would freak them both out, and Owen would probably assume he was hurt himself.

There was a store still open nearby, it's North African owner standing by his tourist-oriented merchandise of t-shirts and bags and sunglasses, but looking curiously at the spectacle still unfolding along the street.

Jay said, "I need a t-shirt." He looked down. "Maybe some shorts, espadrilles."

The store owner looked at him as if he'd seen it all before, and gestured into the cramped interior space, saying, "Please."

"And do you have a bathroom where I can change?"

"Please," said the storekeeper again, gently, as if making clear he knew Jay's night had been a tough one, but that he'd do his best to make it better.

He showed Jay to the small bathroom, then brought him a pair of boardshorts, a pair of striped espadrilles and a t-shirt with the town's name on the front underneath a generic picture that could have been anywhere on the Cote d'Azur. He gave him a plastic bag, too, and held it open for Jay to drop the soiled jacket into it.

"Thanks."

Jay washed his hands and face, then changed, looking in the mirror when he'd finished. He looked like someone heading to the beach for a day's relaxation in the sun, not someone on a late night walk with a bag full of bloodied clothes and a gun that he hadn't had chance to draw.

The storekeeper didn't want to take his money, but Jay insisted, and the guy finally relented. He looked at Jay then with an expression of world-weary empathy and patted him on the shoulder.

Jay left the store, not looking back up the street where the patrol cars were still making a light display, but turning instead for home. When he got there, he dropped the bag in his bedroom before walking through to the living room where Juliette and Owen were playing blackjack.

They turned and looked at him as he walked in, as if he'd walked into the casino in town like that, and after a moment's silence, Juliette burst out laughing.

"Was it a costume party?"

Jay laughed a little too, and said, "It's a long story. But what do you think, could I go with this look?"

"I like your sneakers," said Owen, and Jay was pleased that he didn't seem unduly alarmed by the radically different appearance.

"They're called espadrilles."

"They're cool. Maybe I could get a pair." Before Jay could reply, Juliette gave Owen a stern look, a warning, making clear that espadrilles would be a fashion mistake, even for a ten year old. "Or maybe not."

"Okay, well, I'm back. I'm gonna change out of these things." Juliette stood and Jay said, "Message me when you get back."

He went into his room to change and left Owen and Juliette to say their goodbyes. She called a goodbye to Jay as she left and by the time he walked back through, Owen was in his bathroom.

Jay poured himself a drink, walked out onto the balcony and sat for a little while, but couldn't settle. Sitting with a drink on this balcony had been one of the unsung pleasures of his life here, something he recognized only now as it seemed to be lost to him.

By the time he walked back through, Owen was in bed reading.

He looked up and said, "I'm really tired, Jay. I don't know why."

Jay sat on the floor next to his futon and said, "How much did you sleep last night, at the *sleep*over?"

Owen looked noncommittal, but he was grinning too, hinting at the true answer.

Then he grew serious and said, "Why were you wearing those clothes?" Jay feigned confusion, as if to ask what there was to explain. But then Owen added, "Did someone get hurt?"

"What makes you ask that?"

He pointed. "You have blood. On your nails."

Jay looked down and saw what he'd missed earlier, the final moments of Rich McKenzie's life captured there in the crevices. He saw a flashback to the little white scar again, pointlessly regretting that he hadn't asked Rich how he'd gotten it.

"Yeah, someone got hurt."

"A good guy or a bad guy?"

"One of our side."

Although Jay had to admit, that wasn't really true—he and Rich had been on opposing sides. But Rich McKenzie had been, in Owen's binary terms, a good guy, working for the right people. He'd also been sacrificed by those same people, as any intelligence officer was when they were sent into the field without the information they needed.

"So you didn't kill him?"

"No."

Was Owen troubled by the thought of him killing people? He guessed that was only natural—he was a little kid, with a moral compass, the same moral compass that had made him stick up for that kid who was being bullied.

But Jay reminded himself of the justice Owen had meted out in turn to Isaac Gleick, and at the same moment, Owen said, "Will you kill the people who did it?"

He wasn't concerned now, but apparently looking for more of the moral certainty that had seen him complacent about Isaac's injuries.

Jay said, "It's not always that simple." He was intrigued then, and added, "Would you be okay with it if I did kill them?"

"Like, totally. I told you what Mom said, that you kill people, so it's not like I didn't know about it."

He thought of Harry telling him that Owen saw him as a model, or rather, had seen him as a model before he'd actually met him.

"And I think I told you that your mom was kind of making it seem worse than it really is. Sure, I've killed people, but it's not like that's my job."

"I know." His tone was casual. "Does it make you sad when you kill people?"

He'd asked him that question before and for some reason it made Jay uneasy.

"No."

"What about when people get killed, like people you know?"

Matty Martinez had been a local guide they'd worked with in Guatemala City. Someone—they'd never found out exactly who—had gone to his apartment, killed him and his girlfriend, and dumped their bodies in front of the hotel where Jay and his team were staying. He'd told Jay the week before that his girlfriend was pregnant, and even in death they'd looked so full of promise, as if that whole optimistic future were still opening out in front of them.

"Sometimes. But sometimes life is difficult. So you feel sad, but you also remember that most of the time life is good. You get to hang out in nice places with nice people, and play blackjack with pretty teenagers." Owen sniggered, suddenly looking once more like the small child he was. "All I'm saying is, I don't want you to worry, but at the same time, you can always ask me anything. I might not answer, but I'll never lie to you."

"Thanks, Jay." He frowned. "You're not like other adults. Well, except Harry, I think you're kind of like her. But you're not like the adults back in Denver."

"No? Well you're not like other kids, either, so that makes us a good team." He smiled at that. "Goodnight, Owen."

"Goodnight, Jay."

He left him to read his book, but when he checked in again ten minutes later, he was fast asleep, his face a sea of calm. Jay took his drink back out onto the balcony and this time he sat and finally found some calm himself.

He wished he could feel sad for Rich McKenzie, but he didn't. He knew at some intellectual level that it was sad, that this young man had died, that there would be people learning in the coming hours that someone they loved had been stabbed to death on a French street, but he didn't actually feel it. Maybe he never had, or maybe that part of him had been lost, cauterized in one go, or slowly eroding over the years with each subsequent death.

29

It was a normal morning, or what had come to pass for normal. Jay and Owen had breakfast together, but only because Jay was happy to wait until after nine for Owen to stir, then another twenty minutes before he emerged fully dressed from his room, ready to face the day.

Marion called to say she was running late. Owen talked about sailing and how he'd like to do more of it even after Alexei went back to Minsk. Jay idly wondered where he might go once he left Cotignac-sur-Mer, and if there'd be sailing opportunities.

Owen was in his room playing a game just before eleven when Jay's phone rang. He looked and saw it was Georgy Gumilev and almost didn't answer, thinking he'd just call him back once Owen had been picked up.

At the last, though, he did pick up and Georgy said, "Jay, can you talk?"

"Sure," said Jay, even as he registered how grave Georgy sounded. "Is there a problem?"

"There is. You know I expressed concerns about speaking to Minsk on your behalf." He did, although if Georgy hadn't done that, there was a pretty good chance Jay would have been lying dead on the street alongside Rich McKenzie the night before. "It seems my fears were well-founded. One of the people at Bogdanov's villa was working for Petrov. I only found out this morning. Your cover is blown, Jay. They know you're against them."

He'd always known this was a possibility, but his stomach still hollowed out with the delivery of the news. The game was up. Any lingering hope of undermining Petrov by subterfuge was gone. And at the same time, Jay had removed himself from one target list only to place himself on another.

He heard Owen sing a snatch of some song to himself, and realized there was a more immediate problem. Someone would show up here within minutes to take Owen away and Jay couldn't let him go. He also wondered how long Vitali had known.

Had he been toying with him yesterday? Was the sailing trip a set-up for an ambush? It didn't seem likely somehow, but if Vitali hadn't known then, he must have found out shortly after, and Jay could imagine how furious he would have been. The fact that he'd been able to contain that fury was even more disturbing.

"How certain are you, Georgy?"

"Absolutely certain. I'm so sorry, Jay."

Jay checked the time and said, "Okay, don't worry. We're not done, not yet, but thanks for letting me know."

"Jay, if there's anything I can do—and you know, I mean *anything*—then you just let me know."

"I'll bear that in mind, Georgy. Thanks for calling."

He put his phone away and walked through into Owen's room. He was in the bathroom, still singing the same song even as he brushed his teeth, the words and the tune all mashed up and garbled with toothpaste.

Jay looked from the window down into the street. A car had just parked below and someone had climbed out of the driving seat and was looking at the building. Jay had seen him in passing up at Petrov's place, but it wasn't someone who'd previously come to collect Owen.

The guy checked the time on his watch, and Jay followed suit—it was almost eleven, but the time was just a cover, and so was the sailing trip, even if hadn't been to begin with. Was this a simple hit? Jay doubted Vitali would have waited this long if that was all he'd wanted. More likely, the guy would take Owen, all the better to inflict the most pain on Jay.

Owen came out of the bathroom. Jay turned and they stood facing each other like two men in a standoff.

Owen spoke first, saying, "What's up, Jay?"

Jay glanced back into the street. The guy had disappeared. He walked a few paces, crouched down so he was close to the same level as his son.

"I haven't got time to explain now. You're not going sailing. Someone's coming, but I… Not a good person."

"Is he gonna hurt us?" Amazingly, he sounded curious rather than afraid.

"No. That's what he's here for, but he won't."

"Are you gonna kill him?"

"Yes." Owen seemed unfazed. "But I need you to stay in your room and keep the door closed. Okay?" He nodded, taking the instructions seriously. "Good. I'll be back before you know it."

He felt a powerful urge to kiss the boy's head, but he didn't want to scare him, not now, so he simply patted him on the shoulder and left the room, closing the door behind him.

He went into his own room and took the gun from the bag of bloodied clothes, angry with himself for having left it there. He attached the silencer and moved quickly back to the front door. But even as he opened it, he could hear the elevator in motion.

Jay stepped out, closing the door behind him, then moved beyond the elevator, slipping into the doorway of his neighbor's apartment which was normally empty. Yet, to his astonishment, he heard noise now beyond the door— tinny music, then, unmistakably, the sound of a man singing tunelessly. It only took Jay a second to work out the neighbor was now at home, but listening to music through headphones. Maybe that would be enough.

The elevator arrived and paused. Jay was definitely ready for a change of scene; he'd spent too much of his time killing people in and around this elevator this past week. The door slid open and Jay pressed himself back into his hiding place.

Petrov's guy stepped out, looked briefly right, then headed left, two steps, and knocked on Jay's apartment door. Jay stepped out at the same time and fired his shot as the second knock sounded. The guy seemed to stumble forward, thumping into the door. Jay picked up his pace, pushing in behind him, turning the handle, helping him fall through, and as he landed, Jay crouched and fired another shot close to point blank into the center of his back.

Even then, Jay dropped down onto his knees and pulled up the bottom of the guy's jacket, then his shirt, making sure he wasn't wearing Kevlar. Only with that risk eliminated did he look at his face where it lay uncomfortably in profile against the hard floor. Jay thought of Owen and wanted to put another bullet in the guy's head, but it was also because of Owen that he didn't.

He checked for a pulse to be sure, then pulled the dead man up by the shoulder and reached inside his jacket for his gun. He was wearing a customized holster, the gun with its silencer already attached. The fact that he hadn't drawn it suggested they'd intended to take Owen from him under the cover of the sailing trip, but equally, the choice of man and the choice of weapon made clear what the back-up plan had been.

Jay said, "It's okay, Owen. Stay there, but it's all good."

Owen said something in response but he didn't catch it. Jay put the two guns on the table in the hallway, then opened Owen's door a crack and looked in with a smile. The boy was standing midway between the futon and the bathroom door, looking alert and expectant but composed.

"Is he dead?"

"Yeah."

"It was really loud, Jay. I thought you'd have a silencer."

"I did. So did he." Not that Petrov's man had gotten around to using it. "They're a lot louder in real life than they are in the movies."

He realized as he said it that this was almost the same thing he'd said to Polina, the hooker he'd used to help snare Bobo.

Jay noticed Owen craning his neck this way and that, curious. He was looking around Jay's legs at the body slumped in the hallway beyond. Jay came into the room and closed the door behind him.

"I don't want you to see that. I know you're curious, but—"

"I saw a dead body before. This old man was sitting in the doorway of a store and we ran past because he looked kind of scary and then Walden said that he wasn't scary, just dead. So we turned back, but then this woman ran up and tried to cover our eyes which felt really creepy. But anyway, he was dead. He froze to death."

"A homeless guy?" Owen nodded casually. "That's a real shame. And look, you'll see dead people sooner or later, but right now…"

"It's okay, Jay. I don't wanna see him."

"Good. Stay here for a minute. I'm gonna put him in the bathtub in my room."

"Are you gonna leave him there?" He sounded incredulous, like leaving a body in the bathtub was the strangest thing about his morning.

"For now." Until last night, he'd have called Rich McKenzie and asked for a removal, but that option was gone, and Jay had more pressing issues to deal with. "And we're gonna have to hide out somewhere else for a day or two, so… why don't you pack some clothes and things into your backpack, just like for the sleepover, and we'll get out of here."

"Okay."

Jay left him to it, closing the door behind him. He dragged the guy through into his bedroom, then into the bathroom and heaved him into the tub. He collected the two guns from the table, put the one in the box and kept his own.

There was a small amount of blood on the hallway floor, although not much. But he was still on in his knees cleaning it up when he heard the elevator in motion again. He went back to his room, grabbed his gun and was just stepping out as Marion opened the door and looked at him with immediate suspicion.

"What's wrong?"

"There's been a development. Someone came here to kill me, or take Owen, or…" She raised her eyebrows, but that was the extent of the shock. "He's in the bathtub." She turned and looked at Owen's door. "Owen's fine. He's just packing a few things. We'll have to keep clear of the apartment for a day or two, and that means you, too."

"Do I need to worry?"

"No, but don't come back here until I call you."

She looked at the closed bedroom door again. "You want me to take Owen with me, until you're certain?"

It was tempting. He'd be free to act without limits if Owen wasn't with him. And there'd be less risk for Owen, but more risk for Marion if Petrov found out the boy was staying with her. Above all, he knew that Owen would want to be with him, and tough as it might be over the next forty-eight hours, he didn't want him thinking Jay had abandoned him.

"I'm grateful for the offer, Marion, but I think it's best he stays with me. He'll be fine."

With that, the bedroom door opened and Owen stepped out, wearing his backpack.

"Hey, Marion." His tone was as cheery and casual as if he were still about to go sailing.

She hugged him in response, and seemed unwilling to let him go even as she said to Jay, "So I should leave now?"

"Yeah, I'll message you as soon as it's safe to come back."

"I'll be waiting," she said, and reluctantly let go of Owen and raised a hand in farewell as she left.

Jay looked at Owen then and said, "Ready?"

"Ready."

"Great. I'll just throw some things together. Got your books?"

"I don't believe it! That's the one thing I *did* forget." He traipsed back into his room to get his books and Jay went into his own room and put clothes in a bag, then into the bathroom where the body in the tub looked like someone sleeping off a heavy night.

Owen was once again waiting for him in the hallway, and looked at him with an expression that almost made Jay laugh, as if saying, *Well, here we are, in a fine old mess.*

Jay said, "Let's go."

They took the elevator and Owen said, "Are we taking the car?"

"No, we're walking."

"Where to?"

"Right now we need a friend, so we'll go see a friend, see if she can help."

"Yes!" He punched the air, knowing without asking who it was that Jay was talking about. And Jay envied him, because he still thought this was an adventure—Jay only hoped the illusion would persist over the coming days.

30

Jay was casual as they left the building, but he was alert, too, and didn't fully relax until he saw that the car was empty, confirmation that the dead man upstairs had come alone. They started walking toward the Bellevue.

After a short distance, Owen looked behind before saying, "How did you kill him?"

At first, Jay had thought he was looking behind because he was nervous, but now realized he was checking no one was close enough to overhear. If he was play-acting, he was pretty good at it.

"You know how I did it. You heard the shots."

"Sure, but I mean, like, were you hiding, or did you wait for him to come to the door?"

This whole last week Jay had felt like he was getting sloppy, like the lifestyle down here was making him complacent. As he thought through what he might say in response, he knew that he'd been riding his luck and that there were no great strategic insights to be had from his methods, not even for a kid.

"I heard the elevator, so I walked up the hall and stood in the doorway of my neighbor's apartment. Petrov's guy came out of the elevator, walked up and knocked on the door, and that's when I shot him—"

"Wait! He was working for Alexei's dad?"

Of course, in the rush of dealing with the body and getting out of the apartment, he hadn't explained that fact yet.

"That was probably why I caught him off-guard. He thought he'd catch us unawares, act like he was just coming to pick you up for your sailing lesson, then…" He didn't want to spell out how Owen might have ended up as a bargaining chip, or worse. "Well, I guess he was hoping to kill me. But I'd been tipped off by a friend."

"Harry?"

"No. You remember Georgy?"

"The old Russian man."

"Yeah."

"But. I thought you were on the same side as Alexei's dad. You're trying to help him become president."

"It's complicated." He looked down at him in what he imagined was a reassuring way, but Owen simply looked confused. "I can't explain it all right now. The thing is, for the last six months I've been acting like I was helping Alexei's dad, but I've been working for the other side, to stop him becoming president of Belarus."

"Why?"

"That's one of the things I'll have to explain another time."

"Is Alexei's dad a bad guy?"

Jay frowned, because that binary distinction really broke down when it came to places like Belarus.

"Honestly, I don't know. He's no worse than the guy who's in charge in Belarus right now, but it's also possible he's no better. I don't know enough about him to have a personal opinion. I'm just doing a job, and my job is to try to stop him."

"I understand, Jay. I won't ask any more about it."

Jay was pretty certain Owen didn't understand, but he was smart enough to know that Jay wouldn't be drawn on any of the details. Jay couldn't imagine many kids of his age being willing to park their curiosity like that.

"Like I told you before, you can always ask me anything you like, as long as you know that sometimes I won't be able to answer, even if I wanted to."

"Okay. Do you like Harry?"

Jay laughed. He hadn't expected Owen to take his pledge quite so literally.

"I meant you could ask about professional stuff, not so much personal stuff. But yeah, I like Harry. She's good fun to be around and she's very pretty."

"I think she likes you, too."

"I think she does. But she's also very professional and she doesn't wanna get involved. You know, Harry's likely to move on in the next week or so, and chances are I'll never see her again. That's what this kind of work is like."

"Is that what happened with you and Mom?"

"Kind of. Your mom didn't like the work I did back then. It bothered her. But Harry? I don't think she'd be too concerned that I've left a body in the bathtub."

Owen said, "Seriously? Mom gets mad if I forget to put the toilet seat down."

"Trust me, *all* women get mad if you do that. Body in the bathtub, not a problem, leave the toilet seat up, you're in big trouble."

Owen laughed and couldn't stop, which set Jay off in turn, and they walked some way along the street like that, earning smiles from passers-by.

When they reached the Bellevue he walked up to the reception desk and said to the young woman standing there, "Would you call Ms. Baverstock and ask if she's at home for some American visitors?"

"Of course."

She walked off to one side of the reception desk. Jay couldn't hear much of the brief conversation that ensued, but he heard her say, "yes, a man and a small boy".

Owen said, "Why didn't you message her?"

"I don't know how secure her line is. I'm sure it's good, but I couldn't afford the risk of people knowing we're here."

"What if people saw us walking here?"

"Good thinking. It's possible, I guess, but I think it's less likely. For one thing, they probably don't even know yet that the guy who came to our apartment failed. And it's easier to follow people electronically than in person—that's why I said you and Walden need to be careful online."

"I know." He thought about it. "I kind of miss Walden."

"Maybe when this is all over…"

He left the comment unfinished as the receptionist came back and said, "Miss Baverstock would be happy to see you. She's in 301. Would you like me to show you the way?"

"We'll be fine, thanks."

They headed to the elevator and as they were riding up, Owen said, "Are we gonna stay the night in Harry's room?"

"I don't know. Hopefully we'll stay for a few hours at least. But the Bellevue is an all-suite hotel so she might let us camp out in her living room for the night. You wouldn't mind that, would you?"

"I think it'd be cool."

They stepped out and Jay rang the bell. She opened the door a few seconds later, dressed in shorts and a t-shirt, as if she'd planned to spend the day relaxing on her terrace.

She noticed their bags and said, "Well this looks terribly serious." She smiled at Owen then and said, "Come on in. Are you hungry?"

"No, thank you," he said, almost matching her accent. It was true, he really was a sponge.

"Well sit down, anyway."

Owen slipped off his backpack and sat on the couch. Jay left his bag by the door and took one of the armchairs. Harry came in and took the other. Her legs were long and tan, and for a second or two he was totally distracted.

He came back to himself and said, "We're in a bit of a jam. We can't stay in my apartment for a short while."

"There's a dead man in the bathtub," Owen offered by way of explanation.

She looked at him deadpan and said, "I hate it when that happens."

Owen burst out laughing, chuckling away to himself.

Jay looked at her even as the laughter continued in the background and said, "Rich McKenzie got killed last night."

"I know. And I know I predicted it, but I didn't think it would happen quite so soon."

"He was with me at the time."

"Ah." That gave her pause. "I have to confess, I didn't know that. And the assailants were people from Bogdanov's villa?"

"Correct."

"Did they attack you?"

"No. If they'd wanted to, I'd be dead, too, because they caught us both by surprise."

"And the man in your bathtub?"

"Came for me this morning. Sent by Vitali Petrov."

"Ah." She paused again, but he could see that her thoughts were coalescing quickly. "I'm not sure how much I should say in the present company."

Jay looked at Owen—thinking of what he'd already witnessed and how untroubled he was by it—then turned back to Harry. "I think you can talk freely. If I suspect you're headed into dangerous waters I'll let you know."

"Okay." She glanced at Owen herself before saying, "Rich McKenzie gave you a document, an outline of the latest intelligence on the situation in Minsk, forward projections, that kind of thing."

"Yeah."

"That's what got him killed. Someone in Petrov's camp is reporting back to the regime. Once Minsk knew Rich was offering more than moral support to Petrov, they wanted him gone."

She stopped and looked expectantly. It took Jay a moment to work out what she was probing at, why she'd been reluctant to say these things in front of Owen. Then it fell together.

"I see. But no, that person was not me. I'm not working for the regime in Minsk, just working against Vitali Petrov."

She looked visibly relieved, even as she said, "I thought that would be the case, but I had to check."

"The person working for the regime was a guy called Stas. Vitali knew he was a double, but I didn't. I suspected he was vital to Petrov's plans, and Rich McKenzie told me the same, that Stas was indispensable to Vitali Petrov. Which, of course, is why I killed Stas." From the corner of his eye he caught Owen's surprised expression and Jay looked at him, acknowledging he hadn't been completely open about that. "I also asked the Russians to let Minsk know they should stop targeting me. But as it turns out, Petrov also had a mole in the Bogdanov camp, which is why Petrov is now gunning for me." She stared at him, frowning, trying to put these pieces together in her thoughts. "It's kind of a mess, huh?"

"I thought understatement was meant to be an English trait."

Owen said, "What's understatement?"

Jay said, "When you make something sound much less bad or good than it really is." Owen's face grew serious, which Jay was learning was his expression when he was pretending he understood but didn't. "So, like if you said, Mr Petrov gave me a gold private jet and a million dollars, which was *nice* of him."

"Oh! I get it."

When Jay turned back to Harry she was smiling at him, with a real warmth in it, but then the smile slowly sank away and she said, "Who are you working for Jay?"

"You know I can't tell you that."

"Yes, but I had to ask. Then another question—even though I think I know the answer—how do you plan to stop him?"

"Can we crash here tonight?"

"Of course. There's a sofa bed in the bedroom, for a child presumably—Owen can have that. You can sleep in here. But if you're going to be my house guest, I do expect you to answer my question."

"I'll stop him the only way I can. The intelligence side of things looks like it's failed. Which leaves the option of killing him outright, and that's tough, too, because he has a lot of men up there, but that's what I have to look at."

She looked troubled. "Jay, I'm still here as an observer, not as a participant. As an act of friendship, I'm willing to hold off reporting what I learn today until the end of the week, not that I think it would make a material difference anyway. But even if you can't tell me everything, you have to tell me something. Are you working for Minsk?"

"I already told you. No."

"Are you working for a state actor?" He hesitated and she caught it in time and changed tack, saying, "Are you working against western interests?"

"No, absolutely not."

She seemed reassured, and said, "Not that knowing it helps. Because you're right, of course—the only guaranteed way of stopping Sunday's party is to kill the would-be host."

"So I have to find a way of doing just that. And sure, he's been really careful until now, but I have to rely on him losing focus as he gets closer to the prize."

Harry looked doubtful, apparently not wanting to question his belief, but certainly not believing it herself.

"Well, you know him, Jay, and you know more about him than I do, but the man hasn't left his villa in weeks."

Jay thought about it for a second. The day had taken him by surprise. In fact, the last *two* days had taken him by surprise. But the ground shifting beneath his feet was only part of the problem. Harry was right.

"I'm not sure, either. I just know I have to think of something."

"Why don't you kidnap Alexei?" They both turned and looked at Owen, because it had been his suggestion. And Owen simply shrugged in response to their scrutiny, as if to ask whether they had a better idea.

31

Briefly, as they continued to stare, Owen looked less sure of himself, but he rallied and said, "Only, in movies and stuff, the bad guys always kidnap the hero's wife or kid."

"So you want us to be the bad guys?"

"I'd rather us be the bad guys than they kidnap me."

Harry laughed, and said, "That's just wonderful. But in real life, Owen—"

Jay interrupted, saying, "No, wait, he might be onto something."

She looked at him, like they were a couple and she was giving him a coded look, asking if he realized what he was saying.

"I'm serious. Kidnapping Alexei could be a really good move, in theory, give us leverage, strategic advantage. It could be the smart play." He turned back to Owen then and said, "The only problem is, it's easier said than done. See, if I could get into the villa to snatch Alexei, I could just as easily kill Vitali and then I wouldn't need to kidnap his son."

He already had a way into the villa, something he'd planned months earlier, but getting in and getting past at least a couple dozen armed men was above and beyond what anybody was paying him to do.

Harry said, "I agree—in theory—it could be something to build a strategy on, but you highlight the problem with it perfectly. Getting to Alexei would be as difficult as getting to his father in the first place."

Owen said, "What day is today?"

"Tuesday," Harry and Jay said together.

"So… Alexei has a suit fitting. They measured him all over and they're making this suit that'll like, fit him perfectly, and then he has to go and try it on so they can check it fits in all the right places and they can make changes if it doesn't." He seemed to realize that bespoke tailoring wasn't news to Jay and Harry, so he added, "I mean, I didn't know you could get clothes made like that. But anyway, the suit fitting is on Wednesday at three. That's tomorrow, right?"

Jay said, "Yeah, it's tomorrow. Do you know where it is?"

"Maison something."

"Maison Larenti?"

"That's it!"

Harry threw him a questioning look and Jay said, "It's an old school tailor here in town." He was already thinking about where it was. There was a back alley behind it, not unlike the one in which Stas had died.

Harry interrupted his thoughts, saying, "Surely Petrov won't let Alexei leave the villa now?"

"Because I killed one of his men this morning? No, trust me, he has form on this. The son of the future president of Belarus doesn't hide from anybody. Vitali will send extra security, but Alexei will go for that suit fitting."

Owen looked as if he couldn't believe what he was hearing. "You mean, it could work? I had a good idea?"

Harry smiled at him, looking touched.

Jay said, "You had a great idea, based on good intelligence. And yeah, with some help, it could work. The real question will be what we do with him once we have him."

"You have to chop off his finger and send it in an envelope." They both looked at him, and then his earnest expression collapsed into giggles and he said, like it should have been self-evident, "I'm kidding!"

Harry said, "What a charming sense of humor your son has."

Jay couldn't deny that, but his mind was already racing through the first stages—getting hold of Alexei—even before he'd thought through the best way of leveraging the boy.

"Can Owen stay with you for the afternoon?"

"Of course. Is it safe for us to go out?"

"I'd say so."

"Good. I have two emails to write and one telephone call to make, but then we'll go out. There are dolphin-spotting boat tours from the marina and I've been looking for an excuse to go on one." She turned to Owen. "Looks like you're my excuse."

"Awesome!" He was wide-eyed like only a kid from Colorado could be about the prospect of seeing dolphins in the wild.

She faced Jay again and said, "Can I ask where you'll be spending the afternoon?"

"I'm gonna go back and get my car, then drive out to Bogdanov's villa."

"Is that entirely wise?"

"Well, they're not trying to kill me anymore, and sure, they might not like the losses they've incurred on my account, but I think I'll be able to talk them around. Fact is, I'll need some help, not just to kidnap Alexei, but also to use that to get to Vitali. Do you have any intel on what numbers Vitali has?"

"We think he has about thirty down here on the security side, around a dozen on duty at any one time. Some share apartments in town, but most live in two guest lodges up at the property."

"That tallies with my take."

He'd have to eliminate at least two thirds of them to stand any realistic chance of getting to Vitali, and he wouldn't be able to do that without the help of the people up at Bogdanov's place. True, working with the Minsk regime's forces might upset his superiors. But the whole point of working the way he did was that he could ignore the rules of engagement, that he could ignore all the rules entirely, as long as he got the job done. And the job was to stop Vitali Petrov any way he could.

32

He was cautious on the approach to his building, but relaxed a little when he saw that the car the guy had arrived in was still parked on the side of the street. Inside, he took the stairs, but no one was waiting for him, nor in the apartment itself.

All that did await him was the beginnings of a telltale odor. He checked the time. He had no choice but to make a call to an old friend.

Maisie answered right away, saying only, "Jensen."

"Maisie, it's Jay Lewis."

"This. Can't. Be good." She sounded light-hearted, though, and said, "How the hell are you?"

"I'm good, thanks. And what about you, how's your little girl?"

"Um, not so little any more. She's eight."

So Owen and Maisie's daughter were of a similar age, a realization that left him inexplicably angry. He wouldn't have thanked Megan for turning up ten years ago to welcome him to fatherhood, and yet now he was only conscious of everything he'd missed out on.

"That's incredible."

"Yeah, she has a little brother, too."

"That's fantastic."

He thought about mentioning his own new instant family, but before he could decide that it was probably best left unsaid, she said, "But I suspect you're not calling to catch up on news of my kids."

"No, I'm not, I'm kind of asking for a favor, a removal."

"Um…"

He didn't wait for her to formulate her answer. "Maisie, it's all above board, kind of. I'm on the Cote d'Azur, in a resort town called Cotignac-sur-Mer, and I've been liaising with one of your people, a guy called Rich McKenzie." He wasn't sure if he heard a brief intake of breath with that— they would have heard about his death back in Langley. "The person who killed Rich is now lying dead in my bathtub. If you can arrange a removal, great. If you can't, really, don't worry about it. I'll find some other way."

"Who else is there?"

"No one, and I won't be here for long, either. The apartment will be empty for the next twenty-four hours, maybe more."

"Okay, I'm not promising anything, but give me the address and I'll see what I can do."

"Thanks, Maisie, I owe you."

"Do you have an ID for the individual?"

"No, but I was there when Rich died. I know he's the one."

He didn't like lying to Maisie. Sure, it was true he'd been there, but the guy in the bathtub was not only not the man who'd killed Rich, he wasn't even on the same side. But the circumstances called for it.

"Okay, I'll see what I can do first, then kick a report upstairs."

Jay gave her the address, ended the call and emptied his strongbox.

He headed down to the parking garage for the car, then drove toward Nice a little way before taking the road up to Bogdanov's villa. He pulled up in front of the solid gates, got out of the car with the engine still running, and looked up at the camera that was trained on him.

A few seconds crept past, then the mechanism whirred into life and the gate started to slide open. Jay got back in the car and drove inside, and as he headed up the drive he saw that a decent number of people must have arrived since he'd scoped the place with his drone—there were at least six vehicles visible from the drive, and as Jay pulled up in front of the villa, a dozen men came out to meet him with their guns at the ready.

They bristled as Jay got out of the car, but moved aside as a young woman came out of the house and stood on the steps. She had short, severe blond hair and was dressed in black, in the same vaguely paramilitary style as the others, but she was smiling broadly.

"Mr Lewis, this *is* a surprise." Her accent was solidly American. "Are you committing suicide or did you have something more creative in mind?"

"I'm not the suicidal type."

"I guessed as much, based on my predecessor's inability to eliminate you." He wondered if her predecessor had been one of the men Jay had killed, or if he'd simply been removed because of his failures. "So…?"

"I'm here to discuss my plan for stopping Vitali Petrov, but before I say another word I need to know how well vetted your men are, because news got back to Vitali very quickly that I'm not actually on his team."

She looked at the men flanking her. "As of last night, I can vouch for every one of them personally. My predecessor had a conflict of loyalties which is why he overlooked the traitor in our midst, and also why he was recalled, so both problems have now been dealt with."

"I'm glad to hear it."

"We have suspicions about one or two people in Minsk, too, so if it reassures you, your plan can stay strictly between us for the time being."

He looked at the men himself, recognizing among them the two who'd carried out the hit on Rich—in an odd way, their presence here reassured him.

"Okay, so shall we talk?"

"Please," she said. "And I'm sorry, how rude of me— Valeria Karnitsky."

She shook his hand, her grip deceptively soft, because there was some quality in her that suggested she could handle herself.

"Pleased to meet you, Valeria."

"Let's go to the terrace. Coffee, or something stronger?"

"Coffee's fine."

"Excellent." She started walking without asking anyone to get the coffee she'd just offered.

Jay glanced back at the men they were leaving behind, then said to Valeria, "Your accent—"

"New York. I've spent nearly my whole life on the Upper East Side. I only moved back to Minsk permanently two years ago. And you?"

"West Bedford, New York, but I've spent no more than a few months in the US in the last ten years."

"Then we're both émigrés," she said, turning to face him briefly. As they walked through the house, he spotted more men in other rooms, but she waved at the opulent décor—all gold and crystal—and said as if it were a real estate viewing, "The terrace is my favorite room, because really, all this would have to be remodeled if I were staying here any length of time. Isn't it just ghastly?"

She really had spent her formative years on the Upper East Side.

They stepped out onto the terrace which managed to be simultaneously private whilst offering a spectacular view over the Mediterranean, spreading out below them in a hazy powdery blue. Jay thought of Owen and Harry, out there now somewhere, searching for dolphins.

There were another three men sitting at a table under a large umbrella, deep in conversation, but as Valeria appeared they all stood and acknowledged her deferentially as they walked into the house. She gestured for Jay to take one of the seats and then sat across from him.

"I see what you mean, the terrace is definitely the best room."

"Yes, indeed it is. The Bogdanovs are good people, just a little unreconstructed." She glanced out to sea. "I always had my doubts that you were truly working for Petrov—of course, the KGB created a file on you, and it just seemed out of keeping to me."

"Very intuitive. Do you mind me asking who exactly you work for, Valeria? Are you KGB yourself?"

"I don't mind you asking at all. Just as I'm sure you won't mind when I don't answer."

"Naturally."

"I work for my country, that's all you need to know. And pride in my country requires me to tell you that the men you killed were not... representative of Belarus, nor of the people I now have here."

"I believe it. The people you have here now have a more professional bearing. Which is good, because that's what I need." She seemed cautiously interested in what he had to say. "I want you to help me kidnap Alexei Petrov, then create a diversion so I can get in and kill Vitali."

One of the men who'd been part of the welcoming committee emerged from the house carrying a tray with the coffee on it.

Valeria looked toward him and said, "Ah, good, coffee." She smiled at Jay again, adding, "I have a feeling we may need it."

But he could he see that he'd piqued her interest, and that was all Jay needed right now. Looking at the numbers she had here, she'd probably been considering a full-on assault, but that would still be costly in terms of lives lost, so the prospect of kidnapping Petrov's child no doubt appealed to her just as much as it did to Jay.

33

"All I need for my plan to work is for you to assign two of your men to me for forty-eight hours, to have another half-dozen available tomorrow at three, and that's pretty much it."

"You make it sound very reasonable, but I can hardly be expected to judge until I hear the plan itself."

"True." He sipped his coffee and was momentarily sidetracked by the flavor. "That's really good coffee."

That appeared to please her. "It's from Adriano's in Milan. I never drink anything else."

"I can see why." He took another sip, then put the cup down. "Tomorrow at three, Alexei Petrov has a suit fitting with a tailor in Cotignac-sur-Mer. It's possible, of course, that Vitali will cancel the fitting or have them come to the villa, but I know him, I know how he thinks. He'll send six or seven bodyguards, but the fitting will go ahead as planned. I need your men to attack the guards at the front of the store. Meanwhile, I'll go in the back and I'll kidnap Alexei. Thing is, he won't know I'm kidnapping him. He's friends with my son—he'll think I'm rescuing him." She gave an approving look in response to that detail. "I'll take the boy to a safehouse, with two of your men accompanying me. You'll then tell Petrov that you have his son here and that you'll kill him unless he abandons the planned coup."

"He could call our bluff."

"He could, but he won't, not where his son is involved." Jay thought of the way Vitali lavished affection on Alexei. But even from his own brief experience of parenthood, he already knew that there was nothing he wouldn't do to stop Owen coming to harm. "He won't call your bluff, but he also won't call off the coup. What he will do is have his men stage a raid on this place. He has about thirty up there."

"Yes, that's our assessment. Some are little more than hired thugs, but some are well-trained."

"After the kidnap, he'll know the same is true of the people you have here, so he'll send a sizeable part of his force to rescue Alexei. I guess he'll keep a half-dozen back. That's where the two men you assign to me will come in. They attack the main gate—do they have explosives at their disposal?"

"Of course. We always assumed C-4 would be the best way of getting through the gate."

She gave a minimal shrug, as if she were discussing nothing more serious than party invites with her old schoolfriends on the Upper East Side.

"Good. And while they're doing that, I'll go over the wall. There's one small section at the back of the property where I disabled the sensors four months ago. I go in. I kill Vitali. And we all carry on with our lives."

"Why not actually bring the boy here?"

It was a good question, but one that he'd preempted. "If my plan hits a roadblock, I have Alexei as a human shield."

She appeared to accept that at face value, then said, "Why do I need you at all? And why would you want to be involved? With this information, we could handle it ourselves. Keep it an all-Belarussian affair."

"Why do you need me? Like I said, it makes the kidnap smoother, I know how to get in, I know how to get around. I have no doubt you could do it without me, but it'll cost you more lives, and probably increase the risk of Alexei Petrov getting killed in the process, which is not the kind of PR Minsk wants right now."

"True. You still didn't answer the other question. Why do you want to be part of it?"

Jay said, "Professional pride. I came here six months ago to do a job, and now I'd like to finish it."

"Yes, I can understand that."

She looked briefly out at the distant blue sea. He could tell she wanted to ask who that job was for, given it clearly wasn't for Vitali Petrov, but she had enough self-control to keep her curiosity in check.

"We need to hammer out the details, but I like this plan. For the two men I assign to you, I think the two Dimitris would be best, Dima and Dimka, as long as you don't have a problem with that." He made a show of not following. "You've encountered them before—they're the men who killed your friend, the CIA Officer."

Dima and Dimka. The diminutives didn't match the two men he'd encountered, nor the easy efficiency with which they'd ambushed Jay and Rich on a busy street. If he'd come to know Rich McKenzie a little better he might have had pause, but as it was, he was simply satisfied that she was entrusting him with two reliable men.

"I don't have a problem. They were doing a job, that's all. But for what it's worth, killing Rich McKenzie was pointless. It didn't help your cause one little bit."

"It sent a message." Her voice had developed an edge, but it softened again, becoming lighter as she said, "Sometimes that's enough. You know it as well as I do."

"Yeah, I know it, but it won't be enough this time."

"Exactly, so we need to pin down some details, but first, one more question." He liked that her mind was so lively, prodding at his plan even before she'd heard the intricacies. "If we're going to engage in a gun battle in front of this tailor's, how can we be sure the boy won't be killed in the crossfire? As you pointed out, it would be unfortunate in PR terms, and eliminate the bargaining chip we're hoping to get out of it."

"Sure. I went there to have my tux adjusted. The front of the store is like a regular store. The fitting room is at the back, corridor to one side of it that leads to the back door. So as soon as Alexei gets there, they'll show him through into the fitting room. It doesn't have windows so I guess the security will check it's clear, then have one or two guys guarding the corridor, the rest out front."

She was all concentration, looking as if she might be picturing it in her mind. "So my men attack the front, then you and the two Dimitris go in the back, kill the guards in the corridor, take the boy."

"Almost. The two Dimitris wait around the corner in the car. I go in alone, kill any guards in the corridor, *save* the boy—if it's just me, he'll come without question. Then we drive to the safehouse."

"Which is where?"

"I don't know yet." She did a double-take, and he said, "I have somewhere in mind. I just need to check it out."

"Then we really do need to get busy, but I like your plan. And as it happens, we have two hidden security cameras on the road north and south of Petrov's villa, so we'll even get a heads up."

"How long have they been in place?"

"Two weeks."

Jay was surprised by that, and knew that he shouldn't have been. "Lucky I don't work for him anymore—he might have fired me for not knowing about those."

Valeria looked pleased with herself, then said, "To work."

She gestured toward the house and almost immediately someone came out, while at the same time, Valeria poured more coffee into their cups.

It was another hour before Jay left. He turned right out of the villa and took the back road through the hills, dropping down again as if heading to Vitali's place. But instead of taking that road, he found the other, and the track leading to the unoccupied vacation home where he'd left the first two bodies.

It still looked empty. The car with the two bodies had long gone from the open carport, but Jay walked out and looked around, in awe of the work done by the removal team—there was nothing at all to suggest a vehicle or other people had been here in the last six months.

He worked the lock into the back door of the house. It was spartan inside, a general lack of soft furnishings and ornamentation, speaking of a place that was probably only used for a month in high summer. He guessed it was at least still in some form of use because he was able to turn on both the power and the water.

The house would be perfect. It was more or less hidden from the road, a road that few people used anyway, and they'd probably only need to hole up here for twenty-four hours at most. He left, driving toward town until he saw a supermarket where he called in and bought some supplies—it was probably the same place where the homeowners went for their own essentials each summer.

He dropped the supplies back at the house, then programmed the Bellevue into the satnav and drove into town. He left the car in a multistorey car park a few hundred yards from the hotel and made for the center of town on foot.

Monsieur Larenti was in the store window as Jay approached, adjusting the display, but he waved in recognition and met him with a smile as he stepped inside.

"Monsieur Lewis, what a delight."

"Likewise." He glanced at the racks. "I was hoping to pick up an off-the-peg jacket, white or cream, linen or linen-mix, you know the kind of thing."

"Of course! Summer is here, and I have just the thing."

They embarked on the theater of trying and buying an off-white jacket, with Larenti so happy and solicitous that Jay regretted the damage that would most likely be done to his store this time tomorrow.

Then as Jay made to step out into the street with his bag, he stopped and moved back again, turning to Larenti. "Ex-girlfriend."

"Which is why we have a back door," said Larenti, and gestured for Jay to follow him.

They walked into the corridor, past the open door to the fitting room, then out through the back door itself. Jay thanked him, holding the door as he did so, glancing casually at the lock. The door opened outwards but there was only one locking point, which meant it would be easy to jimmy open.

"Always a pleasure, Monsieur Lewis."

"Pleasure's mine, Monsieur Larenti. See you soon."

He strolled along the alley and back out onto the street, then found a coffee shop, not wanting to return to the Bellevue until Harry and Owen were back. And with that thought, he also felt a pang of regret, ridiculous in itself, because he barely knew Harry, barely even knew Owen. And yet being with the two of them gave him the sense of what it would feel like to be part of a family, something he hadn't truly known for a long time—but the little instant family he was picturing was no less an illusion than the Cote d'Azur itself.

34

"Seriously, Jay, it was like they were *racing* against our boat. And they were so close. Harry even touched one."

"I'm not sure I made contact. But they were very close. It was quite exhilarating."

"I wish I'd been there."

Owen's face lit up. "Maybe we could go again sometime."

"Maybe. I'd like that. I don't think I've ever seen a dolphin in the wild."

Harry looked hopefully at Owen, as if they had some secret code between them, then turned to Jay and said, "But how was your day?"

"Promising. I'll tell you all about it while we're eating."

They ordered from the room service menu and ate at the table on the suite's large terrace. The waiter who brought the food smiled at them warmly, as if he too bought fully into their fake vision of a fantasy nuclear family.

Jay outlined the bare bones of the plan as they were eating.

Harry and Owen listened in silence, then Harry said, "Have you done recon on the tailor's shop?"

"Sure. I know the place anyway, but I went back there today—that bag over by the door contains an absurdly expensive linen jacket. So, it's ideally situated. In fact, if I were Vitali, there's no way I'd have gone ahead with the fitting, not the way things are."

"What if he does cancel?"

"He won't. Six months of knowing him, I'm pretty confident of that. If he did… Well, if he did we'd have to take a more direct approach, but trust me, it won't come to that."

She accepted his word, thinking it over. "You'll have to tell me how to get to the safehouse."

"I used the satnav coming down here, so you can use it to get back."

"Clever," said Owen, raising his finger, as if filing that ploy to memory for future use.

"So we're all good to go," said Harry, sounding uncharacteristically uneasy, and Jay wasn't sure if that was because she feared something would go wrong, or because she was dancing perilously close to the edge of her "observer" remit.

Owen seemed to pick up on it too, and said, "Could Alexei get hurt?"

Harry threw Jay a glance, as if cautioning him against being too honest, but Jay had told Owen at the outset that he wouldn't lie to him, and he planned to stick by that as far as he could. Life could be messy, as both he and Owen already knew.

"If everything goes to plan, no. But sure, if something goes wrong, he could get hurt. And you know, being the son of someone like Vitali Petrov, he'll always be in more danger than the average kid, he'll always have security."

Owen appeared to understand that already, possibly from the conversations he'd had with Alexei.

"What about me? Will I be in danger?"

He didn't seem concerned. It was more like he wanted all the available information so that he could prepare. For once, that was a quality that struck a chord with Jay even from his own childhood—whenever they'd gone on vacation, even as a small boy, he'd wanted all the travel details, information about their destination, all kinds of stuff, not because he was nervous, but because he wanted to know as much as possible in advance.

"No, you won't."

"I don't mind if I am."

Jay caught a smitten expression from Harry in response to that, but he smiled himself, and said, "I know it. But I *do* mind, and you won't be in danger."

Owen looked satisfied with that and went back to his food. He hadn't asked about Jay or Harry's safety, of course, but that was because he obviously never doubted it for a second.

Harry was less certain. After Owen had gone to bed she poured them both a drink and they sat on the terrace, looking out over the larger terrace below and the dark bay beyond.

"You appear incredibly relaxed about tomorrow."

"It's not a complex plan."

"No, I'll give you that. I still wish I could share your sangfroid."

"Oh, I think you'd be calm enough in a crisis. Have you done much fieldwork?"

"I suspect not much of the kind you've done in the past. Or in the past few days for that matter. What I do know is that when bullets start flying, all bets are off, even more so when a lot of the players aren't highly trained."

Jay had to agree with that. "There's a risk to Alexei, of course there is. He could get caught in the crossfire—"

"And if he does?"

"We take the body and claim we've kidnapped him anyway."

She raised an eyebrow. "Wow. You didn't even need to think about it."

"Because I learned a long time ago that you can't afford to think about things like that. Start dwelling on the fact that he's a little boy who could lose his life, you end up frozen. But the risk is slight. As for you and Owen, I don't see any risk at all. You'll be at the safehouse until it's all over."

"And you?"

She looked genuinely concerned, an expression on her face that warmed him.

"Honestly, I'll probably be in less danger than at any point in the last two weeks. The Belarus factions will be shooting chunks out of each other, mostly up at Bogdanov's place, and I'll be dealing with Vitali. He doesn't even carry a gun."

She stared at him for a second, as if trying to read him.

"Have you ever been afraid, Jay?"

He thought back to his first time in the field, in San Salvador, and a raid they carried out on some drug lord's compound—Jay couldn't even remember the details of the mission, so swept up had he been in the reality of it. The place had been in darkness, the corridors maze-like, and he hadn't been scared at all at the time. But one of the team had walked around a corner and right into the barrel of a gun, getting his face blown off in the process. Jay hadn't even seen it, but afterwards he'd had a few anxiety dreams of walking through the corridors of that compound, corridors that became infinitely more complex in his dreams. It had shaken him up for a while.

"I wasn't scared on my first job, but it went wrong for one guy, and I guess I overthought it after the fact, picking over it. We went out again a couple weeks later, similar job, and I was so nervous, sweating, heart racing, edgy. But as soon as we got there, instinct kicked in and that was it. Never bothered me again."

"*That's* your experience of being scared? You were a teeny bit nervous on your second job? You poor lamb."

He accepted the mockery.

"What can I say, maybe you only get scared if you have anything to lose. Back then, I didn't."

"You do now."

"But nothing's gonna happen to him." Yet even an oblique reference to Owen was enough to unsettle him vaguely, so he added quickly, "What about you? Ever scared?"

"You mean apart from right now?" Even as she spoke, she waved her own comment away. "I'm kidding, of course. But yes, I've been scared. Usually when I've been alone in a room with a man, inevitably a dangerous man who doesn't realize we're there for business reasons alone." He had a flashback to Bobo shoving Polina onto the bed, the way she'd staggered off those ridiculous heels. Then Harry said, "The funny thing is, I was in a helicopter once which was taking fire from the ground. Bullets bouncing off it, and then something got hit and the engine started to whine and for just a matter of seconds, it seemed like we'd crash and we'd all be killed. And I was terrified right up until that moment, but as soon as I was certain I was going to die, I wasn't afraid anymore. It was like time slowed down and this total sense of calm and acceptance came over me. I'll never forget that. I don't think I've ever felt so at peace."

He stared at her, transfixed, and in the end she said, "What are you thinking?"

"Oh, only that I'd like to kiss you right now, but parking that thought, when this is all over, could we at least keep in touch? I mean, Owen would like to—"

He was interrupted by her laughter. "You mercenary! Using your son to get what you want!" He couldn't deny it, but she paused then and said, "I'm not going to kiss you, Jay. I have great self-control, but even so, I'm not going to, just in case. But yes, I would very much like to keep in touch. Not for you, of course, only for Owen."

"Good."

She sipped her drink and said, "Where will you go, after this?"

He hadn't given it much thought. "Wherever the work is. I have a feeling I might have trouble getting a reference from Vitali."

"But I presume if everything goes to plan tomorrow, your real employers will be more than happy to give you a glowing reference."

"I'm gonna nod along, but I have no idea what you're talking about."

She was dismissive of his intransigence, but she seemed happy for him to keep his secrets. And he wouldn't have shared them anyway, not even for her, and certainly not this close to the end—he'd come too far, and risked too much, and he still had a job to do.

35

Harry and Owen left just after lunch and she messaged him once they were up at the house. Jay took everything out of his bag except for the guns and ammunition, took a taxi to the Grand and waited in the lobby with a coffee.

The last time he'd been here had been that prickly meeting with Rich McKenzie. And at a little after two, it was Rich's killers who walked in through the main doors, dressed in their all-black paramilitary chic.

They walked over and introduced themselves without sitting down. Dima was the one who'd warned Jay off that night, and he had the more dangerous air about him. Dimka was the one who'd stabbed Rich—he was more solid-looking, but if it came to a fight, Jay was in doubt which one he'd shoot first.

Dima said, "I hope you have no hard feelings."

"I killed some of your people, too. All a misunderstanding. No hard feelings."

Dimka said, "I lived America, two years, Chicago."

His accent was thick, his English apparently limited, but he had friendly eyes, as if he were someone eager to find common ground.

"Did you like it?"

"Is great country. I visited New York City, Los Angeles and New Orleans. New Orleans, I like a lot. I'm sorry to kill your friend."

"He wasn't really my friend, but thanks." He stood and picked up his bag. "Shall we go?"

The two Dimitris were in a silver Range Rover with its windows tinted a smoky dark gray. They didn't drive far, and a few minutes later were parked just around the corner from the back alley to Maison Larenti. Dima gave Jay his comms.

As Jay put in the earpiece, he said, "They know to speak in English, right?"

"Of course. Team Leader One will speak English to you, Team Leader Two. Anything said in Russian will be to the rest of the team or to us. If you speak, only Team Leader One will answer. Miss Karnitsky will not be on the channel—she'll speak to you by cellphone if she needs to."

"Okay. You get the crowbar for me?"

"It's in the back."

Jay leaned over the back seat and reached for the crowbar, placing it in his lap and settling in for the wait.

At twenty to three, Valeria called him and said simply, "Two vehicles just left Petrov's villa, heading into town."

He didn't need to ask if the boy was in one of the cars—he was absolutely certain he would be.

"Good." With the comms line open, he said, "Is Team One in place?"

The answer came through his earpiece, a clean American accent. "Team One in place, awaiting target."

"Good."

Valeria had hung up.

Dima looked in the rearview, catching Jay's eye. "It's all good?"

Jay nodded and said, "Remember, don't say anything to the boy. He'll think I'm protecting him from the kidnappers and there's no reason for him to hear otherwise."

"I understand." Dima spoke a few words to Dimka, explaining what Jay had just said.

Dimka turned and smiled, saying, "He's just a boy."

Jay wasn't sure from the tone precisely what Dimka had meant by that, but the smile suggested benevolence.

They waited in silence, and then the voice sounded in Jay's ear again. "Team Leader One to Team Leader Two. The target has arrived."

"Okay, tell me once they're in the store."

Another minute and the voice came back. "The boy is in the store. Four men inside, one of them just inside the door, two outside."

Jay checked his watch. "We wait ten minutes. I'll give the word. Be ready."

"We're ready."

He settled into silence again, aware of the two Dimitris fidgeting, glancing in the mirror, at each other.

At eight minutes, he said, "I'll be back in no time at all."

He climbed out of the car, carrying the crowbar at his side. Turning into the back alley, he wasn't surprised to see no one standing outside the rear of the store, and wasn't sure that he would have positioned someone there himself—if Jay had been in charge of security, of course, the trip to Maison Larenti wouldn't have gone ahead in the first place.

The ten minutes were up by the time he reached the door.

"Team Leader Two to Team Leader One. It's a go."

Team Leader One responded with a couple of short sharp commands in Russian. For a moment, nothing happened. Then the gunfire started in the next street, sounding like a firework display across town, and from inside the store he could hear shouts and breaking glass.

Jay forced the door with the crowbar, dropped it, drew his gun and pulled the door open. There was someone at the other end of the corridor, but looking into the main part of the store, the deafening racket beyond leaving him oblivious to Jay's forced entry.

Jay shot him in the back of the head as he walked up the corridor. He opened the door into the fitting room and Larenti screamed. He was cowering in the corner with Alexei, who was wearing the new suit and smart shoes, a white shirt and dark blue tie.

"Monsieur Lewis! What's happening?"

"Mr Petrov's enemies, trying to target the boy. Alexei, come with me—you'll be safe."

"Is Owen with you?"

"No, but you'll see him soon. Come quickly."

Alexei jumped up with the urgency of a child who'd probably been used to being ushered about in a hurry by security. It seemed his dad hadn't gotten around to telling him that Jay was no longer working for them.

"Stay here, Monsieur Larenti. You'll be safe."

He didn't wait for a response, moving quickly to the door, one hand on Alexei's shoulder. He looked out, but as he did, a few rounds in succession tore through the air and peppered the wall opposite, then more. Jay pushed Alexei back. Larenti cried out again. Jay couldn't work out why so much fire was finding the corridor, but for the moment, they were as good as pinned down.

Then he understood why. He poked his head around the doorframe, just enough to see one of Petrov's men had taken cover in the doorway between the corridor and the main store, standing just in front of the guy Jay had already shot.

Jay raised his arm and shot him in the back. He fell forward, the movement bringing about another volley of shots. The shooting continued even after he fell but no longer toward the corridor—it seemed another of Petrov's men had taken cover somewhere within the store itself.

Jay turned, saw Alexei was right behind him, and ushered him along the corridor. Alexei let out a small cry, but Jay kept pushing him forward and out of the door. He closed it behind him, picked up the crowbar and ran along the street, urging Alexei to keep up with him. The boy seemed to be hobbling in his stiff new shoes.

"Just around this corner, Alexei."

"Where's my father?"

"I don't know, but you have to keep running." The boy tried to pick up his pace in response, the clumsy percussion of his footsteps audible even over the increasingly isolated gunshots. "But I'm taking you to a safehouse until we know everything's secure. Owen's there already."

Alexei pushed on harder and within seconds Jay was bundling him into the back of the car.

He climbed in behind him and said, "Okay, drive slowly. Nobody's chasing us, we don't want to draw attention."

Dima glanced at him in the rearview and set off, and only now did Jay notice that Alexei was gasping.

"Are you asthmatic, Alexei?"

He shook his head, but there was no question he was hyperventilating. Dimka looked round, concerned.

Jay loosened the boy's tie and collar, then took hold of his shoulders and said, "Okay, Alexei, I want you to breathe with me, okay, just copy me." Alexei nodded, scared, and Jay breathed deep slow breaths and watched as the boy struggled to copy him. "Good, you're doing fine, and again." He kept going like that for a minute or so, until finally he was calm again and started to sob. "It's okay. Don't cry now. You've been so brave. Just keep breathing the way I showed you, and put on your seatbelt."

He put on his seatbelt and breathed in the same slow exaggerated fashion, stifling little sobs.

Valeria rang and when Jay answered she said, "Success. We lost one man."

"And the others?"

"We killed all six. You have the package?"

Jay was overly conscious of the boy breathing his deep meditative breaths next to him, but Alexei seemed oblivious to everything around him.

"Yeah, we'll call you once we're safe."

She hung up. Jay noticed that the comms line had gone flat so he took out the earpiece, then looked across at Alexei who smiled, apparently relieved to be breathing normally again.

"Is Owen better now? Papa said he was sick. That was why he didn't come sailing."

Jay said, "Yeah, he's better now. It was just a migraine, like a really bad headache."

"My mother has migraines."

Jay didn't doubt that. He sent a message to Harry, telling her to prep Owen to back up Jay's lie. That probably constituted yet another parenting failure—encouraging his child to be dishonest as a cover for his own falsehood—but then, he guessed it would take him a while to turn that particular ship around.

36

When they got to the house, Harry and Owen came out to meet them. For some reason, Jay expected the two boys to hug each other, but they simply exchanged friendly nods like old comrades and went inside together.

Harry gave Jay a friendly acknowledging nod of her own.

He returned it and said, "This is Dima and Dimka. This is Harry." Dimka looked confused, and Jay added, "It's short for Harriet, like Dimka is short for Dimitri."

"Ah!"

They said hello to each other, then Dima turned to Jay and said, "We'll get everything ready for the next stage. You think tonight?"

"Probably, and definitely before daybreak."

"We'll be waiting."

Harry and Jay walked toward the house, but didn't go inside, carrying on to the old collapsed trampoline on the scrubby lawn.

When they were out of earshot, Harry said, "It all went to plan?"

"I'd say so. Petrov sent six men and they're all dead, which is six fewer for us to worry about tonight."

"And the other side?"

"Lost one. I don't think Petrov's men were expecting an attack. It's one of Vitali's weaknesses, this secrecy, never wanting anyone to know everything he knows."

"It's how men like him maintain power. Divide and conquer."

"Yeah. Owen's okay?"

She frowned. "So relaxed it's almost uncanny. I thought perhaps he didn't understand what was going on, but… I don't know, he just seems to have an ability to take things in his stride. Like father, like son, I suppose."

He felt flattered by that comment in some way he couldn't quite pin down, but said, "I don't think I was as cool as him when I was ten. I had to learn it."

"Maybe so did he." She left that thought hanging, hinting at the unknown nature of Owen's relationship with Megan, at the way his life had really been through those first ten years. "We should go in."

They walked into the house, and Jay heard Owen saying, "You don't have to worry. Jay will fix everything. That's what he does."

There was no answer and then as Jay stepped into the room he saw that the two boys were sitting at the kitchen table with juice and cookies, Owen playing the ten year old's version of the good host. Alexei looked up at him and smiled, looking reassured, which was all the answer he needed. Whether he'd look so trusting this time tomorrow was another thing.

It was an hour later before Valeria called back.

Jay answered but said, "Wait a minute." He walked outside and across to the old trampoline. "Okay, go ahead."

"I spoke to Vitali Petrov, told him we have his son, that we'll kill him if he doesn't change his plans and publicly endorse the President."

"How did he react to that?"

"As you might imagine. He's a vulgar man at heart, not really our kind of person at all." He was amused that Valeria was talking as if she and Jay were part of the same social circles back in the US. "The police have also been to Petrov's place, but we've been listening in on the police radio—he hasn't told them his son was kidnapped, and it seems he's insistent he has no idea who was behind the attack."

"Which confirms he's taken the bait. He doesn't want the police involved because he's gonna come after you."

"Good, we'll be waiting for him. And you?"

"We're all set."

"Then I'll speak to you when there's movement."

They ended the call, but before Jay could move away from the trampoline he had a second call, this time from Benny.

"Hey, Benny, what's up?"

"Hmm. I was hoping you'd tell me. How, for example, a mysterious group of armed men attacked a tailor's shop in Cotignac-sur-Mer and left six of Vitali Petrov's men dead, before disappearing into thin air. Or how one of Petrov's employees—who the tailor recognized but didn't know by name—managed to spirit Petrov's son to safety even as the attack progressed. It's a mystery, no?"

Jay admired Monsieur Larenti's old school discretion, refusing to name a client even when his store had been shot up.

"I don't work for Petrov anymore."

Benny found some humor in that. "Newsflash—you never worked for Petrov." He became serious again, saying, "But I have to warn you, Jay, this is messy, and if gets much messier, the authorities won't sit back. You understand what I'm saying to you?"

"Yeah, I get it, Benny." He checked the time. "And I have to tell you, my reading is that things *will* get messier. But it'll be self-contained from here on in, no members of the public involved, and twenty-four hours from now, it'll all be done. That's all I can promise you."

"Then I'll have to take that. What about your boy?"

"He'll be fine. I'm really nothing more than an impartial observer right now. And that's what you should be. I know if reports come in, you have to respond, but take my advice, be slow about it. Let these people kill each other and by tomorrow they'll be out of our hair altogether."

There was a pause, maybe a sigh, before Benny said, "Many more days like today and I won't have any hair."

Jay finished the call, but stood for a moment or two looking at the house, unsettled. Was it because Benny had asked about Owen? There was no danger, he was convinced of it, but maybe he was being too complacent. His whole adult life, he'd made plans and carried them through, and he saw no reason why this one would be any different. The only real difference was that in the past, all he'd had to lose was himself.

37

One of the bedrooms was downstairs and the two Dimitris made that their base. It was easy to forget most of the time that they were even in the house, although Jay checked in on them now and then. After dark, the two men took it in turns to sleep.

The boys camped out in one of the upstairs bedrooms, with all thoughts of the day's events briefly banished when a bat flew in through the open window and had to be coaxed and shepherded out. Harry took the other upstairs bedroom.

Owen said, "Where will you sleep, Jay?"

"On the couch downstairs."

But in reality, he didn't sleep for more than a few minutes at a time—always tuned in to the sounds of the house and the night beyond—and he was fully awake long before it was light.

He went into the kitchen and scouted around until he found an old packet of coffee in a sealed plastic container. It still smelt like coffee so he made a pot, and Dima came through as if drawn by the aroma. Jay poured him a cup.

"Thanks."

The stairs creaked and they both looked in that direction as Harry came down. Jay poured a cup for her too, and the three of them sat around the littered kitchen table, not speaking, just drinking one and then a second cup of coffee each, waiting for dawn or a call.

Finally, Dima said, "I would have gone at two."

Jay checked his watch. "It's a couple of hours till sunrise. If he doesn't go by then, he won't go today."

But Vitali thought his son was being held captive in Bogdanov's villa, so Jay was confident. He'd attack before sunrise.

The next hour crept by. None of them opted for a third cup of coffee. They sat instead in silence, contemplative, like people awaiting news from a sickbed. And then Valeria called.

"Six vehicles just left Petrov's villa."

"Heading north or south?"

"North."

"So they'll be there in fifteen to twenty minutes. Call me once the attack begins."

He slipped the phone into his pocket and responded to Dima's expectant expression with a nod. Dima stood and went to rouse Dimka. Jay stood and Harry stood with him. She gave him a quick hug, then took hold of his shoulders.

"A son's going to lose his father today. Just make sure it's not yours."

"It'll be fine." He kept her gaze. "Still no kiss?"

"Maybe a peck on the cheek."

She leaned in and kissed him on the cheek. Her lips lingered for a tantalizing moment before she stepped back and let go of his shoulders.

"I'll call once it's all clear. Oh, I've left you a gun in the cupboard there."

"Will I need it?"

"No, but better to have it and not need it, than… you know."

They left that thought hanging.

Jay and the two Dimitris left in the Range Rover. He guided Dima to a spot in the road that was close to the point where Jay would be going over the wall and they parked up.

It was full night around them, but Jay could already detect a hint of the coming day in the sky to the east. He experienced a brief surge of memory, thinking back to the last night he'd spent with Amandine, standing on his balcony as the sun was about to rise—the beginnings of a day that would see him become a father.

It was almost an hour since the first call when Valeria called again.

"They've started. We thought they'd come through the gates but they've scaled the walls, maybe twenty men in all."

That was good, meaning there were probably only half a dozen left at Petrov's place, just as he'd hoped. Jay was surprised he couldn't hear any gunfire in the background.

"Have you engaged them yet?"

"No, they're closing in on the house from three directions." She sounded faintly mocking as she said, "I imagine they're aiming at stealth. But we're watching them. Another minute."

"Good. See you on the other side."

He patted the two Dimitri's on the shoulder.

"See you soon. I'll wait for the explosion. No comms until you've neutralized everyone. And don't shoot me. I'll be cutting across the lawns and into the house at the side or the back."

"Kill him good," said Dima, and Dimka chuckled as if his friend had coined some genius phrase.

Jay left them and as they drove on he made his way down through the trees and scrub in the dark and climbed over the wall. He waited there, probably only a couple hundred yards from the villa, but lost in the dense cover of trees and shrubs. He could hear the Range Rover's progress to begin with, but after a minute the engine noise ceased and there was silence. And then the night tore open as the C-4 did its work on the gate.

Jay started running, even as the explosion died away and gunfire popped and clattered out by the gate and at least two car engines revved wildly. The villa was lit up, every window shining bright, but he guessed nobody would have been sleeping here tonight, not knowing what was planned.

The only open ground Jay had to cover was the lawn at the side of the house, but as he ran onto it the security lights burst into life, and then Jay caught sight of a figure emerging from one of the villa's side doors. He didn't wait to see who it was, just started shooting and only stopped when the figure slumped to the floor.

When Jay reached him he saw in passing that it had been a good call—the guy's Heckler & Koch was lying by his side. Then he noticed it was the guy who'd been looking at the map of Minsk with Vitali and Stas. Jay had never spoken to him directly and didn't know his name.

Moving on, Jay stepped in through the door, but then hesitated as silence fell. He stopped, listened. One more shot sounded out by the gate, a sole shot, like someone finishing off the wounded.

A moment crept past, the stillness unnerving, and then Dima's voice sounded in his ear. "We're all clear out here. Five dead."

Jay stepped back outside for a second and said, "One more dead in here. Hold by the gate."

"Okay, boss."

Jay stepped in again. He didn't know this corridor, but he had a feeling it led past some of the service rooms into the main hall. He didn't like that everywhere was lit up like this, but he moved quickly along the corridor, paused for a second to listen, then opened the door and stepped through.

He'd guessed right and was in the hall with all its marble and excess. He stopped again, and then a door opened, and the polite young flunkey walked through, immaculately dressed as usual, as if he never stepped down from his duties. He walked toward Jay as if about to ask how he could help him.

Jay pointed his gun casually and said, "You don't need to be involved in this. The—"

Jay didn't even see the kick, it came so fast. He felt the young flunkey's foot make contact with the side of his head, and he felt himself launch across the hall and onto the floor. He felt the second kick, too, into his ribs, but he intercepted the third and brought his other hand round and shot the flunkey in the gut.

The young guy staggered backwards and fell as Jay jumped to his feet. To his credit, the guy tried to get up again, even as he held the wound in his stomach. It was insane—he'd looked so much like someone with a future in politics or finance, or anything other than this. And that had been one hell of a kick, the side of Jay's head still throbbing and tingling with the power of the impact.

"This was nothing to do with you. You should have laid low."

He spat out some words in Russian and Jay shot him again.

He paused and listened then. There didn't seem to be movement anywhere else in the house. He guessed the remaining guards had all been killed, and the rest of the staff were doing what the flunky should have done, keeping out of the way.

Jay moved silently across the hall to the study. Vitali wouldn't be in his bedroom at a time like this. He'd be in the study, where he'd most enjoyed planning and strategizing and acting like a president in waiting.

He took hold of the door handle, readied his gun, but waited another second. The silence was finally broken by a yell from inside the study, Vitali in full throttle, shouting, belligerent and wheedling all at once. And then a gunshot sounded beyond the door and a woman let out a small scream of anguish and the silence resumed.

38

Jay knew where Vitali's regular armchair was in relation to the door, and his voice had seemed to be coming from that direction, so Jay aimed the gun there as he pushed the door open. He knew immediately that there was no need.

Vitali was slumped, a bloom of blood across the chest of his white shirt. Jay stepped cautiously into the room and took in the woman standing in front of Vitali, a gun hanging casually at her side.

He guessed it was the elusive Mrs Petrov, dressed incongruously in white jeans and sneakers and a fitted white hoodie. Her hair was a striking blond, piled up on top of her head. She looked like a soap opera character from the 1980s.

As if in a state of deep confusion, she appeared to become aware that someone had entered the room, and turned slowly and raised the gun in half-hearted fashion.

"It's okay, Mrs Petrov, it's me, Jay Lewis."

He wasn't even sure if that would mean anything to her, but the fog seemed to clear from her vision and she offered a slightly deranged smile and let her arm fall again.

"I killed him."

She had an accent but it was lilting, almost musical.

He crossed the room and took the gun from her hand. She let it go willingly.

"I can see that, but no one needs to know it was you."

She started nodding, and only stopped when she turned to look at the body of her husband.

Jay looked at the body, too, trying to imagine the chess-playing boy finally taking a stand against his father—the old Belarus—but he wasn't there, and maybe hadn't been for a long time.

Mrs Petrov said, "He wasn't a bad man, not really. He wasn't cruel, he just…"

She ran out of steam.

"So why did you kill him?"

She looked at Jay, wistful. "For my son. I don't want him to grow up like this." She waved her hand in the direction of Vitali. "I never wanted the things Vitali wanted. But this last week, seeing my Alexei with Owen, how happy he was, how much like a boy, it made me see. I want Alexei to be like your son, not Vitali's."

Jay felt a swelling of pride at that, and yet it was totally misplaced, because Jay had played no part in making Owen the person he was. For better or worse, Megan was the one who could take that credit, whether or not she'd want it.

"I hope your life will be better now. But you need to lock the door to this room, and then I want you to go to your bedroom, just until we're sure it's all clear."

"But what about Alexei? I have to get him back."

"Alexei's fine. I have him. He's with Owen and he's safe. Someone will bring them down to the house as soon as we're sure it's clear."

She gripped his arm, her fingers surprisingly vice-like, and said, "Please, bring him to me now."

"I will, as soon as it's safe."

She still had a pleading look in her eyes, as if it were a cruelty to keep her waiting any longer. Her grip remained fierce, her need for her son so visceral that once again it made him think of Megan and what demons could have possessed her to give up on that bond.

"Please!"

He relented a little. "Lock this door, then wait in your room. I'll go outside and if it's clear, I'll call for him to be brought down."

She appeared to take that as a promise, and finally released his arm.

"Thank you, Mr Lewis. For everything."

"I didn't do very much." And in truth, she was thanking him only for bringing his son into their life.

He guided her toward the door, then left her as she removed the key from the inside and locked the door behind her. He moved quickly through the hall and out onto the front steps.

Everywhere was bathed in a pallid light now, but it was clear looking up at the sky that it was going to be another sun-drenched day. The gravel in front of the villa was still scored with all the tire tracks of the vehicles that had headed across to Bogdanov's.

To the left of the main door, a jeep was parked sideways on, riddled with bullet holes. Jay stepped closer and saw the driver slumped inside, hidden from view where he'd collapsed dying onto the passenger seat. Jay couldn't work out how it had come to be there, unless the driver had tried to get back to the house and been hit by the two Dimitris.

At the end of the drive, a hundred yards away, he could see the gate and the silver Ranger Rover. It looked like the gate had only been blown partly free and the Dimitris had pushed it the rest of the way with their SUV. They were standing at the back of the car now. A body lay on the grass next to the security lodge nearby.

He waved and as they waved back, he spoke through the comms. "All clear up here. Petrov's dead."

Dimka's shout of triumph was deafening in the earpiece. Dima upbraided him but was laughing at his friend's jubilation, too.

Dima said, "The one in the jeep?"

"Yeah, he's dead too."

"Good. I knew we hit him. So, mission completed."

"I guess so. I'll call Valeria, then I'll call Harry to bring the boys down. Don't shoot at the Mercedes."

He was half-joking, but Dima said, "I hear you, boss."

He called Valeria and as soon as she answered he said, "We're done. Petrov's dead."

"Confirmed?"

"Confirmed. And you?"

"It's all over."

"Good. Speak soon."

He called Harry and told her she could bring the boys down.

She said, "We're on our way. They were up and about as soon as you left. All okay?"

"Yeah, like I told you, it wasn't a complex plan."

"Yes, you might have mentioned it."

He walked back into the house, checking the other downstairs rooms. There was a family kitchen which he'd been in before, but he was surprised to find a larger kitchen at one end of the villa, where a half dozen people sat around a table in pensive silence.

They didn't seem alarmed at the sight of him standing there, but he said, "Is everyone okay?"

There were a few mumbles of assent, then an older woman said in a French accent, "Can you tell us what's happened?"

"Mr Petrov's dead. Mrs Petrov's fine, so is Alexei. It's all over now."

They took the news blankly. He guessed they were more concerned about what would become of their jobs. He left them and made his way back outside, stopping to check first that Mrs Petrov had locked the study door.

The sky had inched another step toward beauty by the time he stepped out again, and he could hear the familiar sound of his Mercedes heading along the road.

Harry slowed at the gate and exchanged a few words with the men there, then drove up and parked to the right of the door. The boys got out before she did.

Owen looked back toward the gate and said, "Wow, Jay, they blew the gate up!"

"They sure did."

The boys walked over and started looking at the bullet-riddled jeep, quietly discussing some aspect of it, apparently oblivious to the body inside it. Harry climbed out of the car and immediately looked out beyond the gate as the sound of sirens broke through the morning calm.

She held the gun out. "You better take this back if the police are on the way."

He took the gun off her.

The sirens were approaching at speed, the car engines audible too now.

"You killed him?"

Jay looked over his shoulder at the boys who were deep in conversation like crime scene officers, and said, "His wife killed him." He responded to her look of shock. "She really didn't wanna go back to Minsk."

One of the police cars seemed to be ahead of the pack, closing in now on the gate. Jay's phone rang and he answered to Valeria.

Her tone was urgent. "Jay, there are only five cars."

She didn't have to repeat herself. He handed the gun back to Harry who took it without question, then he turned to face the gate. Six cars had gone to Bogdanov's but Valeria had only found five abandoned on the other side of the wall. Which meant this wasn't over yet, not quite.

39

Too late, Jay realized that the sirens were coming from one direction, the speeding car from the other. The thought had only just registered when tires screeched and a black BMW flew through the gate. Dimka arced into the air as it hit him, looking from this distance like it was an acrobatic trick he was performing.

Gunfire sounded.

Jay shouted at the boys. "Get down! Behind the wheels!"

Owen almost threw Alexei behind the front wheel of the jeep, then scrambled behind the other himself. There was an explosion—a grenade by the sound of it—more gunfire. He saw Dima lying on the grass next to the drive, and the car was speeding the final hundred yards. Harry had already taken cover behind the Mercedes.

Jay aimed at the driver and fired, once, twice, a third time. The car suddenly lost speed and veered left, coming to a crunching stop in some bushes. But the other two were out and behind it quickly, and Jay had only just dropped alongside Harry as the first shots were returned.

The sirens, which had seemed so close, now seemed distant again, maybe only because of the gunfire bouncing on the cars around them.

Harry said, "We have to get the boys in the house. Can you cover me?"

"Of course, but—"

Glass shattered above them, then the shooting stopped. The lull lasted a second, maybe two. Jay looked across at the boys, making themselves small. And then something dropped out of the air and fell like a hard apple into the gravel in front of Alexei and Owen.

Jay knew instantly what it was, and so did the boys. A grenade. They stared at it, wide-eyed. For one sickening fraction of a second, Owen looked as if he was about to throw himself on top of it. Jay's heart carried out some wrenching maneuver inside his chest and he was scrambling to his feet before he knew it.

He heard the gunshots as he broke cover. Heard more behind him, Harry giving cover fire. He dived, the world slowing around him, his brain stubbornly trying to count the seconds he had. He landed in the gravel, scooped up the grenade, small and firm and without substance in his hand, and hurled it the only way his body position allowed, over his own car to the lawns beyond.

He wasn't even conscious of getting back to his feet, but as the grenade exploded, still sounding too near, he was sprinting toward the BMW. A bullet flew past, so close he could feel it, then he was on them, shooting even before he could see them. He shot the first one twice, in the neck and face, turned. The other was replacing his magazine, fumbling. He looked up as Jay shot him clean in the head.

He stood then—breathing deeply, his heart pounding— looking from one to the other, then to the driver, wanting to be sure the threat had been dealt with. His body felt like it was twitching with the flood of adrenaline. Once more, the sirens swelled in the morning air.

Jay turned and started back to the others. Harry was already ushering the two boys into the house, just as Mrs Petrov came out and sank to her knees in front of her son, throwing her arms around him.

Owen saw Jay and peeled away from Harry, running over and hugging him, laughing and crying at the same time as he said, "That was amazing, Jay! The way you got that grenade and you killed them all. *So* amazing!"

"You were amazing, too."

He rubbed the back of Owen's head as Harry walked over to join them. And he was grateful for Owen's enthusiasm, but he was angry with himself. He should never have been in that position in the first place. He should never have yielded to Mrs Petrov's need for her son, not until he was completely convinced the danger had passed. How close had he come?

Harry looked to the gate and said, "It doesn't look good for the two Dimitris."

"No, I'll go and check on them. And I'll need to speak with the police when they get here. Can you take Owen inside to Alexei and his mom?"

"Of course."

She handed Jay the gun for the second time. He walked up the drive as Harry and Owen went inside. Dima was dead, hit by four or five rounds, including one to the head, and maybe shrapnel too. Dimka was still alive, though, lying in the gateway, struggling with his breathing, grimacing with pain.

Jay crouched down next to him, and for all his discomfort, Dimka tried to smile. This was the man who'd been so brutally methodical in his dispatch of Rich McKenzie and yet there was no mistaking the kindness of his eyes.

"How you doing, Dimka?"

He merely looked pained in response and winced as he said, "Dima?"

"No."

Jay looked at him, trying to see if he could tell what was broken. Dimka was blocking the drive, but Jay didn't trust himself to move him, and then he caught movement from the corner of his eye and the first two police cars screeched to a halt in front of him.

The officers were drawing their guns even as they got out of the cars. They shouted commands, but Jay stayed where he was, only looking back passively, and as they walked over they appeared to sense he was no threat and holstered their weapons again.

There were plenty more sirens approaching and Jay said, "Is there an ambulance coming? He was hit by a car. I don't think we can move him."

"An ambulance is coming," one said, while the other spoke urgently into his radio.

"Good. I'm Jay Lewis, I was Vitali Petrov's security adviser."

The officer who'd answered him first said, "I know who you are. I kept watch outside your apartment one night."

"I appreciate it."

He looked nonchalant in response, as if to say he'd only been doing his job, then said, "People are coming. They'll want to talk to you." He glanced over Jay's shoulder at the house. "Is it safe now?"

"Yeah, I think so."

More police cars arrived, then the ambulance. Once they started to treat Dimka, Jay walked back toward the house. He saw Harry outside, talking on the phone.

She finished the call as he got there and Jay said, "Dimka's still alive. They're treating him now."

"Wow." She looked toward the ambulance, as if remembering the sight of Dimka hurtling through the air. "My superiors are keen for me to talk to the police. What's our story?"

"Petrov attacked the regime element and they hit back harder. As Petrov's security adviser, I got his son to safety. You happened to be with me when it all went down and had no choice but to accompany me."

"Good. That's more or less what I just told London." She poked him in the chest, playfully, and said, "And I'm not about to get quite as enthusiastic as Owen, but that was some trick with the grenade."

"Yeah. You asked me the other night if I'd ever been scared. Well, right then, I was more scared than I've ever been in my life."

"Welcome to humanity, Mr Lewis, we've been expecting you."

He laughed, because she was right, and it had been a long time coming.

They were distracted by the sound of cars. The ambulance crew had finally moved Dimka and a convoy of police cars—both patrol cars and unmarked vehicles—were crawling along the drive toward them.

In the ensuing confusion, Harry went off without speaking to him again. He saw her climbing into the back of a patrol car which immediately drove away.

Then Jay heard someone say, "So, you promised me it would get messier."

He turned to face Benny. He hadn't even seen him arrive. And for all Benny's claims that he might lose his hair, he looked as immaculate and stress-free as ever.

"It's not as bad as it might have been. What about at Bogdanov's place?"

Benny pulled a face like he'd eaten something sour, and said, "We're not aware that anything has happened at Bogdanov's villa. Should we be?"

Jay made a point of looking equivocal, knowing there was a distinct possibility Valeria would simply make the bodies disappear.

"Who knows? Possibly not. All I can tell you is that Petrov sent around twenty men to attack the regime forces at Bogdanov's." He pointed at the BMW. "And only those three came back."

"Okay. And here?"

"The regime hit back. Petrov is dead. His wife and son are unharmed. It's done."

"And Owen?"

Jay was touched that he would ask.

"Owen's just fine. He's with Alexei Petrov."

"Good. I'll need you to come into Nice with me. Let's see if we can get this cleaned up as quickly as possible." He gave Jay a knowing smile. "So that you can go back to doing whatever it is that you do."

"Sure, give me a few minutes and I'll be back with you. Oh, Petrov is in his study. I got his wife to lock the door but I'll get you the key."

"I'll be waiting."

Jay went back inside and hesitated. A police officer was looking at the body of the flunky, but otherwise all was still. Then he heard the faint sound of voices from upstairs. He followed them and found Mrs Petrov with the two boys in what he guessed was Alexei's room.

Alexei was sobbing as his mother helped him pack clothes into a small case. Owen was sitting in an armchair and tipped his head in a comically world-weary fashion when he saw Jay.

Mrs Petrov acknowledged Jay's arrival and said, "I've called a cab. I can't stay here. I'm taking Alexei to the Grand Hotel for the next few days and then we'll decide what to do."

"That makes sense. Maybe Owen could go with you for a little while. I have to go into Nice with the police, just to give a statement."

"Yes, of course."

Owen cut in, concerned as he said, "They're not gonna arrest you?"

"No, nobody's getting arrested. Harry's gone with them already. They just need a full version of what's happened, but I could be a few hours." He looked back to Mrs Petrov. "I'll pick him up later this afternoon."

"It's the least we can do. And it will be good for Alexei. He's had a terrible shock."

Alexei looked at Jay in response to that comment, his face tear-soaked, and Jay said, "I'm sorry for you loss, Alexei. Your dad was a good man."

"Thank you."

"Oh, Mrs Petrov, I also need the key, for the police."

She reached into the pocket of her hoodie and gave Jay the key. Her own eyes were rimmed with tears, too, but he could see a determination in them. Maybe Vitali Petrov *had* been a good man, but Jay had no doubt, given a hundred chances to relive that moment, she'd have shot him every time, and all for the sake of her son's future. He didn't know much at all about her, but he admired her for that.

40

It was after two before Jay was finally finished in the police station. Benny acted like an anxious host the whole time, keeping him fed and watered, apologizing for how long things were taking. When he was finally told with one more apology that he was free to go, Benny even offered to drive him to Cotignac-sur-Mer but Jay told him he'd make his own way back.

As he stepped out of the station he noticed a black limousine with tinted windows, brazenly parked behind a couple of patrol cars on the cramped lot. His first thought was that Valeria Karnitsky might have sent it, but for all her talk of "our kind of people", Jay had probably already ceased to exist in Valeria's world.

Instead, the window lowered and Georgy Gumilev looked out with a smile.

"Care for a ride?"

Jay walked over and climbed in and Georgy handed him a glass of champagne.

"What are we celebrating?"

"You tease! But I think we can all be happy with the results."

They were already driving away smoothly into the traffic, the champagne barely moving in their glasses.

"Sure. Some people died, but we averted a coup, and who knows how many more would have died if that had gone ahead."

"Or what greater conflicts might have resulted." Jay had to accept that there was some truth in that. "Do you know where you'll go next?"

"No, I was thinking after six months on the Cote d'Azur I could probably use a vacation."

Georgy laughed heartily, then reached into his jacket and handed two business cards to Jay. One was Georgy's own, the other plain white with a Moscow phone number on it.

"I know you didn't do it for our benefit, but you've done my country a great service. If ever you need anything, I personally am at your disposal. But you can also call that other number, any time. They'll know your name and they'll know to offer you every assistance."

"Thanks, Georgy."

Yet Jay felt a little fraudulent even as he thanked him, because he had a feeling Mrs Petrov might well have killed her husband anyway. For all Jay's machinations, introducing his son into the Petrov family had ultimately been enough to convince her that Vitali should die.

Georgy dropped him at the Grand and Jay made his way to the suite she was in with the two boys.

She seemed more composed now, and so did Alexei, but she said, "If you have no plans, Mr Lewis, I was hoping Owen might spend the day with us tomorrow, as well. Owen was telling us about a dolphin watching trip, and there's a light show in the marina tomorrow evening. I thought it might be nice."

It was clear she was trying to keep Alexei busy and distracted from what had happened. The woman herself seemed to be flowering and gaining confidence by the minute.

Jay felt like he wanted to keep Owen close right now, but even so, he said, "Sure, if Owen would like to. I can bring him in the morning, pick him up around ten tomorrow evening."

Owen gave Jay a clandestine nod, but after they left and were walking back to the apartment, Jay said, "You don't have to spend the day with Alexei tomorrow if you don't want to."

"No, I do want to. I think I should, anyway. Like, he's just lost his dad and everything. And I'm his only friend." Jay sensed he was mimicking expressions he'd heard in a movie or TV show, but he admired the sentiment all the same. It was possibly the same characteristic that had seen him sticking up for a smaller kid back home in Denver.

Then Owen said, "So I guess we have to walk everywhere now that our car's been shot up."

"I guess so, until I get a new one. Fortunately, I had gunfight coverage on my insurance."

"Is that a real thing?" He sounded both excited and incredulous.

"No, I'm kidding."

"*Jay*!" He started laughing then and couldn't stop for a minute or so. Finally, when he'd calmed down, he said, "I really liked that car."

"Yeah, me too. You can help me choose the next one."

"Cool!"

And for the rest of the way home, Owen talked about the cars he liked with the obsessive detail only a ten year old could muster.

The apartment smelt fresh when they got inside, but Jay still went to check the bathroom before they settled. Maisie Jensen had been good to her word and the bathtub was pristine and unoccupied.

Owen and Jay settled in, then looked at what was in the fridge that was still fresh and set about making dinner together. They'd only just started when Jay's phone buzzed. It was a message from Harry—*I'm about to knock on your door. Don't shoot me.* He was amazed by how good it made him feel to know that she was right outside, that she'd soon be in here with them.

The knock sounded and Jay said, "Why don't you go get that?"

Owen pulled a face. "Is it safe?"

"Safer than a grenade."

Owen laughed and went off to get the door, coming back almost immediately, excitable, dragging Harry by the hand.

"I thought I'd hang out with you gentlemen while I can." Jay looked questioningly. "I'm flying back to London day after tomorrow."

Owen added, "But we're keeping in touch."

He went back to mixing the salad as Jay said, "So… this is all we have to offer tonight, but maybe tomorrow evening, I can repay you that dinner."

"I'd like that. I mean, perhaps we could all go."

"I have plans," said Owen, as he continued to mix the salad.

She looked at Jay as if to say, "so it's just us." He looked back, holding her gaze, wondering what she was really thinking, why she was so determined nothing would happen between them. But in truth, he knew the answer.

She wasn't looking for a brief fling or a bit of fun, she was looking for stability, a future, and if Jay was honest with himself, he didn't have much to offer in that regard.

41

They went to the Yacht Club and ate against a backdrop of the light show that was illuminating the marina and hopefully keeping Owen and Alexei entertained. One of the laser lights briefly bounced off the windows on that side of the restaurant and Harry looked out before turning back to Jay.

"I don't have much experience of children in these situations, but Owen doesn't seem in the least bit traumatized."

"No, he's a composed little guy."

"But when you think about what they witnessed yesterday morning. I just think, perhaps you need to keep a watch on him, you know, in case he's more disturbed by it all than he's letting on."

"Sure, I mean…"

What? He didn't think it healthy to dwell on it or go over it, not unless Owen started having nightmares or something like that, and he couldn't see that happening— there was just something about the boy's psychology that would see him take it in his stride, Jay was certain of it.

Possibly so was Harry, because she said, "On the other hand, children deal with this stuff. Why keep going over it?"

"That's my thinking. And it all ended well enough."

"That's one way of looking at it."

He topped up their glasses and said, "Are your people satisfied with what you've done down here? You were only an observer, after all."

"I'm sure they will be. And what about yours? I note that Georgy Gumilev brought you back from Nice this afternoon."

There was that flirtatious glint in her eye, but at the same time it was almost as if the professional barriers were beginning to go up again.

"It seems I'm the least-informed person down here. Georgy apparently knew I was leaving the police station before I did. And you knew he gave me a ride."

"I wouldn't really be doing my job as an observer if I didn't." She sipped her wine, then said, "To answer your question, all my superiors will expect of me is my assessment of what happened here. My reputation's good enough that they'll give weight to whatever I have to say, use it accordingly."

"Let's hear it then."

"Okay." She took another sip of wine. He was pretty confident that she'd intended to give him her own version of events from the start. "You might think this a bit fanciful, but bear with me. I think the US Government had to publicly show moral support for Vitali Petrov—pro-Western, pro-democratic, promising a popular overthrow of the old autocracy. They sent a CIA Officer down here as a subtle indicator of that support. Very subtle—it's wrong to speak ill of the dead, but he wasn't exactly Langley's finest." Jay acknowledged that fact. "But here's the thing. Secretly, the Americans—and the British for that matter—didn't want Petrov to succeed at all. Their priority is to stabilize relations with Russia, not make them worse than they already are, which is what would happen if another former-Soviet domino fell right on the Russian border. Let's be honest, the Russians are skittish enough as it is. So the CIA sent someone else down here, someone much more highly-regarded, under deep cover, with the sole objective of ensuring Petrov didn't succeed, using all means necessary, with complete deniability." She smiled. "It needs some finessing, but that's more or less the gist of what I'll say in my report."

He made a look of considering her assessment and said, "I remember a station chief I met early in my career, told me that within every intelligence organization there are two types of information—hard facts and hard fiction."

"Are you suggesting I should go and write novels, Mr Lewis? How very patronizing of you." She was in good humor though. "I wouldn't expect you to accept or deny any of what I've just said, and I'll be the first to admit that it's based on intuition rather than hard facts. But you also have to admit that fiction often contains more than a grain of truth."

"Most definitely. And who knows, if we keep in touch, one day I might tell you how close you were."

"Deal." Another blaze of light appeared over the marina, what appeared to be the crescendo of the show. Harry looked out, then said, "I'll come with you to the Grand, if you don't mind, just to say goodbye to Owen."

"Sure, he'd like that, and so would I."

It was a little after ten when they walked to the hotel. Owen looked tired but he perked up at the sight of Harry. He extracted an additional assurance that she'd be keeping in touch, but otherwise seemed relaxed that Harry was saying goodbye.

It was only when they parted outside the hotel and stood for a minute watching Harry walk gracefully away into the Mediterranean night that Owen said, "I'm really gonna miss her."

"Yeah, so am I."

"You think we'll see her again?"

"I hope so."

He looked down and saw that Owen's eyes were moist with tears.

Jay gently wiped them away and said, "Come on, let's go home."

They started walking, and after a few steps, Owen reached up and held his hand.

42

The next morning, Jay found an A4 manilla envelope pushed under his door. He picked it up but didn't open it. Instead he made his coffee and went out to sit on the small couch on the balcony, putting his feet up on the railings.

The sky was clear, but the air was already warm, the town and the sea looking like a painted backdrop, full of the promise of the day ahead.

He opened the envelope and studied the contents. First off were the results of a DNA test, confirming that Owen was his son. Why had they taken it upon themselves to do that? And how had they gotten hold of Owen's DNA in the first place? He'd never been in any doubt anyway, and yet, now, retrospectively, he felt nervous for the result.

What would he have done if the test had come back indicating no match? He liked to think it would have made no difference, that he'd already bonded with the boy, but he couldn't know that for sure, and he was angry that they'd risked even putting him in that position.

The next couple of sheets gave him the address of an apartment in Lausanne, the location of a safety deposit box in the city, and various other pieces of crucial information, including the fact that Owen was enrolled in the American

School there for the coming fall. He shook his head in disbelief. *That* was why they'd done the DNA test— because they didn't want to spend government money educating someone who wasn't Jay's child!

He heard Owen come out of his room and he slipped the sheets of paper back in the envelope. He heard the boy's bare feet slapping on the floor, then he emerged onto the balcony in his pajamas.

"Morning, Jay."

"Morning, Owen."

Owen climbed onto the couch next to him. Jay realized that in all the nights he'd stayed here, this was the first morning that he hadn't come out of his room fully dressed. Was that a sign that he was settling, feeling more like this was his home, with Jay?

"You want some breakfast?"

"In a little while." He glanced to the side. "You had a letter."

He didn't miss much.

"Yeah, just about the next job. Did you learn to ski in Colorado?"

"Sure." He looked apologetic. "I'm not really that good at it. I'm pretty good at snowboarding, though."

"That's just as good. We're moving to Lausanne for a while, in Switzerland. So you'll be able to ski or snowboard in the winter. And it's right on a lake so you'll be able to sail, too."

Owen gave the air a little victorious punch.

"What about school?"

"Funny you should ask, but you're enrolled in the American School there, this coming fall. It's an English-speaking school, kids from all over, not just America. But they speak French in Lausanne, so you can keep learning French as well."

"So I'm staying with you?"

"It looks that way. Is that okay?"

"Duh. *Yeah*! The last few weeks have been amazing."

"Okay, the last few weeks have been pretty unusual, but…"

He stopped there, knowing that he could hardly predict what might lie ahead in Lausanne.

"What's the job? In Switzerland, I mean. What will you be doing there?"

"I don't know. Probably just security consultancy. I'll find out more when I get there." Owen looked up at him, skeptical. "What's that look for?"

"Dad, I know you're still in the CIA."

"Oh, do you now?" Jay laughed. "And how do you know that exactly?"

"Walden. When he found out where you were, he said you're still on the payroll, even though everyone thinks you left."

Walden, of course.

"Wow. You know, maybe Walden should be in the CIA." Owen laughed as if Jay had just said the funniest thing ever. When he calmed down, Jay said, "You've known all this time?"

"Yup."

"So why didn't you say anything?"

"I guessed it's meant to be a secret."

Jay looked at him, and suddenly felt suffused with love for this boy. He put his arm around him and kissed the top of his head, and Owen snuggled in against him. He started laughing his infectious laugh.

"And don't think I didn't notice. You're calling me Dad now all of a sudden?"

That set Owen off laughing even harder and Jay found himself laughing with him. So they sat there on the couch together like that, laughing sporadically, looking out over

Cotignac-sur-Mer and the beginnings of another beautiful day, and for the first time in many years, certainly for the first time in his adult life, Jay felt complete.

Printed in Great Britain
by Amazon

38625259R00198